"Are you afraid of me, Melissa? Afraid of what I'm making you feel?"

"The only thing you're making me feel is uncomfortable."

"That's a lie. Don't you think a man knows when a woman is feeling all fluttery and excited because of him?"

Melissa's eyes suddenly blazed. "What you're interpreting as fluttering and excitement is incredulity that you'd have the brass to come here in the first place. I don't want to be your friend, Wyatt North. I don't want—"

Her words stopped abruptly because his mouth was suddenly on hers. Sputtering, she pushed against him. But his hands were cradling her head and holding it right where he wanted it. His lips moved on hers, gently, then roughly, then gently again.

Her lips felt swollen and softly sensual when he finally stopped kissing them and raised his head to look into her eyes. "I didn't intend doing that when I came here tonight," he whispered. "I never expected to see you again, and apparently you never expected to see me again. But it happened, and I'm not going to lose you a second time."

Jackie Merritt

and her husband live just outside of Las Vegas, Nevada. An accountant for many years, Jackie has happily traded numbers for words. Next to her family, books are her greatest joy. She started writing in 1987 and her efforts paid off only a year later with the publication of her first novel. When she's not writing or enjoying a good book, Jackie dabbles in watercolor painting and enjoys playing the piano in her spare time.

Jackie Merritt

THE RANCHER TAKES A WIFE

Silhouette Books

Published by Silhouette Books

America's Publisher of Contemporary Romance

Special thanks and acknowledgment to Jackie Merritt for her contribution to the Montana Mavericks series.

Text and artwork on page 8 is reprinted with permission from NEVER ASK A MAN THE SIZE OF HIS SPREAD: A Cowgirl's Guide to Life, by Gladiola Montana. Copyright © 1993 Gibbs Smith Publisher. All rights reserved.

 SILHOUETTE BOOKS

ISBN 0-373-50169-2

THE RANCHER TAKES A WIFE

Copyright © 1994 by Harlequin Enterprises B.V.

Printed in U.S.A.

MONTANA
Mavericks

*Welcome to Whitehorn, Montana—
the home of bold men and daring women.
A place where rich tales of passion and
adventure are unfolding under the Big Sky.
Seems that this charming little town has some mighty
big secrets. And everybody's talking about...*

Charlie Avery: Years ago, all of Whitehorn thought he'd deserted his wife and family. But now his bones have been found on the Laughing Horse Reservation. Was Charlie murdered? No one wanted to know more than...

Melissa Avery: One mystery in her life was solved—and another begun. Yet the rumors *never* seemed to stop about her father and the notorious...

Lexine Baxter: Seems the town hellraiser skipped out of Whitehorn just about the same time Charlie disappeared. What ever became of her? Nobody knew better than...

Mary Jo Kincaid: Not even her good marriage could save her from suspicion. But her pretty smile and cunning manner could win her a whole lot more. As long as she steered clear of...

Winona Cobbs: Wily old Winona, town seer, knew more than most. And with a little help, she might just make sense of her haunting visions. But was anyone in Whitehorn ready for the truth?

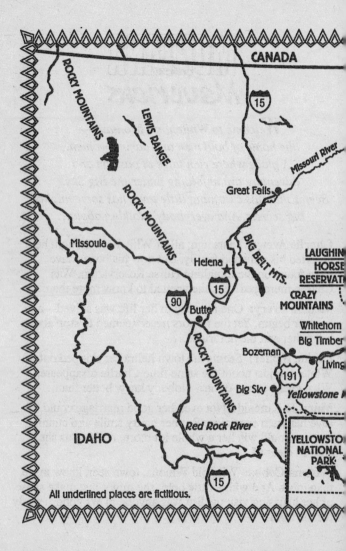

CANADA

ROCKY MOUNTAINS

LEWIS RANGE

ROCKY MOUNTAINS

Missouri River

Great Falls

15

Missoula

Helena

BIG BELT MTS.

LAUGHIN
HORSE
RESERVAT

CRAZY
MOUNTAINS

90

Butte

15

Whitehorn

Big Timber

Bozeman

Livin

191

ROCKY MOUNTAINS

Big Sky

Yellowstone

Red Rock River

IDAHO

YELLOWSTO
NATIONAL
PARK

15

All underlined places are fictitious.

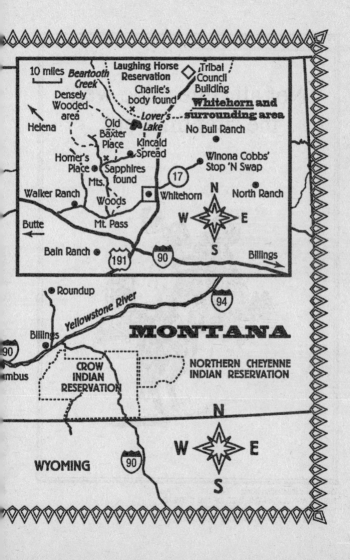

10 miles

Beartooth Creek

Laughing Horse Reservation

Tribal Council Building

Charlie's body found

Whitehorn and surrounding area

Densely Wooded area

Helena

Old Baxter Place

Lover's Lake

No Bull Ranch

Kincaid Spread

Homer's Place

Sapphires found

Winona Cobbs' Stop 'N Swap

Mts.

17

North Ranch

Walker Ranch

Woods

Whitehorn

N
W E
S

Butte

Mt. Pass

Bain Ranch

191

90

Billings

Roundup

Yellowstone River

94

MONTANA

Billings

90

CROW INDIAN RESERVATION

NORTHERN CHEYENNE INDIAN RESERVATION

mbus

N
W E
S

WYOMING

90

Not all fillies ride well the first time out.

Quote and Illustration from:
NEVER ASK A MAN THE SIZE OF HIS SPREAD,
by Gladiola Montana. Illustration by Bonnie Cazier.
Copyright © 1993 by Gibbs Smith Publisher.

One

It was a hot day in August. Melissa Avery opened the front door of her restaurant, the Hip Hop Café. The ceiling fans were stirring the inside air, but she hoped to catch a breeze from outside. Her building didn't have air-conditioning, which was a problem she intended to rectify when her expansion plans came to fruition.

It was midafternoon, the least busy time of day for the café. Melissa turned to one of her waitresses. "I'm going to leave the door open, Wanda." She smiled teasingly. "This heat makes me feel like playing hooky."

Wanda merely laughed. Melissa could play hooky any day she pleased, but she rarely did. Wanda had never worked for anyone so dedicated to her business as Melissa was. But it was probably that very dedication that explained the Hip Hop's success. Of course, the town of Whitehorn, Montana had never had a restaurant quite like it before, either. Wanda loved the way Melissa had decorated the place, and so, it seemed, did the Hip Hop's many repeat customers.

Melissa returned to the booth she'd been using before opening the door. On the table was a scattering of notebooks, cookbooks and grocery lists. It was at this time of day that she often planned menus and food purchases, enjoying the task with a cup of herbal tea she bought specially blended from a company in San Francisco. Today the tea was in a tall glass, sharing space with a half-dozen ice cubes.

There were only a few patrons in the place, and Melissa smiled at the couple seated at a table in the far corner.

Picking up her glass, she took a sip of tea and looked at the bright sunlight outside. She really did feel like doing something silly on this beautiful day, like maybe scampering through a field of wildflowers. Shaking her head at the inane image, though with good humor, she set down her glass in preparation for getting back to work.

At that moment a man appeared in the doorway, a tall man with broad shoulders and long legs. He was dressed in jeans, boots and a white, Western-cut shirt. There was a big hat on his head, and dark sunglasses concealed the upper half of his face.

It had been almost ten years since Melissa had set eyes on Wyatt North, but she recognized him immediately. She became statue still, not by choice but because of utter shock. Wyatt walking in like this had never once entered her mind. He didn't even live around here anymore, or so she'd heard. Since his marriage six years ago he'd been living in Helena.

To her intense relief, he never even glanced her way. He walked over to the counter, sat on a stool and picked up a menu. Wanda was there immediately. Melissa could hear every word they spoke.

"Hi," Wanda said. "Coffee?"

"Iced tea, I think, and..." Wyatt took off his dark glasses and tucked them into his shirt pocket. "What kind of pie do you have?"

"Apple, cherry and banana cream. Homemade."

Wyatt grinned dubiously. "I've heard that one before."

"Not from me, you haven't. I remember faces very well, and you've never been in here on my shift."

"Never been in here on anyone's shift. Seems like a nice little place, but—" he leaned forward "—do you mind telling me who decorated it? It's got something from every decade of the twentieth century. Couldn't the owner decide what he wanted it to be when it grew up?" He chuckled at his own wit.

Wanda's chin lifted, as though instead of making a joke, he'd insulted her. "Our pie is homemade and delicious. Do you want some or don't you?"

Melissa gave Wanda a mental pat on the back. The Hip Hop *was* decorated eclectically. But she hadn't wanted just another run-of-the-mill, small-town café, and she thought she had blended the antique and modern pieces quite tastefully. Besides, she didn't care if Wyatt North liked it or not. Much more important to think about was if it were possible for Wyatt to sit there, eat a piece of pie, pay his tab and leave without noticing her. If she got up and left the booth, there was no way he would miss seeing her. Maybe she could crawl under the table until he left.

God, she silently groaned, dropping her forehead into her left hand to hide her face, just in case he should glance over his shoulder. It wasn't that she was afraid of seeing Wyatt, she just didn't *want* to see him. She didn't want to be polite to him, to smile and pretend that she didn't despise him. Worse, to pretend that there wasn't any reason why she *shouldn't* despise him.

"Give me a piece of the banana cream," Wyatt said to Wanda, who dutifully wrote his request on her order pad.

"Iced tea and banana cream pie," she mouthed as she wrote. "Coming right up." She walked away.

Wyatt began looking around. The long chrome counter amused him, though it had to be forty years old and was probably quite valuable. He recalled that the place used to be owned by a grumpy old guy who'd made it clear to the high-school crowd that he didn't like teenagers hanging around. Not that Whitehorn teenagers had wanted to hang around. Back then the café had been dingy and colorless, and had served greasy hamburgers and soda in the can. There'd been much better places to buy burgers and sodas— the Whirl-In Drive-In, for one.

A nostalgic smile tipped the corner of Wyatt's mouth. He hadn't thought of the Whirl-In in ages. Was it still there? Maybe he'd drive by the site and find out after he left here.

Wanda delivered his order. "Here you are, sir. Enjoy."

Melissa was all but holding her breath in the booth. Wyatt not turning enough to spot her when he'd looked around must qualify as a minor miracle. But just then the telephone rang. She closed her eyes as a horrifying premonition hit her. Sure enough, after answering the phone, Wanda called, "Melissa, it's for you."

There was no eluding a face-to-face now, Melissa thought disgustedly as she slid from the booth and walked behind the counter to the telephone.

Wyatt had a bite of pie halfway to his mouth. His hand stopped in midair, though he gulped as though he'd taken that bite and needed to swallow it. Melissa had turned her back on him to speak into the phone, but his wide, startled eyes were taking in her long lean build in a flowing print skirt and blouse. Her hair was in a French braid, its tip almost reaching her waist. Melissa...dear God...it was *Melissa*.

He slowly lowered the fork to his plate. He couldn't take his eyes off her. He'd walked in here and missed seeing her. Where had she been sitting? Swiveling his stool, he spotted the booth with the papers spread across the table. She'd seen him come in—how could she have not?—and had given no sign. Swiveling back, he locked his gaze on her again.

His stomach muscles ached with tension. The pie was good, homemade as the waitress had promised, but there was no way he'd be able to finish eating it. A hundred, a thousand times he'd thought of someday seeing Melissa again, but not like this, never like this. Not in a public place with neither of them prepared. When had she returned to Whitehorn? What was she doing in this little café, with papers and books strewn on a table?

"Thank you," Melissa said quietly into the phone. "Goodbye." With deliberate caution, she placed the handset onto the receiver. Her stomach was cramping. She had to turn around and face Wyatt. She had to say hello, and maybe ask how he was. A chill went up her spine, causing her skin to ripple with goose bumps. The air no longer felt warm.

As she turned, she was aware of him getting to his feet. "Hello, Melissa."

Her gaze flicked over his face, then dropped to his shirt-front. "Hello, Wyatt."

"How are you?" *Look at me! Look into my eyes!*

"Just fine. And you?" *How dare you enter my café and expect courtesy from me?*

She was so beautiful, Wyatt realized, unable to stop staring at her. As a girl she'd been pretty, but her beauty now stunned him. Her coloring—gleaming dark hair, deep blue eyes and skin like rich cream—was a shock to his nervous system. Had it always been so?

Something else was stunning him—the unexpected situation?—making him feel as though his feet had lost the strength to carry him out of there and that his brain wasn't functioning well enough for him to speak intelligently.

"Uh...you're looking well," he stammered. Then, miraculously, he thought of a reasonable question. "Are you living in Whitehorn again?"

Melissa was aware of Wanda and the other waitress standing at the opposite end of the counter, furtively watching and listening. Naturally, they were curious, since she was behaving so differently than she normally did with customers.

But she couldn't smile at Wyatt. She just couldn't, even if she had been forced to speak to him. "I've been back for about eighteen months. About a year and a half," she added unnecessarily.

"I'm living here again, too," Wyatt said, his voice low and laden with tension. "On the ranch, I mean. Not in town."

"Oh?" *Why would you think I'd be interested?* "You'll have to excuse me, Wyatt. I have a hundred things to do before the dinner rush." Melissa walked around the end of the counter and continued on to the booth she'd been using. Nervously, she began gathering up her books and papers.

"Melissa..." She whirled, startled to find that he was right behind her. "Give me ten minutes," he said softly. "Outside."

She flushed. "I don't *have* ten minutes. I told you—"

"I know what you told me. Melissa, I'm so surprised to see you. Couldn't we talk for just a few minutes?"

Everyone in the place was watching, she realized, not only the waitresses. Her chin rose. "Some other time, Wyatt." With her books and papers stacked in her arms, she swept past him and kept going through the swinging door to the kitchen.

Wyatt stood where she'd left him, near the vacant booth. Memories bombarded him, and he couldn't escape them to think clearly. Several moments passed while he tried to get his bearings, but finally he realized that the café was deathly still and the handful of patrons and the two waitresses were all staring at him.

Walking over to the counter where his half-eaten pie and tea were waiting, he dug into his jeans and came out with a ten-dollar bill. "That should cover my order," he said to Wanda. "Keep the change."

Crossing the room to the door, he stepped outside and stopped in the sunshine to put on his dark glasses. As shocks went, the past few minutes had been a beaut. Looking up the street, then down—why, he didn't know—he strode to his pickup and got in. Starting the motor, he pulled away from the curb and drove to the edge of town, where he turned into the large parking lot of a farm-equipment dealer. Parking as far from any other vehicle as he could get, he switched off the ignition and at long last permitted the pain in his gut to spread throughout his body.

Groaning aloud, he put his arms around the steering wheel and buried his face in them. *Melissa... Melissa... I'm so sorry, so damned sorry.*

* * *

There was a minuscule, windowless—which was why she rarely used it—office off the kitchen, and Melissa went into it, snapped on the ceiling light, closed the door, dropped her books and papers on the tiny desk, then fell into the chair behind it. Every cell in her body was trembling. Her hands, shaking so badly she couldn't keep them still, traveled from her face to the arms of her chair, then fluttered over the items on the desktop.

She finally clenched her fingers into fists, forcing them to stop quivering. But she couldn't stop the turmoil inside her and eventually she put her head down on the desk and collapsed into tears. She'd walked right past her employees without a word, something she never did. What must her staff think?

But was that why she was crying—because her cook and waitresses and a few customers had witnessed her unfriendliness with Wyatt? That was an absurd idea. Everyone was entitled to an occasional lapse of good manners.

Eyes dripping, Melissa got up. With her arms wrapped around herself, she paced the floor of the small office. How could he speak to her as though they were merely old acquaintances running into each other? How dare he ask for ten minutes of her time to talk? What did he think they had to say to one another? Remembering that he'd said he lived on the ranch again, she groaned. They were bound to end up in the same place at the same time on occasion in this small town. She had to keep her wits about her and react more normally the next time they met. He knew he'd hurt her; he didn't need to know that the pain had never subsided.

Her trembling had, however, she realized gratefully. In fact, she felt much calmer, even deep inside where the pain resided so tenaciously. She sat at the desk and took a long, slow breath, calming herself even further. Without the agony that her brain had suffered only a few minutes ago, she was able to relive the scene in the café from a less-personal point of view. In retrospect, she hadn't behaved *that* badly.

She had said a civil hello and asked how he was. It was sufficient conversation for a first meeting after so many years, even if her normal buoyancy had been completely absent.

Besides, she thought with a toss of her head, she really didn't care how anyone in the café—especially Wyatt—had interpreted the episode. Hopefully he'd gotten the message that she had no intention of *ever* having that talk with him. Let him go home and talk to his wife. Let *her* soothe his ego. Never was Melissa going to tell him that what he'd done six years ago was all right; maybe his wife could reassure him on that subject.

Eventually Wyatt's blue funk diminished enough for him to start his truck and leave the equipment dealer's parking lot. Before stopping at the Hip Hop, he'd been driving around Whitehorn checking on the changes that had taken place during his absence. He'd been enjoying himself, admitting that from the moment he and Shannon had agreed on a divorce he'd felt as if a ten-ton burden had vanished. Moving back to the ranch for good about a week ago had been one of the high points of his life, and he'd just been enjoying this beautiful summer day, breathing in the warm air and reveling in his sense of freedom.

He was no longer reveling. He was no longer enjoying the weather or the innocuous tour of Whitehorn. Melissa was back, and that was something he couldn't have dreamed up in a million years. What fate had decreed he should notice the Hip Hop Café's sign, think it a clever name and decide to stop for a cold drink?

While he no longer enjoyed seeing the sights of Whitehorn, he didn't want to go back to the ranch—Melissa was here, in town—so he kept turning corners and listlessly checking out whatever street he was on. Instinct—or some mysterious malady—brought him to the high school, and without plan or reason, he pulled the truck to the curb and turned off the motor.

For a while he merely stared blankly at the silent school, then old memories began churning in his brain. He sighed heavily and despondently. He had started dating Melissa when he was a junior and she a sophomore. They had clicked in so many ways, liking the same kind of music, the same dumb jokes. She was pretty and smart, and he'd fallen hard for her long legs and wry sense of humor. Because his last name was also a direction—North—she would pretend to forget *which* direction, and in passing each other in the hall she'd often call out, "Hi, East," or "West" or "South." He'd laugh and she'd laugh, and he'd go on to his next class feeling good.

That year and the following flicked through Wyatt's mind—the dances, the football and basketball games, the dates that had consisted of a movie and a stop at the Whirl-In before he'd taken Melissa home to meet her curfew. Melissa's father had disappeared when she was a little girl, and Nan Avery, her mother, was overly strict with her only daughter. At least Wyatt had always thought so. His own dad was a widower, but Simon North never had imposed a curfew on *his* only child. Still, the North and Avery families were too dissimilar to make comparisons. Beneath Melissa's jokes and laughter lay a sadness that very few people ever got to see. Wyatt had seen it, and after they had dated for a long time, she had talked about her father. She would never believe he'd just up and deserted his family the way her mother insisted he had, she'd told him. *Something else happened, Wyatt, I know it, and someday I'm going to find out what it was.*

Wyatt suddenly sat up straighter. That was why Melissa was back in Whitehorn! He remembered reading that Charlie Avery's remains had been found buried on the Laughing Horse Indian Reservation. Melissa had come back to unravel the mystery of her father's death—he'd bet on it.

Wyatt's shoulders slumped again. No. The bones had been found in the spring and Melissa had already been here for over a year. Still, she was probably digging out the truth.

The poor kid. She'd been so positive that Charlie would come back to her someday, and all along he'd been dead.

Absently he watched an unfamiliar car use the school parking lot to turn around. Was there any chance at all that Melissa would ever forgive him? There was so much he yearned to tell her, if she would just talk to him. So many times in the past six years he'd thought of contacting her, or attempting to. Something had always stopped him. Call it honor, or a sense of responsibility, but after his son, Timmy, was born he'd felt duty bound to make his marriage work. Timmy had been the only bright spot during those years. Shannon, his soon-to-be ex-wife, was a shallow, selfish woman with a cutting personality that only softened when everything was going her way. Why draw Melissa into his misery? Even if he had decided in favor of contacting her, she probably wouldn't have talked to him.

Wyatt's expression became grim with the memory of how she had treated him in the Hip Hop. Yet he couldn't blame her for wanting nothing to do with him. He'd hurt her in the worst possible way a man could hurt a woman. Not by choice, for God's sake. If he'd had any other option...

Sighing, Wyatt turned the ignition key. There was little point in sitting here feeling sorry for himself. And he was tired of sightseeing, too. He decided to head on home.

Melissa had fixed up the old apartment above the café as her living quarters. She had painted every wall eggshell white, and hung white shutters on the windows so she could push them open and bring in the sun. Decorating the apartment simply, with overstuffed furniture in pastel colors and lots of green plants, she had created a pleasant, comfortable home for herself.

When the café closed at ten that evening as usual, Melissa wearily climbed the inside staircase to the apartment. There was also an outside staircase, which was handy at times, but mostly she used the one inside the building. Ordinarily she didn't find 10:00 p.m. late, usually staying up until midnight. Tonight, however, she went immediately to her bathroom, threw off her clothes, took a shower and crawled into bed. From the time she entered the apartment until she pulled the top sheet and summer-weight blanket up to her chin, no more than ten minutes had passed.

She closed her eyes and saw Wyatt North. Sudden fury engulfed her, and she got up, opened the window about six inches, climbed back into bed and glared at the dark ceiling. Damn him! Why had he moved back to the ranch? His wife was in some way involved with state politics, she'd heard, and the Whitehorn area wasn't exactly a hotbed of political activity. One would think that Mrs. Wyatt North would find the ranch rather dull.

Frowning, Melissa speculated on that idea. Maybe Wyatt had insisted on moving back because of his child. Maybe there was more than one by now, and he wanted to raise his children on the ranch where he'd grown up.

But she knew for sure only about his first child and couldn't help wondering, as she'd done many times in the past, if it was a boy or a girl. When she'd returned to Whitehorn, she'd thought of going to the library and looking up old editions of the Helena paper to see if there were any photos published of Wyatt's wedding, just so she could get a glimpse of his wife. She'd been so tempted, in fact, that one day she'd found herself on the steps of the library. For some reason she'd come to her senses before going inside. It didn't matter if his wife was beautiful or plain, damn it— it simply didn't matter. What was wrong with her?

That had been Melissa's one and only serious lapse into the past. She'd gotten on with her own life, buying Billy Struthers's old café and refurbishing it into something not only tasteful but attractive. Restaurant work was what she'd done in California, eventually becoming manager of a small but chic café, so it only made sense to her to continue doing what she knew best. Until today she'd been ... well, almost happy. Not with the investigation of her father's death—that was moving so slowly Melissa could hardly bear it. But her work was satisfying and she even had plans to expand her business.

Now, she thought, staring into the dark, nothing would ever be the same again. She would be forever looking over her shoulder, dreading another confrontation with Wyatt. Worse, a confrontation with Wyatt and his wife. The thought of meeting the two of them on the street was horrifying. She didn't want to be introduced as an old friend, and what else would Wyatt be able to call her? *"Honey, this is the woman I was engaged to before you and I got married."*

It was a preposterous supposition, but heartrending. Tears filled Melissa's eyes again, angering her. She'd done her crying six years ago, and she wasn't going to spend the rest of her life shedding tears every time Wyatt invaded her space.

Brushing them away with a hardened expression, she turned over in bed and forced her thoughts to go elsewhere. She had lots to think about, the expansion of her café and the unsolved death of her father in particular. Wyatt North was not going to disrupt her life, and that was a vow.

Two

At least twice a week Melissa put aside her duties at the café and drove to the sheriff's office to converse with Sheriff Judd Hensley about the death of her father, Charlie Avery.

"Of course it was murder," Melissa said with some pique, when Judd announced the possibility again, as though for the first time. "The whole town knows it was murder. My father didn't bury himself out there on the reservation. But Judd—" she leaned forward "—there *has* to be some clues to who did it, and nobody's found anything substantial."

Judd sighed. He understood Melissa's persistence and at times even admired it, but he couldn't manufacture clues just to appease her. "Melissa, it's been over twenty years since whatever happened out there took place. Besides, you know that Tracy's in charge of the investigation. She's the one you should be talking to."

Tracy was an FBI agent and Judd's wife. Theirs was a convoluted story. Married to each other at a young age, they had divorced when the death of their son had driven them apart. Tracy'd left Montana and, to Judd's surprise, had joined the FBI. Many years passed until, because she was familiar with the area, she'd been assigned to work on the mysterious human bones found by George Sweetwater on the Laughing Horse Reservation. Judd really had no authority to get involved in Indian affairs, but it had come as no small shock to him that the FBI agent sent to investigate the old murder had been his ex-wife. It still amazed him that they'd fallen in love again and remarried, though he was certainly happy about it.

"I do talk to Tracy, which I'm sure you know very well," Melissa replied. Tracy's office was just next door to Judd's. "I also talk to Sterling McCallum, Rafe Rawlings and anyone else who has the remotest connection to the investigation. I just can't understand what's taking so long."

"Real-life murder investigations aren't like TV shows, Melissa."

"Well, of course they're not, but one would think…" She closed her mouth. Maybe she was haranguing Judd and Tracy too much. They were both experienced, capable officers of the law and were undoubtedly doing their utmost to solve the long-ago crime.

"I'm sorry, Judd." Forcing a smile, Melissa got to her feet. "Is it all right if I keep coming around? I know it's an obsession on my part, but I have to keep abreast of the investigation."

Judd stood. "Come around anytime you want, Melissa, but I guarantee you'll be the first to know if and when we find out anything important."

"Thanks, Judd."

Every time Melissa talked to either Judd or Tracy, she left the meeting feeling frustrated. It was true what she'd told Judd about being obsessed with the investigation. Even though she sometimes sensed annoyance from him, Tracy or anyone else in the law-enforcement community she could pin down to discuss the case, she couldn't stay distanced from it. From the day of her father's disappearance she hadn't believed that he'd merely run off and deserted his family. But by the same token, she hadn't imagined him as a murder victim. Someone had killed him deliberately, purposely taking his life. It was so abhorrent to Melissa, so difficult to accept, that she often had nightmares about it.

Her mother, on the other hand, had received the news quite calmly. "Mark my words, Missy. When the law uncovers the murderer, there'll be a woman involved." Nan always had felt—and never hesitated to say—that there must be a woman somehow connected to the mysterious disappearance of her husband.

Nan Avery had been unabashedly relieved when Judd Hensley had telephoned her in California with information about the body's identification. "Now we can collect on your father's insurance," she had told Melissa. Charlie had possessed a sizable, paid-up life-insurance policy. However, it contained a clause that stipulated benefits would be paid to his beneficiaries only upon presentation of a death certificate.

Now she had access to that all-important death certificate and could file a claim on the policy. Unquestionably, Nan needed the money. But Melissa had found her mother's attitude crass and unfeeling. She'd grown up with Nan's bitterness over being abandoned by her husband, and often Melissa and her brother had been at odds with their mother because of that bitterness. "Can't you give Daddy the benefit of the doubt?" Melissa had often asked. "He wouldn't just go off and leave us, Mother. And think about it. He didn't take anything with him—not his clothes, no money from the bank, nothing."

Maybe she had always suspected some sort of foul play, Melissa thought with a sigh while getting into her car outside of the sheriff's office. *Oh, Daddy. What really happened to you?*

Wyatt couldn't get Melissa out of his mind. He thought about her while riding his favorite horse, Sasha, to check on his cattle. Melissa's image was in front of him when he sat down to eat, or when he was talking to his ranch hands, or when he spent time in his office paying bills. It didn't matter what he did or where he went, Melissa was with him.

He wanted to see her. He wanted her to smile at him with her old smile, the one that had made his heart sing. He wanted her to talk to him, to listen to all he had to say to her, and he wanted, desperately, to remind her of that evening so long ago when she'd called him, weeping and panicked because her mother was moving them to California.

Melissa had just started her senior year of high school. Wyatt had started college in Missoula. He'd been called to the phone in his dorm.

"Wyatt North here."

"Wyatt... oh, Wyatt."

"Melissa? What's wrong?"

It took a minute for her sobs to slow down enough to speak. "Mother... Mother is moving us to California."

Wyatt remembered that his knees had gotten peculiarly weak. He'd asked her when this was going to happen, trying to sound calm and sensible.

"The moving truck will be here tomorrow," Melissa sobbed.

"Tomorrow! That's impossible. When did she decide?"

"I don't know. She only told me about it tonight. Oh, Wyatt, what are we going to do? I'll miss you so. And I won't even see you to say goodbye."

"Yes, you will. I'm on my way. Watch for me."

Wyatt had driven the nearly three hundred miles at top speed, risking a ticket every mile of the way. It was one o'clock in the morning when he pulled to a stop in front of Melissa's house. Everything was dark, but he knew she would see his car. He switched off the headlights and waited. Then he saw her coming around from the back of the house, walking very quickly. He pushed the passenger door open and she got in.

"Go somewhere," she said, her voice husky from crying.

Wyatt drove away. "How're you doing?" he asked quietly.

"Terrible." Melissa began weeping again. "I'm sorry. I can't seem to stop crying. I don't want to move to California. I don't want to move anywhere. I want to finish school here, and what if Daddy comes back and he can't find us?"

"And what about you and me?"

She slid across the seat to lay her head on his arm. "I don't know," she whispered raggedly.

"Melissa, I love you."

"Oh, Wyatt, I love you, too."

Wyatt kept thinking of that evening all of one day, and that night he poured himself a scotch and water and sat in his den, staring broodingly into space as he sipped and remembered.

They'd been odd kids by today's standards, he realized. They had dated for several years—gone steady—and had never made love beyond kissing and mild petting. But that night, holding Melissa—feeling both their pain over a separation beyond their control—he'd let their kisses evolve into a passion that neither had put the brakes on. It was a beautiful memory for Wyatt, full of youthful awkwardness and inexperience, but so tender, so genuine.

Afterward they had talked. *"Melissa, you can come back to Whitehorn after you graduate. We'll only be apart until next spring."*

They'd made dozens of promises and vows that night, about getting married the following summer, about loving each other into eternity.

"We were so damned naive," Wyatt mumbled before tossing back the remaining scotch in his glass and getting up for a refill.

Melissa hadn't come back in the spring as they'd planned. They talked on the phone. *"Wyatt, I have to stay with Mother awhile longer. She has a job, but gets such low pay that she needs what I'm earning just to exist."*

"It's okay, honey. My father is very ill and I've got to take care of the ranch. This isn't the end of our plans, just a temporary setback."

Simon North had never been a robust man, as his son was. Frail from birth, Simon had concentrated on academics and earned several degrees. While attending Stanford University in California, he'd met and married Sheila Winston, a soft-spoken, intelligent woman who loved him exactly as he was—a kind, mild-mannered, gentle man who had been completely honest with her about his short life expectancy. For reasons Simon never fully explained to his son, he and Sheila had decided to make their home in Montana. Simon had inherited a fortune from his grandparents and parents, so money wasn't a problem. After a leisurely tour of the state, they'd chosen the Whitehorn area and had purchased two thousand acres of undeveloped land thirty-five miles east of town.

They'd had a beautiful, sprawling home constructed on their property, along with barns, corrals and other structures necessary to a cattle operation. Yet they purchased a very small herd—about a hundred head—and ranched rather lackadaisically, enjoying each other and their large library instead. Simon hired two men to take care of the ranch work and two women to manage the house. Wyatt's parents had been happily married for five years when Sheila became pregnant. In later years Simon told his son that he had felt a joy he never could have believed possible. He said that all during Sheila's pregnancy he had prayed openly for a healthy child and secretly for a son. His prayers had been answered; Sheila gave birth to a lusty, eight-pound boy, whom they named Wyatt Simon North.

Wyatt's birth changed everything for the Norths. Simon built up the ranch to its maximum potential—for his son. When Wyatt was old enough, Simon bought the best horses available for his son to ride. He was profoundly thankful that Wyatt was all-boy and possessed the health and strength that had bypassed him, and he encouraged and supported Wyatt's athletic abilities.

Then, when Wyatt was twelve, his mother died. It was so ironic that Simon had been the unhealthy parent and Sheila, who had always enjoyed good health, died suddenly and without warning of a massive coronary. The light went out of Simon's eyes after that, and though it wasn't noticeable at first, his own health began deteriorating.

The summer that was supposed to include Wyatt's and Melissa's wedding passed in hard work for each of them. Letters flew back and forth, and Wyatt ran up huge telephone bills calling California. Simon insisted adamantly that his son return to college in the fall. *"I'm feeling much better and your education is important, Wyatt. You must see to it."*

Wyatt appointed what he considered the best man working on the ranch to act as foreman in his absence. *"My father is to do absolutely no physical labor. If you see him overdoing in any way, you are to call me at once."*

So Wyatt returned to school in Missoula worried about his father, about the ranch and most poignantly about Melissa. Her problems were financial, and he could have solved them so easily if she would only allow it. But he'd broached that subject one time on the telephone and heard the immediate deep freeze in Melissa's reply. *"I will never take money from you or your father, Wyatt, so please don't suggest it again."* He hadn't.

Another year passed. Melissa was taking business classes and holding down a full-time job. Wyatt's spare time was spent at the ranch. They were still very much in love and in almost-constant contact, either by telephone or through letters. They were both locked into situations not of their making, and their most enjoyable telephone conversations were when they lightened up and cracked silly jokes about themselves, their plans and their respective parents.

But it was serious business, all the same. Simon's health was failing. Wyatt's nerves were stretched wafer thin. The ranch required his attention, and he couldn't disappoint his father by dropping out of school to be there. As for Melissa, all Wyatt had of her were memories, photographs, her voice on the telephone and a small mountain of letters.

Sipping his second scotch, Wyatt put his head back and permitted the final episode of their relationship to run through his brain.

Overwrought and strung out over classes and worry, he'd let himself be dragged to a party by his college roommate. It was a semiformal affair and Wyatt had objected to dressing up, but even he knew that he needed a break from the stress he'd been living with. So he'd put on his best suit, shined his shoes and gone with his friend.

It was the biggest mistake of his life. He'd met a girl there, Shannon Kiley, the daughter of State Senator Wilbur Kiley. Shannon lived in Helena and was in Missoula specifically to attend that party. She was vivacious, dazzlingly beautiful and sexually aggressive. Wyatt had never met anyone like her. She was so confident, so sure of herself, and after he'd had a few drinks she seemed like the only woman in the world. He ended up in Shannon's motel room that night, and awoke the next morning with a pounding headache and a realization of the enormity of what he'd done.

Sick at heart, he had explained his situation to Shannon. *"I'm engaged to a woman I love very much, Shannon. I'm sorrier than I can say about last night."*

She had looked pensive, then sighed. *"Don't take it so hard, Wyatt. You're only human, like the rest of us. For my part, I'm not at all sorry we made love. It was a wonderful night and I'll never forget it."*

Neither would Wyatt ever forget it. A month later Shannon called him. *"Wyatt, we have something of great importance to discuss. Come to my apartment this evening."* She gave him her Helena address.

He'd gone. There had been something in Shannon's voice that had him sweating. With good reason, he realized after she'd talked for a few minutes. *"I'm pregnant, and since you're the only man I've slept with in months, it's your child. I will not have an abortion, nor will I embarrass my father by having a baby without a husband."* She paused. *"It's your move, Wyatt."*

Like hell it was his move. He wanted to run, to go back in time and refuse to attend that party, to do anything but what he knew he was going to be forced to do. His own father would expect him to do the honorable thing. But what about Melissa? What about his own plans?

Weak kneed and nauseous, he'd sunk into a chair. Shannon's apartment was large and elegant. The Kileys weren't paupers by any means, and Shannon lived the role of a wealthy state senator's daughter to the hilt. Right now she was dressed in a stunning black dress that nearly reached her ankles. Below the swirling hemline was sheer black hose and high-heeled black pumps. Her blond hair was arranged dramatically, brushed to the left side of her head and held by an ebony comb. Why was she all in black? Wyatt wondered. Was she deliberately setting a somber scene to underscore the seriousness of her situation? Of his?

"You, uh, want us to get married," he mumbled.

"Can you think of another solution that won't damage my father's career?"

"That's your criteria for a shotgun wedding—your father's career might be affected?"

"Don't be crude, Wyatt. Do you think I'm any happier about this than you are?"

He looked into her eyes and saw a spark that belied her question. She was *happy* about this! How could she be?

He dropped his head in his hands, covering his face. His heart was hammering with remorse, with grief, with misery. Then he stood up. *"I'll marry you. Make the plans and let me know. I'll be there."*

He had driven back to Missoula in a state of numbness. For hours afterward he'd lain on his bed in the dorm and thought of Melissa. He had to call her; a letter would be too cruel. He wept, silently so his sleeping roommate wouldn't hear. It was three in the morning, too late to call tonight. He would do it tomorrow....

A log fell in the fireplace, sending a shower of sparks up the chimney and jerking Wyatt back to the present. His expression became grim and determined. The past was set and irrevocable, but he still had a future. Someway, somehow, he was going to see Melissa and get her to talk to him.

* * *

The serenity he had derived from moving back to the ranch had completely vanished, Wyatt realized a few nights later. He was in a particularly disgruntled mood. Actually, all of his moods were disgruntled in one way or another since he'd seen Melissa in the Hip Hop and she had cut him off so coldly. Despite his vow to see her again and get her to talk to him, he hadn't come up with any feasible way of doing it. Oh, he could walk into the café again, but what would that accomplish? As well as the waitresses, there were bound to be customers. Forcing a public meeting would be wasted effort and probably even cause Melissa to become angry with him. That was one thing in his favor, he felt: Melissa hadn't seemed angry that day in the Hip Hop, merely stunned.

Well, he'd been stunned, too. If he hadn't been, he probably would have handled the situation much better than he had.

What was so frustrating was that he knew so little about Melissa's status. Where did she live? He'd tried to get her telephone number from information and was told it was unlisted. There was a listed number for the café, but he recalled how public the phone there was.

Pacing and stewing, he finally had an idea. Was it possible that Nan Avery still had the same phone number that he had called so many times when Melissa was living with her in California?

He eyed the telephone almost cautiously, pondering this course of action. If he lucked out and actually got to speak to Nan, how would Melissa take it?

But if he didn't do something, he and Melissa could both grow old living within thirty-five miles of each other and never have a conversation.

Drawing a deep breath, he strode to the phone and dialed the number that was etched in his brain. It rang once, twice, three times. Wyatt held his breath.

"Hello?" a female voice said.

THE RANCHER TAKES A WIFE

"Mrs. Avery? Nan?"

"Yes. Who's this?"

"Wyatt North, Mrs. Avery."

"Wyatt who?"

"North. I'm calling from my ranch in Montana. You must remember me."

"Wyatt North. Of course I remember you. How are you?"

"Just fine, Mrs. Avery. How are you?"

"Well, I don't like complaining, but I can't really say I'm fine. Terrible bursitis in my shoulders, and I had my gall bladder removed last spring. I still have the same symptoms that I had before surgery, so I have to wonder about the medical profession. Also—"

Wyatt cut in. "I'm sorry to hear you're not well, Mrs. Avery. The reason I called was to ask you a few questions about Melissa."

"About Melissa? Well, good heavens, she lives in Whitehorn. Why don't you just ask her whatever it is you want to know?"

"It's like this, Mrs. Avery. I only moved back to the area myself a few weeks ago. I'd like to call Melissa, but I've been told she has an unlisted telephone number. Do you have it?"

"Yes, of course I have it. Have you got something to write with?"

"Right here, Mrs. Avery."

"Her number is 555-2888. I'm sure she'll be pleased to hear from you. I wasn't too happy about her moving back to Whitehorn, you understand, but there was no stopping her once she had the financial means to do so. She'd been saving up to go back to Whitehorn for years. I couldn't understand why she wanted to go back there, since California is so wonderful. But she really thought her father would come back one day. Well, I guess you heard that he'd never left. At least I had the sense to keep up on that insurance policy. Now that there's a death certificate I'm finally getting some money out of these bureaucrats."

Wyatt was listening with one ear as he stared down at the number he'd written on a small pad...Melissa's number. His heart was in his throat, but he had to ask one more question. "Do you have her address, too, Mrs. Avery?"

"If you want to see her, Wyatt, just go to the Hip Hop Café. She lives in the apartment on the second floor."

"And she works at the café?"

"Works at it? She owns it, Wyatt, and she lives for it. She rarely dates and spends too much time working. She keeps trying to get me to come for a visit. Can you believe that she has plans for a funeral service when the law releases Charlie's remains? Guess they're doing tests or something. Anyway, I told Melissa not to expect me to be there. That long trip? Oh my no, my health just wouldn't permit it. Anyhow, tell me what you've been doing since we left Whitehorn."

It hit Wyatt like a ton of bricks: Melissa hadn't told her mother anything about their past. Nan didn't know about his marriage, that he'd been living in Helena or anything else of his history.

"It's a long, dull story, Mrs. Avery, and I really have to get off the phone for now."

"Well, call me again sometime and we'll have a nice long chat."

"I'll try to do that. Thanks for talking to me."

"Say hello to Melissa for me."

"Will do. Goodbye, Mrs. Avery."

After hanging up, Wyatt fell into the nearest chair. His pulse was beating a mile a minute. Melissa didn't work at the Hip Hop Café, she owned it. And she lived above it, in an apartment. He had her telephone number in his hand, which was utterly amazing. After fretting and fuming for over a week, one telephone call to California had cleared up all of his questions.

Now all he had to do was pick a time to call Melissa.

Or would it be better to just knock on her door?

Three

After thinking about it, Wyatt decided against calling Melissa. She could hang up and that would be that. He planned another course of action.

Around nine-thirty on Wednesday evening, he drove to town and parked on the street a short distance from the Hip Hop. A telephone call to the café—he had no idea who had answered—had resulted in his receiving information on the café's hours: Melissa would be through working at ten.

Now that he had something concrete to go on, he wasn't nearly as keyed up as he'd been before. They were both adults and he had always known she was intelligent. Surely she'd had time to recover from the shock of him walking into the café without warning, and would permit a discussion between them.

Laying his head back while he waited for the last few customers to leave and Melissa to lock up for the night, Wyatt let his mind wander. His thoughts touched on high school, and the football games in which he'd scored well and become the hero of the hour. He smiled wryly, because what had been so crucially important in those days meant so little in the long haul. Those events and times were pleasant memories, nothing more. Kids in high school were only that—kids, with absolutely no idea of what adulthood signified. He had learned about it the hard way, and probably every other kid he'd gone to school with had gone that route as well.

Before running into Melissa, Wyatt had been planning on checking around to see if any of his old friends still lived in

the area. He would still do that, he thought, but later, after
he had made some headway with her.

He was damn lucky, he decided. Not in his personal life,
for God's sake. No one could have made a bigger mess of
personal relationships than he had. But because of some
smart, shrewd, hard-working ancestors, he would never
want for money, and he had the ranch, which he loved beyond description. Looking back, he wondered how he had
ever let Shannon keep him in Helena for six long years,
when every day he had ached to get back to the ranch.

It wasn't Shannon keeping you there, it was Timmy.
Wyatt sighed. His son, Timothy Wyatt, had held him in a
loveless marriage, not Shannon. Timmy was five now, and
Wyatt had demanded equal custody in the divorce proceed-
ings. Shannon had put up a fight on that point, until Wyatt
threatened to file for full custody, which would have meant
a court battle and too much publicity for her taste.

But other than his love for his son, his marriage had been
a sham and a day-by-day fight against misery. He was married, he had hurt Melissa beyond redemption and he really
had tried to make the best of things with Shannon.

No more. Not ever again. Discovering that Shannon was
playing around on the side had been the biggest blessing of
his life. He hadn't been angry, he'd been relieved. Caught
red-handed, she'd had no choice but to agree to an amica-
ble divorce. Daddy's career, you know.

In the third year of his marriage, Wyatt's father had died.
He'd tried then to get Shannon to move to the ranch. Her
refusal had been coldly put and final. Helena was her home
and where the action was. Bury herself on a ranch in the
middle of nowhere? *"Forget it, Wyatt. I wouldn't even
consider it."*

Now he was glad she had refused, because the ranch
wasn't tainted with any sordid memories.

Wyatt's gaze wandered and his thoughts moved on. The
town had changed in six years, grown a great deal. He
wasn't parked directly in front of the Hip Hop, but rather

at the curb of the vacant lot directly abutting Melissa's property. It was a good lot, he thought, noticing the For Sale sign on it. Amity Lane was a good street. Over the years he had developed an interest in real-estate investments and owned several nice parcels of land that he felt could only go up in value. This lot could be a smart investment. Searching the glove compartment for a piece of paper, he wrote down the telephone number that he could barely make out on the sign.

Then he forget the lot and everything else. The lights had just gone out in the Hip Hop. His heart began a faster beat. He could see the outside staircase to the building's second floor, and any minute now Melissa would be coming out to go to her apartment.

But ten minutes later he was frowning and wondering what she was doing in that dark café. Glancing to the upstairs windows, which were lighted, it dawned on him that there must be an inside staircase.

Okay, North, this is it, he told himself, rubbing his mouth in a burst of anxiety. He sat there another few minutes to calm his racing pulse. She could slam the door in his face, but would she? His feelings for her had never died; maybe she still cared for him in some small way, despite the pain he'd inflicted on her six years ago.

Taking a deep breath, he got out of his pickup and quietly closed the door. He had never been a fearful man, but right then he felt as though a band was around his chest, tightening with every breath. Was it fear, he wondered, or excitement? Unquestionably he was excited over seeing Melissa again, even for a moment, if that was all she allowed.

He climbed the stairs, a long flight of wood steps with a wooden railing. There was a small light burning next to the door. On the landing he stopped, hearing music from within the apartment. Nostalgia hit him. He had forgotten Melissa's collection of Billie Holliday records, which she had valued highly even though she and everyone else had been bopping to rock-and-roll rhythms at school dances.

There was a window in the door and he moved closer to peer into the apartment. The entry was also a laundry room, he saw, and beyond that was the kitchen. His heart skipped a beat when Melissa momentarily appeared in the doorway between laundry and kitchen. She was wearing a blue robe.

Swallowing nervously, he rapped on the door.

Inside, Melissa became very still. No one knocked on her door at this time of night. Peeking cautiously around the kitchen doorframe, she saw a man's silhouette. "Wyatt," she whispered with a sinking sensation, though she was identifying him from form alone. But she *knew* it was him. For a minute she couldn't think.

He rapped again. "Melissa?"

She drew a shaky breath. "Who is it? Who's there?"

"Wyatt. Please open the door."

A crazy thrill shot through her body, alarming her. He was married and he had hurt her, and why in God's name would she feel anything but revulsion for him?

Stay calm, she told herself. Apparently he was going to have to be told how distasteful she found a late-night visit, and probably a few other things as well.

Entering the laundry room, she crossed to the door, unlocked it and opened it a few inches. "What do you want, Wyatt?" The light near the door revealed his handsome face and his eyes, which she had once used to gauge his moods. A dark, chocolate brown, Wyatt's eyes had always silently spoken his thoughts. Right now they contained an impassioned plea.

"Just some conversation. A few minutes of your time. Please let me come in."

She looked away. "We have nothing to talk about. Why are you doing this?"

"Melissa, please don't send me away." Her hair was loose and he could see the hairbrush in her hand. Standing this close to her was a sweet kind of torture. He had loved her so much—her laughter, her kisses—and as easily as striking a match it could all be ignited again. On his side, anyway.

"I only want to talk," he said quietly, which was the truth, for now. But if she refused even that small concession, any other hopes for the two of them had no chance at all.

What he wanted to do, Melissa thought unhappily, was apologize in person for marrying another woman. Did she want to hear that? Could she bear hearing it? What difference would another apology make, anyhow?

"Wyatt, I'm tired. I work long hours, and . . . I'm tired."

"Then you're not going to let me come in?"

The saddened, disappointed look on his face tweaked Melissa's innate generosity. She had never really hated anyone in her life, and while she'd told herself for years that she despised Wyatt because of what he'd done to her, it was obvious that she didn't despise him at all. He was still Wyatt, the boy and then the man she had loved with all her heart and soul. Cruelty wasn't in her nature, and she could be only so hard.

She stepped back and opened the door wider. "Come in. But only for a few minutes."

Enough relief invaded Wyatt's system to make him feel light-headed. "Thanks, Melissa. You won't regret it."

That was a debatable point, she thought while leading him to her living room. "Sit down, if you like."

"After you."

Neither of them sat. They stood there, quite some distance apart, and looked nervous. Wyatt gave a sickly grin. "I had so much lined up to say to you, and now I can't think of what it was."

"Try," she said coolly.

He took a slow, uneven breath and pretended interest in her living room. "You've done a lot work in here. This is nice."

"It's comfortable," she agreed. Obviously he wasn't going to sit unless she did, and she was feeling embarrassed and out of place in her own home with both of them standing there so awkwardly. Moving to the sofa, she perched on a cushion. Wyatt sat on a chair.

He had filled out, she realized. He'd never been skinny, but there'd been a youthful angularity to his body that was missing now. Not that he was fat. He looked just about perfect, in fact, which she found discomfiting. He shouldn't look perfect. He should look . . . married.

He smiled at her, and she didn't know whether to laugh or cry over the jump in her pulse rate because of that marvelous smile. Fortunately one's pulse rate didn't show, and her expression became deliberately cooler.

"What did you want to talk to me about?" she asked, rather brusquely.

Wyatt raised one booted foot to rest on his other knee. "Have you heard about my divorce?"

Melissa's eyes widened. "When did that happen?"

Wyatt cleared his throat. "Actually, it's in progress. It won't be final for a few more weeks."

Melissa's mouth was suddenly dry as dust. Surely he wasn't thinking that his divorce would mean something to her, like maybe she would be glad to hear about it. She wasn't. There was at least one child involved, and having grown up as an "abandoned" child—other people's opinion, not hers—she hated the idea of Wyatt abandoning his children just because he and his wife couldn't get along. Unless he had them at the ranch with him.

Still, she knew now why he was here. Did he actually have the gall to think there could ever be anything between *them* again?

"Melissa, I never stopped...missing you," he said softly.

She got to her feet. "That's unfortunate for you, Wyatt. I stopped missing you about six years ago. Now, if you'll excuse me?"

Wyatt got up slowly. "You don't understand. I'd like to tell you everything."

"I don't want to hear it, Wyatt." She didn't like him very much right now, but even upset with him as she was, something inside of her was responding to his good looks—his long, lean body and his eyes. *Damn* his eyes for being so expressive. "Wyatt, we are not going to be friends," she said.

"You were always special to me," he began.

"Yeah, right," she said coldly. "You proved *how* special, Wyatt, so please don't lay any phony lines on me."

Color rose in his face. "That's one of the things I'd like to discuss with you."

"No, I don't think so. I really have no interest in the past." She thought a moment, remembering that she had an *enormous* interest in the past—but only where it concerned her father. Her and Wyatt's "past" had come to a screeching halt six years ago.

She became aware of his gaze on her robe and defiantly tugged the sash tighter. "Go home, Wyatt. There's nothing for you here."

"Nothing at all, Melissa? Not even friendship?" He didn't want only friendship with her. She was beautiful and bright and he had never stopped loving her. True, she wasn't the same sweet, malleable girl of his memory. Her air of independence and self-reliance was obvious. But just being in the same room with her made his blood run faster.

"You never married," he said softly.

"That's right, I never married. But don't make the mistake of thinking it had anything to do with you." She was getting nervous again. "Wyatt... please go. It's late and I have several things to do before bedtime." She began inching toward the doorway to the kitchen. Gratefully she registered the fact that he was following.

Turning her back on him, she passed through the kitchen and laundry room to open the outside door. Tucking the hairbrush into the pocket of her robe, she reached for the doorknob.

But she hadn't realized how close he was and nearly jumped out of her skin when she felt his hand in her hair. For the merest fraction of time she permitted the thrills to compound in her body. His fingers moving in her hair felt like heaven on earth.

Then she whirled around, showing him an angry face. "How dare you touch me like that?"

His eyes were dark and hooded. "You've never cut it. I'm glad."

"Of course I've cut it," she said sharply. "It would be down to my hips if I hadn't. That's not the point. You have no right to touch me. I know what you want, Wyatt, and it isn't going to happen."

"What do I want? If you know so much about it, tell me."

"Don't play coy, Wyatt. Please move back so I can open the door." He was crowding her, standing much too close, and she was finding normal breathing difficult.

But he was emboldened by the sexual tension between them and stayed where he was. "Will you go out with me?" he asked.

"No, absolutely not."

"Are you afraid of me, Melissa? Afraid of what I'm making you feel?"

She tried to scoff. "You have way too much ego, Wyatt. The only thing you're making me feel is uncomfortable."

"That's a lie. Don't you think a man knows when a woman is feeling all fluttery and excited because of him?"

Melissa's eyes suddenly blazed. "That's enough! How dare you come to my own home, act like I should be glad to see you, and then have the bloody gall to suggest . . . to suggest . . ." She couldn't say it. But he was talking about sex, damn him! As though she didn't have the strength of will to resist him.

She angrily poked him in the chest with her forefinger. "You might be in the process of a divorce, but you're still a married man in my book. Putting everything else aside, just the fact that you're still married would preclude any sort of foolishness between us. And what you're interpreting as fluttering and excitement is incredulity that you'd have the brass to come here in the first place. I don't want to be your friend, Wyatt North. I don't want—''

Her words stopped abruptly because his mouth was suddenly on hers. Sputtering, she pushed against him. But his hands were cradling her head and holding it right where he wanted it. His lips moved on hers, gently, then roughly, then gently again. She thought she might faint from shock and fury, when she'd never fainted in her life. But she was suffering from waves of darkness and a sensation of lifeless limbs, which had to be signs of an encroaching fainting spell.

Her lips felt swollen and softly sensual when he finally stopped kissing them and raised his head to look into her eyes. ''I didn't intend doing that when I came here tonight,'' he whispered. ''But I'm not sorry about it. Melissa, you can deny it till hell freezes over, but there'll always be something between us. What I did to you can never be undone. God, if only it could. I never expected to see you again, and apparently you never expected to see me again. But it happened, and I'm not going to lose you a second time.''

''And I have nothing to say about it?'' She had tried to speak forcefully, angrily, but her voice sounded weak and fragile.

His hands gentled on her head, his fingers twining into her hair. ''You have everything to say about it. All I'm asking for is a chance. See me, Melissa. I'm not even asking for forgiveness, just a chance.''

''Hurt me once, that's your fault. Hurt me twice, that's mine,'' she said huskily. ''No, Wyatt, I'm not giving you anything, least of all a chance to prove again what a bastard you really are. And guess what? I do forgive you. But forgiving isn't forgetting, and that's something I'll never be able to do.''

His gaze roamed her features. "You kissed me back."

"You're not going to argue me into anything, so you may as well stop trying."

"Do you really expect me to walk out of here and pretend nothing happened tonight?"

"Nothing did, except in your own mind."

For a minute there, when he'd been kissing her, he'd felt her approval, her acceptance, her response, and now he felt her slipping away, backing off. "Melissa, you mean so much to me," he whispered raggedly. "Don't be hard, please. You were never hard. You were—"

"Stupid," she put in bitterly. "Take your hands off me, Wyatt. I'm sure you can find any number of women who would just love to fall into bed with you. I'm not one of them and I never will be."

He realized that he wasn't going to change her outlook tonight. But whether she would admit it or not, they had taken a step toward a relationship. He was going to have to be very patient with her and hope that time and tenderness would reduce the pain of the past.

But she was badly mistaken on one point. "Do you honestly believe that all I want from you is sex? You're right about there being a lot of willing women out there, Melissa. That's not why I'm here."

"From where I'm standing right now, it's sort of hard to tell," she retorted. "I stopped believing in fairy tales a long time ago, Wyatt, and what you just said sounds like one. You kissed me. Look me in the eye and tell me it wasn't a sexual kiss."

He looked directly into her eyes for a long moment, but he couldn't lie about it. "It was a sexual kiss. But try to remember I didn't come here with any such thing in mind. It just happened." Dropping his hands from her hair, he took one backward step. "All I can do is apologize. I'm sorry."

"I'll just bet you are," Melissa muttered. At least he'd given her space enough to open the door, which she did promptly. "Good night and goodbye. And please don't do this again. The next time I won't open the door, Wyatt. I mean it. I think our best course is strict avoidance. I'd appreciate your cooperation in that effort."

He shook his head. "That I can't give you."

Melissa's mouth thinned. "So you're planning to harass me at every opportunity? I won't stand for it, Wyatt. If necessary I'll file a complaint with the sheriff."

"Oh, great," Wyatt groaned. "Well, I guess that says it all, doesn't it? Don't worry, I won't 'harass' you again." He stepped out onto the landing and looked at the sky. "The weather really turned in the last few days," he said. "Fall's on its way. Looks like we're in for some rain." His eyes dropped from the cloudy night sky to her. "Have a good life, Melissa. I wish you the best of everything." His trip down the stairs was accomplished with as much dignity as he could muster.

Melissa shut the door, then leaned her back against it and closed her eyes. She felt choked up and her stomach ached. Actually, her entire body ached. The last twenty or so minutes had been an unbelievable ordeal. And regardless of her threat to register a legal complaint should Wyatt bother her again, and his display of resigned defeat, she was positive he'd find a way to see her. Probably when she least expected it, and she'd be off guard again.

Snapping off lights as she went to her bedroom, Melissa sat on the edge of the bed and rocked back and forth with her arms around herself. How could he be so crass? His divorce wasn't even final and he was already out looking for another woman.

Wait a minute, she thought with a frown. It didn't take long for Montana residents to obtain a divorce. Was it possible that Wyatt had broken up with his wife *after* he'd learned about her return to Whitehorn?

The speculation was horrifying, and after a few moments Melissa ridiculed her own wild imagination. "Enough of that," she mumbled, getting up to take her nightly shower.

Then, standing under the spray, it all caught up with her, and she broke down and cried. Sobbing with both the shower water and tears streaming down her face, she gave in to anger and called Wyatt a whole slew of foul names. Every one that she knew came spewing out of her mouth. Standing in the shower and swearing like a sailor was pure idiocy, but it was also healing, and when she finally turned off the water and got out to dry off, she felt much calmer.

Slipping into a fresh nightgown, she turned off the lights and crawled into bed. Her first thought as she lay down was that he'd kissed her. He'd kissed her and she hadn't scratched out his eyes or kicked him in the shins. Instead, she'd stood there and *let* him kiss her. Not only that, she'd kissed him back.

"You damn fool," she mumbled to herself. "What would a man have to do to you before you wouldn't open your door for him at ten-thirty at night?"

Her mood changed, becoming very sad and broken-hearted. Never would she forget Wyatt's telephone call six years ago. She had been baking cookies and reading a marketing-class assignment at the same time. With a batch in the oven, she was at the kitchen table with the marketing text-book when the phone rang. She'd smiled. This was usually the time of day Wyatt called.

"Hello," she said cheerfully.

"Hello, Melissa."

"I knew it was you. How are you?"

"Uh... fine, I guess."

This was not the Wyatt she was accustomed to hearing on the phone. This Wyatt was very upset and down in the dumps. "What's wrong?" *she asked gently. Her thoughts went to Simon North, who'd been ill for so long.* "Is it your father?"

"Dad? No... no. Dad's fine. He's not fine, but he's no worse. This isn't about Dad."

A chill went up Melissa's spine. Never had she heard the lifeless, defeated tone in Wyatt's voice she was hearing now.

"What is it, Wyatt? Tell me." It frightened her to catch what sounded like a sob in her ear. *"Are you crying?"*

He cleared his throat. *"There's something I have to tell you. I thought about just writing a letter, but I couldn't do that to you. Melissa, do you believe I love you?"*

"Of course I believe it. Wyatt, you're scaring me."

And then he blurted it out, his words running together. *"I got a girl pregnant and I'm going to marry her."*

She was struck dumb, unable to grasp what he'd said.

"Melissa? Did you hear me? Do you understand?"

She was beginning to. While she'd been holding down a full-time job and going to classes at night, while she'd been turning down every young man who did more than smile at her, while she'd been worrying and planning and living for the day when she could finally leave her mother alone and return to Montana to marry him, Wyatt had been sleeping with another woman.

She suddenly felt old beyond her years, and shriveled. *"I understand,"* she whispered.

"No, you don't really," Wyatt groaned. *"How could you? Melissa . . ."*

"Please. There's nothing more to say. I really don't care to hear the details. Goodbye, Wyatt." She hung up. He called back. She hung up again, then took the phone off the hook.

In her bed she huddled into a ball of misery. Wyatt had written several letters, which she had burned unopened. Now he had the audacity to try and pick up where they had left off. Didn't he have a conscience?

Even if she wanted to leave Whitehorn to avoid Wyatt, she couldn't—not until her father's murder had been solved. Then . . . well, she'd cross that bridge when she came to it. Her business was doing well and Whitehorn was home. She had never liked California, and she wouldn't have any idea where to go from here.

Besides, the thought of allowing Wyatt to chase her out of the area raised her hackles. To hell with him, she thought vehemently. If he continued to pester her, he was going to find out that she had learned how to fight for her rights as a human being.

Four

Melissa carefully studied the blueprints that had just arrived in the mail from the Billings architect whom she'd hired to draw up a plan for the café's expansion. The vacant lot next door was for sale, and had been since her return to Whitehorn. She had spoken to the owner a few weeks back, and the price was well within reason, though she hadn't yet made an offer to purchase. The share she had received from her father's life-insurance policy had paid off her mortgage on the Hip Hop. Even though the café was making a nice profit, Melissa was putting as much of it as she could into a savings account each month, so buying that lot and constructing the addition she was admiring on the blueprint would require much more money than she had. She had two options, she figured—borrow from the bank or take on a partner. The thought of a partner made her uneasy, so she geared herself up for a visit to Paul Rodell, the loan officer at the local bank.

She made an appointment, and a day later put on a beige linen business suit for the occasion. Her hair was neatly arranged in a fashionable bun at her nape. For jewelry she wore small gold earrings and her watch. Her mirror told her she looked quite smart and like a serious businesswoman, which was the effect she wanted.

Satisfied with her appearance, she took her briefcase, drove to the bank, parked her car and went in. Paul Rodell had a small office off the lobby, and Melissa was shown into it immediately after speaking briefly to a secretary. The young woman introduced her. ''Mr. Rodell, Miss Melissa

Avery." A tall, nice-looking man with thinning, light brown hair rose from behind the desk. "Hello, Miss Avery."

Melissa offered her hand across the desk. "Hello, Mr. Rodell. Thank you for seeing me."

"Seeing clients is my job, Miss Avery. Please sit down."

"Thank you." There were two upholstered chairs in front of Rodell's desk. Melissa chose the one on the right and set her briefcase on the floor beside it. She smiled. "Since you're the bank's loan officer, you have to know why I'm here."

Rodell gave her an acknowledging nod. "You own the Hip Hop Café, don't you? I've eaten there a few times and have always found the food and service head and shoulders above any other restaurant in Whitehorn."

"That's very nice to hear. Business is good, Mr. Rodell, so good that I'm planning to expand. The lot next door is for sale and I hired an architect to draw up plans. I have them with me." Melissa reached for her briefcase.

"Before we get into that, Miss Avery, let me explain bank policy. We do not make loans on undeveloped land. In order for anyone to secure a loan for the construction of any sort of building, they must own the land free and clear."

"Oh." This was an unexpected blow. Melissa thought for a moment. "If I manage to buy the land on my own, then I would be eligible for a construction loan?"

"Actually, that's not quite the correct terminology for what you would need. A construction loan is normally a temporary loan and is paid back upon completion of the building. Spec home builders use this form of loan all the time. Then they sell the house and the new owner takes out a long-term loan, which pays off the construction loan. Do you follow me?"

Melissa cleared her throat. "I wasn't familiar with the different types of loans, but yes, I understand." How on earth would she raise the money to buy the land for cash? "Mr. Rodell, could I borrow on the existing building to buy the land, then . . ." She stopped, because Paul Rodell was shaking his head.

"I'm afraid that would put you in an overextended position, Miss Avery. You would end up with two loans on virtually the same business."

Melissa frowned. "Yes, that's true." She felt rather stupid right then. She had thought everything was pretty well lined up, and in reality nothing was.

The loan officer leaned forward and folded his hands on his desk. "It's really quite simple, Miss Avery. If you're truly serious about this, my advice is to go ahead and buy the land. If it takes you some time to pay for it, the bank will still be here and willing to discuss an expansion loan."

His smile was very open, very friendly, Melissa noted. His age was probably around thirty-four, thirty-five. He was an attractive, pleasant man, and if she was any judge of males, she was on the receiving end of Paul Rodell's admiration. She had dated no one since returning to Whitehorn, and she couldn't help glancing at his left hand, which was ringless. Another quick glance around his office revealed no family pictures. Dare she come right out and ask if he was married?

Why not? she thought recklessly, though doing it with a little subtlety would make a better impression.

She smiled warmly. "Do you and Mrs. Rodell live in Whitehorn proper?"

Paul looked very pleased. "I'm not married, Miss Avery."

"Please call me Melissa."

"Thank you, I will." Paul leaned back in his chair. "So, do you think you'll go ahead with the lot purchase?"

"Definitely. I'll speak to the owner today."

"Good, glad to hear it. Here, let me give you these." From a desk drawer he took out a sheaf of papers. "This is a loan application. From the questions contained in it, you'll be better apprised of what the bank requires from a loan applicant."

Melissa accepted the papers and tucked them into her briefcase. "Thank you. I appreciate your time and courtesy."

They both got up. "Well," Paul said with a dazzling smile. "It's been a real pleasure meeting you, Melissa."

"Thank you, Paul. The next time you stop by the Hip Hop, be sure and say hello. Maybe we can have coffee together sometime."

"If that's an invitation, consider it done."

Melissa left feeling both disappointed and elated. Obtaining a bank loan was not going to be a simple exercise, but she had not only learned the requirements, she had met a man she could like. Paul Rodell would be around for coffee, she was sure.

Wyatt was going to discover there were more fish in the sea than one, and it might be petty of her, but she wished she could be a fly on the wall when he heard that she was going out with another man. It was precisely what he deserved.

Wyatt shook hands with John Hendrix. John had Wyatt's cashier's check and Wyatt had the deed to the lot next to Melissa's building. The deal was final.

"Good doing business with you, John," Wyatt said over the handshake.

"Same here. Got any plans for that land?"

"Not at the present. I'll probably just sit on it for a few years and see what happens."

"Can't go wrong investing in real estate," John said.

"I feel the same way. Well, thanks again. I'd say we'll be seeing each other again, but since you're leaving the area, we probably won't."

Wyatt left the Hendrix home feeling good. He had gotten the lot dirt cheap, as John and his wife were selling everything they owned in Whitehorn to retire in Arizona. They were an older couple, very nice people, but because they were anxious to be on their way, they had set their prices below the current market rates. They already had a buyer for their house, so they would be leaving in a few weeks.

Whistling through his teeth, Wyatt got in his pickup and headed back to the ranch.

It was late afternoon before Melissa found the time to call the telephone number on the For Sale sign next door. "Hello, Mr. Hendrix. This is Melissa Avery. I called a few weeks ago about the price of your lot on Amity Lane. Do you remember my call?"

"Sure do, Miss Avery."

"I'm prepared now to make an offer, Mr. Hendrix. I could put ten thousand down and—"

"Miss Avery, the lot is already sold."

Stunned, Melissa fell silent. "Uh . . . when?"

"Just this morning."

"I missed it by a few hours?" Oh, damn, she groaned internally. What in God's name had made her think she was a businesswoman? Why hadn't she gone ahead and tied up that lot with a deposit, if nothing else? Now her expansion plans were in the ash can, and she had only herself to blame. "Would you mind telling me who bought it, Mr. Hendrix?"

"Well, guess he never said I should keep it a secret. It was Wyatt North. He owns a ranch outside of town. Maybe you know him."

"I know him," she said in a voice so weak it was barely audible. "Thank you, Mr. Hendrix." She hung up.

Melissa was so upset she didn't know where to put herself. She had made the call to Mr. Hendrix from her apartment, and she walked circles in her living room, trying to get her bearings. Why would Wyatt buy property in town? Had he somehow learned of her plans to expand the café and deliberately purchased the lot to deter her? But why would he do that?

Frowning, she tried to recall whom she might have mentioned her expansion plans to. She hadn't said anything to her staff about it, she knew, but what about some of the old friends she had run into? The Billings architect knew, of course, but who else? Oh damn, she thought. News traveled fast in Whitehorn and her plans were probably common knowledge.

This was a nightmare. It couldn't possibly be mere coincidence that Wyatt had bought the one parcel of land in all of Whitehorn that she wanted and needed. Why had she procrastinated on making Mr. Hendrix an offer? It should have been her first step in the process, certainly taken before she spent money on blueprints, which hadn't been inexpensive.

Maybe Wyatt thought he could use the land as leverage in their personal relationship. Instantly Melissa shook her head at that theory. In the first place, they had no personal relationship, and Wyatt was certainly smart enough to know blackmail wouldn't work with her.

Or he used to be. God only knew what kind of man he was these days. For that matter, had she ever really known him? Wouldn't she have sworn on a Bible at one time that he was the most honest, straightforward, loyal, kindhearted and trustworthy man who'd ever lived? And hadn't he proved how wrong that opinion had been?

What should she do? What *could* she do?

Wyatt told himself repeatedly to forget Melissa. And yet she constantly crept into his thoughts. She had definitely kissed him back that night in her apartment. Obviously the wound he'd inflicted six years ago had never healed, but she had still kissed him back. That was what he kept remembering—that kiss; her incredible scent; how her lips, soft and womanly, had yielded to his; the blue robe she'd been wearing; the way her hair had felt in his hands.

Would she really file a complaint if he paid her another visit?

Something within him said no, that she had merely used a threat out of desperation. Her pride was denying any warmth between them, and pride was a powerful influence on anyone. He knew all about pride; Shannon had all but destroyed his.

But that was over. He had survived six years of unhappiness and felt now like the trees must when their sap rose in the spring. Okay, call it what it was, he thought laughingly. He was horny, but not for just any woman. There was only one woman he wanted—Melissa Avery.

Now all he had to do was figure out a way to see her again without ticking her off.

The weather had indeed turned. The day was gloomy, with drizzling rain and a heavy cloud cover. Business at the café was slow after lunch, and Melissa couldn't sit still. "I'll be gone for a few hours," she called to Wanda on her way out.

She hadn't taken the time to go upstairs for a jacket, and she felt chilled clear through by the time she got in her car. Starting the motor, she turned on the heater. It would take a few minutes to warm up, but then the car would be comfortable for a drive.

A drive where? An immediate answer came to mind. Every week or so she drove out to the Laughing Horse Reservation to look at the spot where her father had been buried. It was cordoned off with yellow tape bearing the inscription, Crime Scene. No Trespassing. But she stood outside the tape and tried to imagine what had happened there so long ago.

Today, as chilly and damp as it was, she probably wouldn't get out of the car, she thought as she started the thirty-mile drive. But her mind was filled to bursting with questions about Wyatt's motive in buying that land, and since her other major concern was her father's murder, it only seemed natural to make another visit to the scene of the crime. One crime at a time was all she could attempt to

solve, she thought wryly, which might take her thoughts
away from Wyatt's treachery.

The only conclusion that made any sense about Wyatt
beating her to the punch on that property was that he had
found out she wanted it. So what did he think—or hope—
she would do about it—go to him? Try to buy it from him?
Beg a little, grovel a little?

The mere thought made her nauseous. He had her over a
barrel. He was even more deceitful than she'd thought, and
already she thought him the worst kind of beast there was.

Damn it! Why had she let him kiss her? Why hadn't she
thrown a fit—yelled and screeched and fought like a tiger?
Instead, mealymouthed and acting as if she were completely brainless, she had stood there and let him play with
her hair.

There was little traffic on the road to the reservation, but
she kept to the speed limit because of the wet asphalt. She
turned on the radio, then found it intrusive to her present
state of mind and turned it off again. Sighing, she wondered why everything in life was such a problem. She had
tried almost desperately to talk her mother into moving back
to Whitehorn with her. Nan had refused and wouldn't even
discuss the possibility. Her mother's show of independence
didn't stop Melissa from worrying about her, however. The
only good thing in her own life at the present was the café,
and she wondered how she had lucked out with that success.

Well, luck really had very little to do with it, Melissa had
to admit. She had worked nonstop for weeks after buying
the place, painting, wallpapering, decorating and cleaning.
Everything in the entire building had been coated with about
twenty years' worth of grime. Actually, she had gutted the
restaurant and started from scratch. The kitchen equipment was old, but most of it had only needed a scrubbing
down. She had added a few modern conveniences such as a
microwave and a convection oven. But there were really no
secrets to running a successful restaurant. As Paul Rodell

had pointed out, the Hip Hop provided good food and service, which were what patrons were looking for in an eating establishment.

Passing the reservation's boundary line, Melissa continued on to the area where her father's remains had been found. Changing her mind about not getting out, she left the motor idling and walked from the road toward the taped-off area. The police, the sheriff's department and the FBI kept coming back whenever they got a chance—though a twenty-odd-year-old murder wasn't a high priority. Nobody was out here today, though. It seemed impossible that no real clues had been discovered, but then, as Judd had said, twenty-seven years was a long time. The changing seasons alone would have destroyed footprints, tire tracks and deteriorative items such as a dropped matchbook or a piece of paper.

Melissa felt the sting of tears. She never failed to shed a few when she came out here. Most of her life she had been told that Charlie Avery had deserted his family, and it was such an abysmal departure from the truth that she couldn't help crying.

Finally, feeling chilled to the bone and damp from the misty rainfall, Melissa returned to the warmth of her car. Deciding to return to town the long way, via a road that would take her past the Kincaid Ranch, she made several turns and eventually left the reservation.

She was several miles past the Kincaid spread when she felt the bump, bump, bump of a flat tire. "Oh, hell," she groaned, and pulled over to the side of the road. Her tires were practically new, so she must have picked up a nail somewhere. "Damn!" she exclaimed when she got out and saw that her right rear tire was as flat as a pancake.

She wasn't dressed for changing a tire in this weather. Someone would come along, she told herself, shivering and returning to the car. After a minute she got out again, raised the hood—a distress signal—and hurried back to the heater's warmth.

* * *

Wyatt shook hands with Dugin Kincaid, the only surviving son of Jeremiah Kincaid. Jeremiah had been a strong, influential rancher in the area. He had died a few months back in a bizarre accident: he'd slipped in the shower, hit his head and drowned in his own bath water. Jeremiah had been one of Simon North's few friends, as unlikely as the liaison had been. Wyatt's visit to the Kincaid Ranch had arisen out of a sense of duty to his father's and Jeremiah's memory. Personally, he had never cared for Jeremiah, whom Wyatt had always felt to be too hard on not only his hired help, but on his son, Dugin.

"It was good of you to come by, Wyatt," Dugin said over the handshake. Just as Wyatt hadn't been particularly fond of Jeremiah Kincaid, he had never really liked Dugin, who had always struck him as soft and effeminate. But that didn't prevent him from sympathizing with the man over the death of his father.

"Just paying my respects, Dugin. I apologize for missing the funeral." The truth was, the news of Jeremiah's death hadn't reached him in Helena until some time after the funeral.

"You missed my wedding, too," Dugin pointed out.

"Yes, yes, I did. What's it been—about a year now?"

Dugin nodded, and the expression on his face didn't impress Wyatt as being that of a happily married man. As if on cue, a woman flitted into the room. "Dugin, darling, why didn't you tell me we had a guest?"

"Sorry, Mary Jo. This is Wyatt North. Wyatt, my wife, Mary Jo."

Mary Jo held out her hand with a brilliant smile. "So happy to meet you, Wyatt. I like knowing all of Dugin's friends."

Wyatt took her hand. "Nice meeting you, Mrs. Kincaid." Actually, he could hardly believe his eyes. Mary Jo Kincaid didn't look like a rancher's wife, at least like none that he'd ever met. Her hairdo was so perfect it looked unnatural. Her face was layered with makeup, well done but still very obvious. She was wearing a frilly flowered dress and high-heeled shoes in a shade of pink that matched some of the flowers in the fabric of her dress. Her fingernails were outlandishly long and painted a bright pink.

But it was her eyes that bothered and embarrassed Wyatt. He had met gushing, overdressed women before, but Mary Jo's eyes were sending him messages that could only be described as flirtatious. And right in front of her husband.

He pulled his hand back. "I was just leaving, Mrs. Kincaid. Dugin, I'll be seeing you around." He started for the door.

"Please don't rush off," Mary Jo said in a sugary-sweet, little-girl voice.

Wyatt paused with his hand on the knob. "Thanks, but I really have to be going."

"In this rain? At least stay until it stops. We'll have coffee."

Dugin wasn't saying a word, Wyatt noticed. "Some other time, Mrs. Kincaid. Goodbye."

Mary Jo rushed to the door before Wyatt could close it behind him. "Call me Mary Jo, Wyatt," she called as he dashed through the rain to his pickup.

He pretended not to have heard, climbed in and hastily closed the door. That woman was a pickle short of a full barrel, he thought, cranking the key to start the motor. Poor Dugin. Where in hell had he found her?

Mary Jo closed the door and went to a window to watch Wyatt's pickup leaving the compound. Her eyes narrowed menacingly. She hated what had just happened. In fact, she hated Wyatt North. Who in hell did he think he was, snubbing her the way he had?

At that moment she became her real self, Lexine Baxter. Raising her hand and pointing her forefinger at the back of Wyatt's pickup, she said, "Pow!" in an undertone, as though she'd been firing a gun at the truck. She had owned

a gun once, she recalled. She had bought it during her years
as a prostitute, after she had been severely beaten up by a
John.

A cold smile twisted her lips. Everyone in this whole
damn area would probably die from shock if they knew who
she really was, especially if they had any inkling of the life
she had lived after leaving Whitehorn.

The smile became confident, no one would ever know.
She was much too clever for the horde of hicks who occupied the town and surrounding countryside.

Driving away, Wyatt thought about his father's and Jeremiah Kincaid's longtime friendship. They couldn't have
been more different from each other. Jeremiah had been a
big, gruff, physical man, while Simon had been seeker of
knowledge, a savant, a man who had studied and pondered
the works of the great philosophers. The only physical activity that didn't sap Simon's fragile strength had been fish-
ing, and perhaps it was a common affection for the sport
that had been his and Jeremiah Kincaid's connection.

At any rate, Wyatt had felt the need to call upon Dugin
and pay his respects, which he'd done. After meeting Mary
Jo, however, he was glad it was over.

It was raining, all right—coming down in sheets. He noticed also that fog was gathering in low points of the terrain, and he switched on his headlights. He was almost upon
the car at the side of the road before he saw it. Its hood was
up, which meant car trouble.

Immediately he steered to the side of the road, pulling to
a stop behind the disabled maroon sedan. The windows of
the car were steamed over. Obviously the driver was running the motor for warmth.

Wyatt got out and hurried to the vehicle, bending over to
peer into the driver's window. Seeing Melissa gave him a jolt
that caused a peculiar reaction: he laughed.

Grim lipped, she rolled down the window a crack. "I'm
so glad to be of amusement to you, Mr. North. What in hell

are you doing on this road? Your ranch is clear across the valley."

"Sorry," he said, though it was tough to maintain a straight face. This was some coincidence, the kind of unexpected situation that made one ponder fate. "What's the problem?"

"I have a flat tire. Right rear. I could change it, but I left without a jacket and I'm wearing a dress." Why hadn't she frozen her butt off and changed the tire herself? Accepting help from Wyatt went against her grain. Well, she wasn't *completely* helpless. Grabbing the keys from the ignition, which shut down the motor, she pushed the door open and got out.

"Hey, you don't have to get wet. What're you doing?"

"I'm going to open the trunk."

"You might find this hard to believe, but I've unlocked a few trunks in my lifetime."

"Don't be purposely irritating, Wyatt." She marched to the back of her car. "You're the last person I would have imagined coming along," she fumed.

"Sorry," he said. "Want me to leave so you can wait for the next passerby?"

"Damn, you're annoying," she snapped. "Deliberately, I suspect."

"You're much too suspicious, sweetheart." The trunk was by then wide open. "Okay, there's the spare and the jack. Now why don't you get your pretty tail back in your car and get the heater going again? Unless you'd like to wait in my truck while I change that tire."

"My car will do just fine, thank you very much." Even though she had been waiting for assistance from someone, Wyatt being that someone was extremely aggravating. It was also unbelievable. How many people lived in the county— twenty thousand? Thirty? The odds of one particular, vexing person being her rescuer had to be astronomical. Shivering almost violently, she dashed for the driver's door and climbed in to restart the car and the heater.

Wyatt was still near the trunk, checking out the spare and the jack. If that spare just happened to be flat, too, Melissa would have to ride back to town with him. This was an opportunity to spend a little time with her, and if he let it pass, it might be an awfully long time before another one presented itself.

Without a dram of guilt, he took his jackknife from his jeans, opened it and carefully pushed the razor-sharp tip into Melissa's spare just under the rim. The air whooshed out of the tire.

He walked around to the driver's window again and rapped on it. She opened it a crack. "I hate being the bearer of bad news, Melissa, but your spare is flat, too."

"It couldn't be!"

Wyatt stared into her eyes with an innocent, forthright expression. "Melissa, your spare is as flat as your right rear tire."

"That's impossible. My tires are practically new, including the spare." Groaning, she held her forehead in her left hand. "I don't believe this."

"Good thing it was a friend that came along, 'cause you're going to have to ride back to town with me."

Her head jerked up. "And, of course, we both know how safe a woman is with you, don't we?"

"Sure do," he said solemnly, as though he hadn't even heard her sarcasm. "Come on, Melissa. It's getting dark. Lock up your car and let's get going. We'll send a mechanic back for the car."

Rain was dripping from the brim of his hat, she saw. His shirt and vest were wet. He had to be uncomfortable. She sighed. "All right." What choice did she have? Wyatt was the only one who had come along, and she couldn't refuse his assistance and risk the possibility of staying out here all night.

He lowered the hood and shut the trunk while she locked the car doors. Taking her purse, she got out and hurried to his pickup. It was colder than before, and raining hard. Her dress and underwear were damp and sticking to her body. She felt utterly miserable, especially about the situation.

They were about twenty miles from town. With every intention of stretching their time together to the maximum, Wyatt drove slowly. "How come you're way out here?" he asked.

Melissa was staring straight ahead, sitting stiffly, unwilling to give an inch where Wyatt was concerned, whether he'd rescued her or not. "I drove out to the reservation."

"Without a jacket in this rain?"

She sent him a scathing look. "I didn't plan on having my tires go flat." His handsome profile caused a reaction within herself she didn't like, so she quickly looked forward again. "How come *you're* way out here?"

"I was at the Kincaid Ranch, paying my respects to Dugin. Jeremiah and Dad used to fish together. It was just a courtesy call."

"I didn't realize you were so concerned with courtesy."

Wyatt grinned. "Be nice, Melissa. Think what might have happened if I hadn't come along."

"Yes, well, I do appreciate your stopping," she said grudgingly. She couldn't resist adding, "But why did it have to be you?"

"Fate? Predestination? Luck?"

"Oh, please," she said with obvious disgust. "It was just some weird coincidence."

"You call it coincidence if you want, but I'll stick with luck."

"You would."

After a few silent moments, Wyatt spoke in a deadly serious tone of voice. "Don't hate me, Melissa." Startled, she turned her head to look at him. "Hating someone is such a waste of time and energy," he said. "Especially when that someone suffered more than you did over the same incident."

"I doubt that."

"You're the only woman I've ever loved."

"How dare you say that! Your interpretation of love leaves something to be desired, and just what makes you think I would even want to hear such an abominable lie? Did you forget you married another woman?"

"Hardly. But did you ever for one moment think I *wanted* to marry another woman? God, I hope not. I did what I had to do, Melissa."

"Oh, come on. You *had* to sleep with another woman and make her pregnant? Wyatt, just drop it. I don't want to have this conversation. I *never* want to have this conversation."

"You'll never get past your hatred if we don't."

"Good God, I don't hate you. You mean nothing to me, can't you get that through your head?"

"I don't believe you."

She took an exasperated breath. "Only because you have an ego the size of Los Angeles. Did you actually think I would be glad to see you again? When I moved back here you were living in Helena. It never occurred to me that *you* might move back, too. Besides, you were married, so if we did happen to run into each other it wouldn't mean anything. I felt reasonably safe..."

"And now you don't. You know why you don't? It's because six years and a lot of mistakes didn't destroy what we had. Melissa, nothing has the power to destroy what we had. The second I saw you again I knew that to be a fact."

Melissa's head dropped to the seat back. "Oh, give me strength. Nothing I say makes the slightest dent in your macho confidence." She lifted her head to glare at him. "Listen closely. I have lived very well without you for six years, and I intend to live very well without you for the rest of my life. Is that concept too difficult for you to comprehend?"

"Not at all. It's just not the truth. You're lying to me and you're lying to yourself. Maybe you don't realize you're lying, but that's what you're doing."

Melissa's anger exploded. "You arrogant bastard! Where's your wife and child now? Did you get tired of married life and just walk off? Did you decide that—"

"Hey, just stop it!" Wyatt wheeled the truck to the side of the road and slapped the shifting lever into Park. He turned in the seat. "You don't have the slightest understanding of what my marriage was like. Maybe I deserved it, but the only reason I stayed in it for as long as I did was because of my son."

Melissa was staring at him. "Your... son."

"Yes, my son." Wyatt dug out his wallet and flipped it open. "Here's a picture of him."

Melissa was trembling. She didn't want to look at a picture of Wyatt's son, but she couldn't stop herself. Her gaze dropped to the wallet in Wyatt's hand, and she saw a handsome little boy with blond hair, brown eyes and an infectious grin.

"He—he's beautiful," she whispered, shaken to her soul.

"Yes, he is," Wyatt softly agreed. "His name is Timmy—Timothy Wyatt—and I'm getting equal custody in the divorce. I want him at the ranch with me during the summers. He'll be spending winters with his mother because of school, but I'll have him every other weekend and for alternating holidays."

He gave Melissa a rather hard look. "So you see, I didn't just walk away and forget my son. And I will never apologize for the divorce." His expression softened. "But I would like to tell you about it. There's so much I'd like to tell you."

Wyatt could see how the subject was affecting Melissa. She had covered her face with her hands, and he wasn't sure if she was crying. "You don't have to hear it now," he said gently. "Not now." Taking her hands, he pulled them away from her face. Moving closer to her, he put his arms around her and cradled her head to his chest. He closed his eyes and savored the sensation of holding her.

Then he tipped her chin and pressed his lips to hers. That was when Melissa came back to life. She jerked her head to the side, breaking the kiss. "No, Wyatt."

"Honey..."

"No!"

He looked at her for the longest time. The cab of the truck was shadowed and lit mostly by the dashboard lights. The wipers were rhythmically slapping the rain from the windshield. "Are you ever going to forgive me?" he asked sadly.

"I already told you you're forgiven," she replied, sounding weak and exhausted. "But I don't want you kissing me."

"You're afraid of—"

"Please don't start that again. Take me home, Wyatt."

He hesitated a moment, then slid back behind the wheel. They drove the last few miles to town in silence.

Five

Seeing that snapshot of Wyatt's son affected Melissa in unexpected ways. For one thing, she wondered if maybe she really had forgiven him. Twice she'd told him that she had already done so, but it hadn't been the truth, or at least not the whole truth. To be factual, if she *had* forgiven him during the last six years it had been on a part-time basis. Sometimes weeks had passed without her spirits taking a nosedive because something would remind her of Wyatt's perfidy, and she supposed now that those times could be construed as periods of forgiveness.

On the other hand, how could anyone truly forgive infidelity? She understood what had taken place six years ago better now than she had then, but still there was Wyatt's unfaithfulness to deal with.

And yet...there was Timmy. Even from a snapshot the little boy had touched Melissa's heart. Tender feelings for the child were influencing her attitude toward his father.

But why, if Wyatt had remained in an allegedly unhappy marriage for six years because of his son, had he suddenly decided on divorce? Was it because he had finally gotten wind of *her* return to Whitehorn?

The possibility was so destructive to Melissa's peace of mind that she couldn't allow herself to dwell on it.

The morning after Wyatt rescued her, Melissa found her car keys attached to her apartment doorknob and her car parked at the curb. There was no bill, no note, nothing to tell her the cost, so she placed a call to the garage that had repaired her tires.

"Mr. North took care of the bill, ma'am."

"Oh. Well, I need to know the cost so I can repay him. Will you look it up, please?"

"Uh...sure. Hold on a minute." The man came back on the line. "It was $126.23, Miss Avery. There was a thirty-dollar charge for my man driving out there."

"I understand. Thank you." Melissa jotted down the amount and hung up. Even with the thirty-dollar charge for the trip, the price seemed terribly high for just repairing two flat tires. But she was in no position to argue cost at this point, so she wrote out a check in Wyatt's name and stuck it in her purse. It wasn't going to be mailed. She was going to gear up her courage and talk to Wyatt about the lot next to the café, so she may as well hand him the check at the same time.

But several days passed before her courage was even close to being "geared up." It was disconcerting and unsettling that she felt so confused about Wyatt now, so uncertain. Was it possible that she had judged him too harshly six years ago?

Still, his admitted infidelity remained an enormous hurdle to even friendship, and she honestly believed suspicion of him was a permanent condition on her part. She had trusted him so implicitly that the idea of him seeking other women during their extended separation had never entered her mind. Learning otherwise, hearing it from his own lips on the telephone, had nearly killed her. Certainly it had destroyed her trust in him, and without trust, no relationship stood a chance of surviving.

She wasn't into risk taking anyway, she told herself pragmatically. Romance with Wyatt was simply out of the question. But she could be a little more civil to him now, and maybe they could even do business together. If he was receptive to a discussion on that vacant lot, that is.

Paul Rodell had started dropping in for coffee everyday. When Melissa was there and not too busy, she sat with him and chatted. "You did a remarkable job with this old building, Melissa," he told her one afternoon.

She smiled. "I hope the bank will take that into consideration when I finally apply for that loan."

"Have you purchased the lot?"

"Um . . . it's in process."

The following afternoon he asked her out. "The Ranchers' Association's annual dinner-dance is coming up, Melissa. Several officers of the bank have been invited, including myself. I'd be honored if you would go with me."

Melissa's heart skipped a beat. The Norths had always been members of the association, and more than likely Wyatt would attend the function. She wouldn't have to be a fly on the wall to see Wyatt's reaction to hearing she was dating another man; she could witness it with her own eyes. What went around came around, didn't it? Eventually? If one waited long enough?

"I'd love to go," she told Paul.

Melissa couldn't procrastinate on that vacant lot any longer. With or without courage, she had to speak to Wyatt about it.

The sky was sunny again, although the air was much cooler than it had been before the drenching the area had received. For the drive out to the North Ranch, Melissa put on jeans, sneakers and a blue cotton sweater. She had no idea if Wyatt would be there, but if he wasn't, she decided, she would merely leave the check and a note about the lot. In fact, the more she thought about it, the more she hoped he wouldn't be there. Then he could digest the contents of the note and give some thought to selling her the lot before they actually talked about it. Assuming, of course, that he hadn't bought the land just to get her goat. She still had her doubts on that point.

Turning into the ranch's long driveway, Melissa stopped the car at a high spot in the road. A poignant sigh whispered through her. She had always thought the North Ranch to be the most beautiful in the valley. The house, especially. It was immense and architecturally perfect. Wyatt had never discussed his parents' wealth with her, but it was obvious to anyone with half a brain that they had been. Since Simon's death it was all Wyatt's, of course.

Melissa got the car moving again. Wyatt's assets meant nothing to her, except for one: the lot he had snatched right from under her nose. What was so vexing was that it was her own darn fault. Wyatt wouldn't have been able to do any "snatching" if she had taken care of business the way she should have.

Following the driveway, she approached the house. Up close it was even more beautiful. Constructed of white-painted wood and some type of striking, silvery gray rock that Melissa knew wasn't indigenous to this section of Montana, it boasted a number of interesting details such as porches, cupolas, frosted glass doors and mullioned windows. She was certain there wasn't another house in the valley to compare.

Parking her car near several other vehicles, she got out and walked to the front door, where she rang the doorbell. A middle-aged woman in a neat cotton housedress opened the door. "Yes?"

"Hello. I'm Melissa Avery. Is Wyatt home?" Melissa felt the woman's eyes go up and down, measuring her. Obviously she was wondering who she was.

But she answered politely, if not with any apparent friendliness. "He's around somewhere. Not in the house, though. Would you like to come in?"

"Oh . . . well . . . there wouldn't be much point if he isn't there." Melissa smiled. "Would you have any idea where he might be?"

"Probably out by the barns or corrals. Unless he's on a horse somewhere. You could go out back and take a look, if you'd like."

"Yes, I'll do that. Thank you." Skipping from the porch, Melissa recalled that the Norths had always had a housekeeper and a cook. As a girl she had thought having a housekeeper and a cook to be the height of luxury. But when, big-eyed and open-mouthed, she'd mentioned it to Wyatt, he'd just laughed. The truth, of course, was that he had never lived any other way, and her awe had tickled his funny bone.

Then, as she and Wyatt became closer, his family's affluence lost significance. He'd acted no different than the other high school kids, and who had what hadn't mattered to those of them who liked each other and hung out together. The boys drove pickups—some old, some new—and the girls usually drove the family car, though there had been a few who had their own vehicle. Melissa hadn't been in that fortunate group. Her mother had made ends meet by doing odd jobs—some sewing, some housecleaning, whatever she could pick up—and by dipping into her savings account when absolutely necessary. THE SAVINGS ACCOUNT was the Averys' one asset, and Nan had spoken of it in reverent tones. Melissa had always seen the term in capital letters whenever her mother mentioned it, and to this day she realized the value of every dollar that passed through her hands.

The major difference between her and her mother was that Nan was content with her savings—now replenished by her share of Charlie's life-insurance payoff—and Melissa had ambition and dreams and the determination to do something about them.

Walking around the house, Melissa put a lilt in her step, when she felt much more like dragging her feet. Her visit was going to be a surprise to Wyatt, and she didn't want him getting any funny notions from it. But it seemed more appropriate to approach him confidently when she was going to instigate a discussion about that vacant lot. Her lighthearted step and bright expression were pure bluff; she desperately wanted that land and didn't want Wyatt to catch on to how *much* she wanted it. Wasn't that how practiced businessmen and women threw their opponents off guard?

Behind the house was a beautiful backyard, with what seemed like acres of green grass, flower beds and artistically placed trees, bushes and shrubs. Farther out were the ranch's barns, corrals and equipment sheds. That was where Melissa headed.

Someone called her name. "Melissa?"

She stopped and looked around.

"Melissa? Over here."

It was Wyatt. He was calling to her from one of the corrals. At sight of him, Melissa felt something inside of her go all soft and mushy. He was wearing a big hat, tan leather chaps over his jeans and a shirt without sleeves. There were leather gloves on his hands and he was drawing a rope into a coil. He was too gorgeous to be believed. Vaguely Melissa registered the horse in the corral with him, but she couldn't tear her eyes from Wyatt. It wasn't fair that he should look like that, she thought angrily, not fair at all.

"Come on over," Wyatt called, because she was just standing there.

She took a deep breath and began walking, too uneasy now to "lilt." But she did manage a reasonably normal, "Hi," before reaching the corral fence.

"Hi, yourself." The corners of Wyatt's eyes crinkled as he gave her a pleased but curious smile. He couldn't believe she was here, but she was, looking radiantly beautiful and a little nervous. "This is a pleasant surprise," he said, walking over to the fence where she was standing.

"Yes, well, I wanted to give you this." Melissa pulled the check from her purse and held it out over the fence.

Wyatt looked at it, then folded it and tucked it into his shirt pocket. "Thanks." He had no intention of ever cashing the check, but explaining that to Melissa wasn't a good idea right now. Eventually, by the time she finally realized that the check hadn't been cashed, things would be much better between them and they could laugh together about him slashing her spare tire.

"That garage charged an awful lot to fix the tires," Melissa remarked.

"Prices are high on everything these days," Wyatt said with a perfectly straight face. The high amount was due to having to purchase a new tire to replace the one he had ruined.

Melissa glanced toward the horse nearby. "What are you doing?"

"Trying to take some of the ornery out of that horse."

"Oh, he's ornery."

"*She's* ornery."

"Oh, it's a mare."

Wyatt laughed. "Yep, that she is." His smile faded as he looked at Melissa. "Do you know that you glow?"

"I what?" Her gaze jerked to his.

"You glow."

"Like a fluorescent worm, you mean?"

"Now why would you think of a worm?"

"Because I had a fluorescent caterpillar when I was a child, I suppose. An orange one."

"Well, a caterpillar isn't a worm, and I wasn't thinking about a fluorescent anything. Your glow is like an aura."

"An aura, huh?" Melissa looked away from his eyes. He wasn't kidding and she didn't want to deal with serious compliments. She had to introduce the subject of that lot he'd bought, but how? Just blurting it out would reveal her intense interest in it. There must be a way to lead up to it that would sound casual, like ordinary conversation.

Inadvertently, Wyatt helped her out. "How about something cold to drink?"

"Yes, thanks," she said immediately and with a brighter countenance.

"We'll go up to the house." He came through the corral gate and they started walking.

Thinking of that stern, measuring housekeeper, Melissa eyed the patio. "Why don't we sit out there?"

"Sure, if you prefer." He took off his gloves and beat some of the dust from his chaps with them. Melissa tried not to stare at his arms, which were tanned and muscular and so blatantly male, the sight of them gave her goose bumps. He had not had arm muscles like that in high school. "What would you like?" he asked. "A soda? Iced tea?"

"Just water, please."

He wished he could give her something special, like nectar and ambrosia, the food of the gods and immortals, but water would have to do. For now.

Melissa was glad when she was sitting on the patio alone and he had gone in for the drinks. He was still the Wyatt she had loved, she thought unhappily. However badly he'd hurt her, some part of her was going to keep her miserable by responding to his good looks and incredible smile, and to memories of times past. She wished passionately that they had never made love. It had only happened once—the night she had called him, sobbing her heart out because of being forced to move to California—but it was one memory that would never become dull or tarnished with age.

Her gaze absently drifting over the patio furniture and yard, Melissa heaved a heavy sigh. She had been so young, so naive, and she had believed in "happily ever after," when there was no such thing.

Wyatt came out carrying two tall glasses, one of which he passed to Melissa before occupying the chair next to hers.

"Thank you," she murmured, taking a swallow. The cold water felt good in her dry mouth. "Your ranch looks wonderful. Just like I remembered."

"*You* look wonderful," he said softly. "Just like *I* remembered. I'm glad you're here." She could have put the check in the mail. Her delivering it in person raised his hopes to new heights.

"Please," she said, looking down at the glass in her hands. "Let's keep this impersonal."

Wyatt's eyes narrowed slightly. Keep what impersonal? Was she here for a reason unrelated to that check?

"I don't want 'impersonal' with you, Melissa." He set his glass down and leaned forward, his forearms resting on his thighs, his expression intense. "I want it as personal as it gets."

Color flared in her cheeks. "Don't say things like that. You're married."

"Not for long. I should be receiving the final decree papers any day now. The Ranchers' Association's annual dinner dance is this weekend. Will you go with me?"

She couldn't meet his eyes, nor could she explain that she was going to the affair with Paul Rodell. Besides, that wasn't the issue. She wasn't going to date Wyatt under any circumstances.

"No."

"Why not?"

"Why do you think?" There was some sarcasm in her voice. Inwardly she winced at the way she'd spoken. This was not the conversation she had come out here to have with Wyatt. She took a breath and spoke calmly. "Wyatt, I am not going out with you."

"Not ever?"

"Not ever," she affirmed.

His features became harder. "Why didn't you just put that check in the mail?"

Suddenly nervous, Melissa stalled on an answer by taking another swallow of water. But the time had come, and she couldn't avoid it by sucking on ice cubes, which was all that was left in her glass. The timing was terrible. Wyatt was angry or hurt or something else now, when he'd been in an upbeat, cheerful mood not more than three minutes ago. She hadn't meant to upset him, but in all fairness he'd done that himself with his suggestive compliments. There really was no roundabout way to approach the subject of that lot, so she may as well just come right out and ask about it.

"I didn't mail the check because of something I need to talk to you about," she said, hoping she didn't sound desperate.

"Which is?"

Melissa cleared her throat. "Um . . . I understand that you've recently purchased the lot next to my building."

Wyatt blinked. News traveled with the speed of light in Whitehorn. He'd forgotten what a gossipy little town it really was. Everyone knew everyone else's business, or thought they did, and were thrilled to pass it on.

"That happens to be true," he said slowly, pondering her interest in the transaction. "It was a good investment," he added after a moment of silence between them. "I've bought a couple of pieces of land lately." Melissa was obviously uncomfortable with the subject, and yet she had felt it necessary to drive out here to discuss it. It puzzled him. "John Hendrix, the guy I bought it from, said it had been on the market for a long time."

"For quite some time," Melissa murmured in agreement. For so long, in fact, she had felt no urgency about making an offer to purchase, a dire mistake in judgment.

"I guess I don't understand, Melissa. Were you interested in that lot?" He noted that she was chewing on her bottom lip rather nervously.

"Actually..." How best to present this without appearing to be begging? "... I've been wondering what you intend to do with it."

Now he understood. She was concerned that he might put up some sort of structure that would detract from her business. "You don't have to worry, I probably won't do anything with that lot for years."

Melissa's shoulders slumped. They were conversing at cross purposes, him saying one thing, she another. But was he speaking a little too smoothly? Toying with her? God, she really *didn't* know him anymore.

She sat up straighter. Beating around the bush was getting her nowhere. "Would you consider selling the lot to me?"

Wyatt looked startled. "You want it?"

"I've been working on plans to expand the café for months now. Longer than that. Almost from the first, actually. I should have tied up the lot with a deposit, but—" she took an embarrassed breath "—but I didn't, and it got away from me." She watched Wyatt's eyes for his reaction to her next comment. "You could have knocked me over with a feather when John Hendrix told me you were the person who had bought it."

With his elbow on the arm of his chair, Wyatt rubbed his chin thoughtfully. "This is a peculiar situation, isn't it?"

"One could say that," Melissa replied dryly.

"Well..." He got up. "You can have the lot."

Melissa gaped. "I can? Just like that? Don't you want to discuss terms? I can't immediately pay you the entire amount, Wyatt. What I have is ten thousand—"

"No terms," he said flatly. "You misunderstood. What I said was that you could *have* the lot. I'm giving it to you."

"*Giving* it to me?" Melissa jumped to her feet. "Absolutely not! Why on earth would you even think I would accept a thirty-thousand-dollar gift from you?"

"Twenty-five thousand. Hendrix was anxious to sell."

Melissa's spine was rigidly stiff and her eyes were blazing. "I have ten thousand dollars for a down payment, and I can pay a thousand a month on the balance. There has to be an interest factor and I'll pay whatever you say, plus, if you want to make a reasonable profit—"

"You may as well stop laying down the law," Wyatt said brusquely. "The only way you're going to get that lot is without payment. Take it or leave it."

"This is absurd! You know damned well I'm not going to take that lot as a gift."

"Why not?"

"Because—because I can't be bought," she retorted with her chin in the air.

Wyatt laughed, albeit humorlessly. "I'm not trying to buy you, for God's sake." His amusement vanished. "But maybe I owe you something."

The color drained from Melissa's face. "You *don't* owe me money!" Whirling, she started across the lush grass toward the parking area and her car.

"Aw, hell," Wyatt mumbled, as realization of what he'd done struck him right between the eyes. For one thing, he had forgotten her chilled reaction to his offer of financial aid when she and her mother had both lived in California.

But what in hell was wrong with a man giving a woman a gift? He could write out a dozen twenty-five-thousand-dollar checks and barely notice a dent in his net worth. In fact, he donated almost that much to charity every year. The ranch just kept on making money; his stocks, bonds, T-bills, real-estate investments and cash accounts just kept on making more money. And he did owe Melissa. But apparently it wasn't a debt that could be cancelled with anything monetary. He should have figured that out before talking about "owing" her.

He went after her, calling, "Melissa, wait. I'm sorry. Give me a chance to explain."

She yanked open the door of her car and hurriedly got in. But her anger was evolving into something much worse—humiliation. Holding back the tears burning her eyes was impossible, and when Wyatt reached her car and pulled open the door, they were streaming down her cheeks.

"Leave me alone," she gasped. Her trembling hands were trying to get the car started, but she could barely see the ignition through the massive onslaught of tears, and her attempts were futile.

"Melissa," Wyatt said, sounding forlorn and helpless. "I'm sorry." He was leaning over, peering in at her.

"You're always sorry after you do something abominable." Ignoring the tears, she glared at him. "Shove that lot up your nose, Wyatt." A glimmer of common sense shone between the clouds of her despair. "Unless you decide to behave like a normal human being and sell it to me for what it's worth."

He looked at her beautiful, teary face and an unaccustomed stubbornness set in. "I told you my deal. I'm not going to change my mind."

Furious words came spewing out of Melissa's mouth. "Fine! Keep the damned thing. You planned this, didn't you? You knew I wanted that land and you bought it just to spite me. Just so you could look benevolent and wonderful by giving it to me. And while we're at it, I wonder about the timing of your divorce. If you left your wife just because I was back in Whitehorn, you're the worst kind of snake there ever was."

She grabbed the inside door handle. "Get out of the way so I can leave."

"You little idiot," Wyatt said through clenched teeth. "You're so far from the truth about the sort of man I am and what I would or wouldn't do, it's almost funny. But I'm not laughing, am I? I think you should get your head examined. A completely sane person would never come up with the kind of accusations you've just thrown at me."

"Go to hell!" Slamming the door as hard as she could, she got the motor going and backed up fast. Turning the car around, she sped down Wyatt's long driveway.

He stared after her, shaking his head.

Six

The cardboard cylinder containing the architectural rendering for the Hip Hop's expansion stood in a corner of Melissa's bedroom. Every time she happened to glance that way and realize it was never going to be used, she got a tight, clenched-fist feeling in her stomach. Wyatt trying to give her that lot was so preposterous, she became angry all over again whenever she thought of it.

He was out of her life, she vowed—this time *her* doing. To be honest, she wasn't sure she would even be able say hello to him should they run into each other.

On the evening of the Whitehorn Ranchers' Association's dinner-dance, she thought about that while getting ready. Wyatt was apt to be there, though now she didn't care *what* his reaction might be to her dating Paul Rodell. Wyatt North was history as far as she was concerned, and his reactions simply didn't interest her anymore.

There were few formal occasions in Whitehorn, and tonight's affair was one of them. Actually, it was more semiformal than formal, but it was reputed that people really dressed up for the event. Melissa was relying on hearsay in that regard. Her family hadn't been ranchers, and she'd been too young to be invited to the event prior to leaving Whitehorn. Last summer, though she'd been in the area, no one had asked her to attend.

She went through her wardrobe carefully, considering the season, the event and her own mood. In a way she wished that she hadn't accepted Paul's invitation, but in another she was looking forward to dressing up and spending the evening with an attractive man. Narrowing her choice of apparel down to three dresses, she laid them on the bed and took a shower.

An hour later her hair was curled and perfect, as was her makeup. Wearing lacy underwear, she was studying the dresses, trying to make up her mind which of them was most appropriate, when the telephone rang.

Rather absently, her gaze still on the garments on the bed, she picked up her bedside phone. "Hello."

"Melissa, this is Wyatt. Please don't hang up."

Instantly angry, she tensed. "How did you get this number? It's unlisted and I know I didn't give it to you."

"I called your mother awhile back. Melissa—"

"You called my mother? Wasn't that rather nervy?"

"For God's sake, I don't want to argue," Wyatt said sharply. He took a breath. "Melissa, please change your mind and go with me tonight. Give us a chance. Give *me* a chance. We haven't really spent any quality time together, and—"

Quality time? That was too much. Rudely, Melissa broke in. "Sorry, I'm going with someone else."

She heard silence, then, "Who are you going with?"

"Paul Rodell."

"I see. Well . . . have a good evening."

"I'm sure I will. Goodbye."

Wyatt put down the phone and sat back in his chair, feeling disappointed and empty. He had been getting ready for the dinner-dance and was wearing his black trousers and white pleated shirt. His jacket was draped around the back of another chair, his tie was on its seat. But did he want to go now? Did he want to see Melissa smiling at Paul Rodell? He knew Paul and, worst luck, liked him. He could understand Melissa liking him. Maybe she'd been dating him all along.

"Damn!" Wyatt shot up and out of the chair. Women had been the bane of his existence for six years now—first Shannon, now Melissa. He'd done his best to atone for his sins with Melissa, trying everything he knew how to make amends with her, all but turning himself inside out to garner a kind word, a genuine smile. She had said several times that she'd forgiven him, but she hadn't, and why didn't he just stop acting like a damned wimp and face the fact that she never would?

He stopped his pacing at a large bureau with a mirror above it and looked himself in the eye. Giving up on Melissa would be like losing a crucial part of himself. Could he do it? He stood there for some time, thinking, pondering the past, present and future. He had everything he wanted that money could buy, but he didn't have the only woman he'd ever loved, the only woman he'd ever wanted. No, he wasn't going to give up on Melissa. Not yet.

And neither was he going to attend that function tonight and pretend it didn't matter that she was there with another man. "No more playing the fool," he mumbled under his breath.

Leaving the bureau and the mirror, he took off his shirt and pants and returned them to the closet. Fifteen minutes later, wearing jeans, boots, a cotton shirt and a denim jacket, he left the house, got in his pickup and started driving. His destination was his cabin in the mountains. It had always been the place where he'd done his best thinking.

At twelve-thirty that night Melissa was saying good-night to Paul Rodell. "Thank you, Paul. It was a very pleasant evening." *Wyatt hadn't been there. Why not?*

"I enjoyed it immensely, Melissa." They were sitting in his car, which was parked at the curb outside her building. The motor was idling. "Tomorrow is Sunday. I'd love to take a drive somewhere. Would you go with me? We could go to Billings, maybe, and have dinner. Or anyplace else. You name it."

"Sundays are the café's busiest day of the week, Paul, so I really can't." It *had* been a pleasant evening. She couldn't deny it. She had said hello to a lot of old friends and met some new people. The food had been reasonably good and the live band had been reasonably talented. Paul had been an attentive, considerate companion, and he had done nothing to alter her original opinion of him. But there'd been the most disturbing hole in the entire affair, and it was unnerving to realize how deeply she had felt Wyatt's absence.

She smiled for Paul's benefit. "It's late. Good night, and thanks again."

"Wait, I'll walk you to the door."

"Not necessary," she said, and opened her door to get out. Peering into the car, she said, "'Night, Paul," and saw the perplexed expression on his face. Sighing inwardly, she closed the door and proceeded to the stairs. Aware that he was waiting until she got upstairs and inside her apartment, she waved from the second-floor landing before going in.

Heading directly to her bedroom, she switched on a light, tossed her evening bag on the bureau and began undressing. That was when the tears started. They dribbled down her cheeks while she hung up her striking red dress with its spaghetti straps and fringed hemline, and put away her stylish, high-heeled red shoes. After Wyatt's call, she had chosen the sexiest of the three dresses on the bed, hoping, she realized now, to make him suffer just a little.

Well, he hadn't been there to suffer. He hadn't seen her in her red dress, dancing and laughing with Paul. He hadn't seen her chatting and mingling and enjoying herself, most of it pretense. *He hadn't been there!*

Crawling into bed, she wiped her eyes and thought about the evening. Not about the party, but about why Wyatt had decided to skip it. Because she had told him she would be there with Paul? Because he *hadn't* wanted to see her with another man?

"Oh, God," she whispered unhappily, turning over in bed to hug her extra pillow to herself. Why was this happening? Why was Wyatt in her blood again when she didn't *want* him in her blood? Why couldn't she fall for a nice, uncomplicated guy like Paul Rodell? Yes, she had enjoyed his company tonight, but there were no sparks between them, no excitement that told a woman this was something special.

Wyatt liked fireplaces, and his mountain cabin had a grand fireplace. At this elevation it was cold enough to build a roaring fire at night, though now, after midnight, it had died down to remnants of glowing logs that occasionally popped and sent sparks up the chimney.

The silence and isolation of the cabin were pacifying to Wyatt this night. His father had had it constructed when Wyatt was still a child. The family used to come up here together, to fish or to walk among the tall pines. Like everything Simon had built, the cabin contained every luxury, though with a purposely rustic design to fit in with the mountain terrain. During his final years Simon had spent much of his time at the cabin, and there was a cupboard, Wyatt knew, that held five or six large photo albums. Those albums, with their hundreds of family pictures, had given Simon great comfort.

Old photos didn't provide the kind of comfort Wyatt was seeking tonight, however, and he hadn't taken out the albums. What he wanted was peace of mind, he told himself. After a moment that thought produced a dry laugh. Peace of mind? Yeah, right. Thinking of himself and Melissa for hours on end wasn't the route to peace, and that was what he'd been doing—studying their situation and diverse attitudes from every conceivable angle. He had come up with only one conclusion: he had to either leave Melissa completely alone or do something drastic to get her attention.

Now...what could that be? What could he possibly do to change her opinion of him that he hadn't already tried?

The Hip Hop was as busy on Sunday as Melissa had told Paul it would be. At one point people were actually lined up outside the front door waiting for a table. Regardless, Melissa's mind wasn't completely on the day's thriving business. She had to approach Wyatt about that vacant lot again, but with what ammunition? No way was she going to accept it as a gift. The mere thought of his ridiculous generosity made her head ache, and she had started the day with a headache to begin with.

By eight that evening, when business began petering out and Melissa's feet hurt and her mouth felt stretched from smiling when she hadn't been in a smiling mood all day, she poured herself a cup of coffee and wilted into a vacant booth. What she needed was a vacation, she thought wearily. She had been working hard for eighteen months, and a few days away from the work and responsibility she had assigned herself would probably do her a world of good. Make that a week, she amended with a sigh. She had excellent help and they could handle the place for a week.

The idea brightened her sagging spirits a little. She could go see her mother. Nan made it abundantly clear in letters and on the phone that she was never going to return to Whitehorn for any reason, so the only way Melissa was ever going to see her again was to make the trip to California. And she'd be able to see her brother and his children, too.

Maybe the change of scene would clear her mind some, which Lord knew she needed. She could even use Nan's car and drive to the ocean for a day. Walking on the beach had always been soothing for her. It just might work, she thought hopefully. Maybe she would come back with all sorts of solutions to her problems.

On Monday morning Melissa made the rounds of Whitehorn's law-enforcement agencies, talking to Judd, to Tracy and to Sterling. There were no new developments in her father's murder investigation, and she returned to the café all but scowling. Instead of immediately immersing herself in work, she went upstairs to her apartment and made reservations for a flight from Billings to Fresno, California for the next day. With that task completed, she picked up the phone again to dial her mother and let her know she was coming.

But then, frowning, she hung up. If by some quirk she had to cancel her plans, Nan would be upset. It was better to just go and take a cab from the airport. There was no doubt in Melissa's mind that her mother would be home, or at least very close to home. The extent of her traveling was to a nearby shopping mall, which held a supermarket and a drug store, so she probably didn't put a thousand miles on her car in a year.

Okay, Melissa thought, she was all set. Packing would take about an hour. Much more important was to let her restaurant staff know her plans. She could speak to the shift on duty right now and the other shift this evening.

On Tuesday morning the sunless, cloudy sky looked as though it could start raining any minute. Obviously the area was in for another drenching.

After standing at the window of his den for twenty minutes staring out at the dark and gloomy day, with his mind at the Hip Hop Café and what Melissa might be doing, Wyatt muttered, "To hell with it," and headed for his desk and telephone. He couldn't vegetate and do nothing about Melissa's attitude any longer. He had a plan in mind, that "something drastic" he'd decided was necessary to his and Melissa's faltering relationship, but he couldn't set it in motion all by himself. Dialing the café's number, he sat tensely, awaiting an answer.

"Hip Hop Café," a female voice said brightly.

"Melissa Avery, please," Wyatt said, sounding almost normal.

"Hold on, please." Wyatt could tell the phone had been set down. "Melissa?" the woman called. "Telephone."

It took a minute, but then the receiver was picked up. "Hello, this is Melissa."

"This is Wyatt."

"Oh." He could hear the sudden chill in her voice. "I don't have time for chitchat right now."

"I didn't call to chat. I need to see you."

She needed to see him, too, Melissa thought with a crease of discomfort between her eyes. About the lot. Somehow she had to make him understand why she couldn't accept it without payment. But her mind was a blank as to how to accomplish that feat. At any rate, she couldn't slam that door completely shut.

She spoke with a little less chill in her voice. "Wyatt, I don't have time to see you this morning, and I'm leaving for a week."

"Going where?"

She hated his nosiness. He had no right to question her about anything she did.

Withholding her impatience, she continued without answering his question. "We can talk when I get back."

"Melissa, what I need to see you about is the lot."

"The lot?" Melissa's mouth was suddenly dry. "Um... what about it?"

"I'll tell you in person. When are you leaving?"

"Around noon. Twelve-thirty, actually."

Wyatt checked his watch. It was eight-fifteen. "You're driving somewhere?"

"Just to the airport."

"I see." Wyatt felt a burst of excitement. This was perfect to his plan, fitting it as though by supernatural design. But he had some important matters to attend to before twelve-thirty and had better get to them. "Okay, fine. Call me when you get back and we'll discuss the lot."

"Can't you tell me what you've got in mind right now?"

"I'd much rather do that face-to-face. Have a good trip."

Melissa hung up, frowning. Now she would wonder what was cooking in Wyatt's brain about that lot all during her vacation.

Melissa's flight was scheduled to leave Billings at 3:10 p.m. Since Billings was a little over seventy miles from

Whitehorn, and she wanted to give herself plenty of time
check in at the airport, she was ready to leave Whitehorn at
twelve-thirty.

She was loading her suitcases into the trunk of her car
when a pickup pulled up right behind her. Glancing up, she
felt her heart do what felt like a double somersault. The
pickup was Wyatt's, and he was getting out.

"Hi," he said casually.

"Hello." She looked at him curiously and with no small
amount of hope. Maybe he'd come to tell her his idea on the
lot. Maybe she *wouldn't* have to wonder and worry about it
for a week.

"Looks like you're all set to leave."

Melissa closed her trunk. "I am." She decided to be cordial. "I'm paying a visit to my mother."

"I hope she's not ill."

"She's fine."

"Just a little vacation, then?"

"Something like that." Melissa walked around her car to
the driver's door. "I really have to be going. My plane leaves
at three." She stood with her hand on the door. "About the
lot..."

"You can buy it."

A crazy joy rocketed through her. She breathed an enormous sigh of relief and her expression took on genuine
warmth. "Thank you."

"On one condition."

Her body stiffened with sudden suspicion. "Which is?"

"That you let me drive you to the airport. Where are you
leaving from, Billings or Butte?"

"Billings. But your driving me would be terribly incon-
venient when I return, because I wouldn't have my car to get
home."

"I'll pick you up."

Melissa looked away from his expectant brown gaze. Why
was there a pocket of excitement within herself because he
obviously hadn't given up on her? She could see it in his

eyes. He still had hopes for the two of them becoming close again. Was that what was behind his complete turnabout on the lot? The question was disturbing. She really didn't want to be indebted to him, except for the payments on the lot, of course. But there was no question that this was a business deal with hordes of personal ramifications.

"You'll sell me the lot if I let you take me to the airport. Wyatt, that doesn't make a whole lot of sense," she said slowly.

"Maybe not, but that's my offer. You can have the lot for what I paid for it."

A bargain. She couldn't refuse it, nor could she waste time in a debate over his very strange "condition," though she did take a moment to wonder what his "condition" would have been if she hadn't been on the brink of a week's vacation.

She inhaled a much-needed breath. "All right, fine. Since my luggage is already in my car, maybe we should just take it."

Wyatt shook his head. "No, I'll transfer your suitcases to my truck. As you can see, I've put the camper shell on the bed of my pickup, so if it starts raining before we get to Billings, your luggage won't get wet. Give me your keys."

Melissa hesitated. This was very peculiar. He would sell her the lot if she agreed to his driving her to the airport. But maybe that wasn't such a bad idea, seeing as how she would be gone for a week. They could get the terms of the sale settled during the drive.

Feeling better about Wyatt's "condition," she handed him her car keys. Then, while he transferred her suitcases from her vehicle to his, she got her raincoat and purse from the front seat. "Oh, just a minute," she said. "My staff will wonder why my car is still here. It'll just take a second to run in and explain."

Wyatt nodded. "Sure, go ahead. I'll wait in the truck." He got in and started the motor while Melissa dashed into the café. Admittedly, his stomach was churning a bit sick-

ishly. But that "drastic" plan he'd come up with was risky
business. If it worked, everything would be great between
him and Melissa. If it didn't, he could find himself in deep
trouble. *Very* deep trouble.

It was worth the risk, he told himself while watching the
Hip Hop's front door for Melissa. He had given up six years
of his life in doing the "honorable" thing, so honor wasn't
all it was cracked up to be. Simon North would never have
agreed with that conclusion, Wyatt realized uneasily.

But then, Simon had married the woman he'd loved.

Spotting Melissa coming through the door, Wyatt got out,
hurried around the front of the pickup and opened the passenger door for her to get in. She did so, rather breathlessly. "Everything's all set," she told him.

Returning to the driver's seat, Wyatt put the pickup in
Reverse and backed away from Melissa's car. Then he pulled
into the street and headed east. "It's starting to sprinkle,"
he commented, turning the wipers on Intermittent, so they
would clear the windshield at fifteen-second intervals.

The normal route to Billings was to take Highway 191 to
the interstate. Melissa sat back when Wyatt made a turn
onto 191. She felt elation over Wyatt having decided to sell
her the lot, though she could only guess at his motive for
doing so.

"I really appreciate your selling me the lot," she said,
while in the back of her mind resided the question, *Why?*
She wouldn't ask, though the matter was definitely hounding her. "As I said before, I can put ten thousand down."

"Any terms you want are fine with me." He glanced at
her. "You know I don't need the money."

"Your net worth has no bearing on it, Wyatt. I pay my
own way. You know that."

He chuckled softly. "Yes, I do. I remember when we first
started dating that you wouldn't even let me pay for your
movie tickets or hamburgers. Do you remember that?"

Melissa couldn't help laughing. "I remember. Guess I
went a little overboard sometimes." Her laughter faded.

"But there was so much talk about Dad deserting Mother, my brother and me that I hated the idea of being labeled a charity case."

"Good Lord, Melissa, no one ever thought of you as a charity case. You were too sensitive about that. Do you think people blamed you because your father disappeared?"

"What I think, what I remember, is that there was so much gossip, so much talk about it that every possible scenario was hashed and rehashed a hundred times. I hated knowing it was everyone's main topic of conversation."

"Well, that's probably true. People do love a mystery."

Melissa frowned. "Why are you making this turn?"

Wyatt had just made a turn onto a gravel road. "Shortcut," he said blandly.

"I don't know of any shortcut to Billings."

Wyatt laughed. "But I do. Melissa, I know every back road within a two-hundred-mile radius. Dad and I fished every creek, river and pond in three counties. You have to remember that."

"Well, yes . . . but the interstate is probably best today. I hate being rushed at an airport."

"You'll get there sooner going this way over taking the interstate."

She blinked, startled, when he made another turn. "Wyatt, I've never been on these roads. Are you sure this will save time?"

"Positive. Relax."

How could she relax when he kept making turns and totally disorienting her? The cloud cover concealed the sun, and she no longer knew in which direction they were traveling.

"I wonder if all the rain this year is indicative of a lot of snow this coming winter," Wyatt mused. "The area could use a heavy snowpack in the mountains. Water is a valuable commodity, and our last few winters have been pretty mild."

"It snowed last winter," Melissa reminded him rather sharply. She was getting worried about time and didn't care how much snow had fallen in the past few winters, or how much might pile up this year. She wanted to get to the Billings airport with lots of time to spare. She liked checking in early, then relaxing with a cup of tea before getting on the plane. "Wyatt, please turn around and go back to 191. I don't want to miss my flight."

He flashed her a grin. "What a worrywart."

"Worrywart? Wyatt, we're in the mountains!"

"You're certainly not afraid of mountains."

"Well, of course I'm not afraid of mountains. That's absurd and you know it. But we just seem to be going higher and higher. Look at how dense the forest is getting."

Wyatt did look, out each of the side windows, as a matter of fact. "This sure is beautiful country, isn't it?"

Refusing to answer a remark that had absolutely no bearing on the situation, Melissa folded her arms across her chest and stared straight ahead while her mind worked. Should she be worried or shouldn't she? Certainly Wyatt had told the truth about knowing every back road within a very broad area. Her knowledge was limited to only a few of the lesser-used roads, all of them very close to Whitehorn. If only the sun were out, she thought, squinting through the rain at the cloud-covered sky in an attempt to pinpoint its location. For some reason she felt turned around, as if they were going in the opposite direction from Billings.

Yet it was such an inane thought that she didn't vocalize it. What possible gain would Wyatt receive from making her miss her plane? She glanced at her watch and saw that it was almost one-thirty. She still had plenty of time to make her flight, though if they had taken the interstate she would know exactly how much farther they had to drive.

Trying to appear rational about Wyatt's almost-frightening shortcut, she returned to the subject of the lot transaction. "What I plan to do is pay you a thousand a month. We should agree on an interest rate."

"You don't have to pay interest."

"But I want to."

"Well," Wyatt said in a casual tone, "the prime rate is low right now. How about five percent?"

Melissa shook her head. "No, that's too low. No one can borrow money at five percent. How about nine percent?"

"Nine seems a little high to me. Make it seven."

Melissa thought for a moment, then nodded. "All right, seven. When I get back from California I'll have an attorney draw up a contract."

"Good idea. Then your purchase will be protected should something happen to me."

Melissa's head came around to look at him. "That wasn't what I had in mind when I suggested a contract."

"I realize that. But it's true, all the same."

She kept watching him. Something about his loose and relaxed posture made her uneasy. She cleared her throat. "How come you changed your mind on the lot?"

He sent her a smile. "Because I finally remembered how upset you got when I offered you money years ago. I guess I'd forgotten your spirit of independence."

"Oh." Just then Wyatt made another turn. Melissa's heart skipped a beat. They were climbing higher all the time, and Billings was *not* surrounded by mountains! If she remembered correctly, the city's elevation was just a little over three thousand feet, and right now she and Wyatt had to be at the five- or six-thousand-foot level.

"Um...does this road make a sudden decline?" she asked.

"Coming up very soon now," Wyatt affirmed. He knew how nervous she was getting, and with damned good reason. They weren't anywhere near Billings, and if the sun had been visible, she'd know that.

But they were almost to his destination. That was when the fireworks would begin. What he didn't know was just what form those "fireworks" would take. Would Melissa lose her temper and scream at him? Maybe she'd cry. He was prepared for whatever reaction his surprise might cause, and whether it was screeching or weeping or merely stunned silence, he wasn't going to back off from his plan.

All of a sudden there was a clearing. Melissa saw a large, beautiful cabin ahead. "My goodness, would you look at that!" she exclaimed. "Who do you suppose lives way out here?"

Wyatt said nothing. They were at the end of the road, which wasn't yet apparent to Melissa. He pulled up next to the cabin and stopped the truck.

She gave him a puzzled look. "Why are you stopping?"

Wyatt switched off the ignition and turned in the seat to face her. "Because we're here."

A look of panic entered Melissa's eyes. "We're where?"

"At my cabin. I'm going to say it straight out. You've been kidnapped, Melissa, and for the next week this is where we'll be staying."

She was too shocked to speak. She stared. He stared. Then she exploded. "Have you gone crazy? I have a plane to catch!"

"Want to know something, honey? I think maybe I am a little bit crazy." Reaching out, he touched the tip of her nose. "It's your fault."

She jumped back as though burned. "Don't you dare lay a hand on me, you—you maniac. Get this truck started and take me to Billings right this minute."

"Nope." Nonchalantly Wyatt took the keys out of the ignition and opened his door. "I'm going in. What are you going to do?"

"I am not going into your cabin!"

He paused, then nodded. "Suit yourself." He got out and looked back into the cab at her. "Incidentally, don't try to

walk out of here. You'd be hopelessly lost in ten minutes.''
Giving the pickup door a push to close it, he sauntered to the
porch of the cabin, climbed the three steps, crossed the
porch, opened the door and went inside.

Seven

At first Melissa was too dumbfounded to even think. Wyatt had actually gone inside and left her out here alone. What was wrong with him? My Lord, what was she doing here?

The cab of the truck was cooling down rapidly and she wriggled into her raincoat. Then she began to look around. The clearing was only slightly larger than the cabin. Surrounding it on all sides was forest—thick, dark, dripping-wet forest. She shivered just from looking at it.

And then it sank in, hitting her peculiarly. *Wyatt had kidnapped her!* Her eyes widened at the same time as a hysterical urge to giggle welled up in her throat. Her fingers rose to her lips. Should she be scared? She wasn't, not of Wyatt. He hadn't brought her out here to harm her, the conniving sneak—he'd brought her here to convince her of what a great guy he was and always had been, and of how badly she had misjudged him all these years.

Now she was thinking. Fury nearly choked her. How dare he ruin her vacation? How dare he intrude on her life at all, but particularly in this manner? He had used her need to own that lot against her, and like a fool she'd fallen for his charming generosity and friendly smile.

She wasn't an ordinary fool, she was a *terrible* fool. She had learned six years ago not to trust Wyatt, and putting her trust in him was exactly what she had done today. Groaning, Melissa shivered, not sure if it was from the cold or from frustration.

Years ago Wyatt had occasionally mentioned his family's mountain cabin, but he had never brought her out here. Just exactly where "here" was, Melissa had no idea. She racked her brain, trying to recall if he had ever indicated a location when talking about the cabin, and came up empty. There could be a direct, simple route back to 191 for all she knew, but he had thrown her off balance by making so many turns, most of which had probably been unnecessary. He had deliberately addled her sense of direction, and done it so calmly, so coolly, that she hadn't caught on, the snake.

Gritting her teeth, she wished she had the physical strength to walk into that house and pop him one right in the nose.

But he might pop her back, and the thought of her and Wyatt in a fistfight created another nervous giggle.

Why on earth was she giggling? she thought disgustedly. She was stuck out here until Wyatt decided to take her back to town.

Melissa checked her watch and felt anger rising again. She would stay right where she was, she decided furiously—in the truck, shivering and shaking from the dropping temperature. Eyeing the ignition, she wished she knew how to hot-wire a vehicle. Oh, how she wished it, with every fiber of her being. Wouldn't she just love to drive Wyatt's own truck away and leave him stranded?

She shot the ignition a dirty look, then turned her attention to the cabin, which was much nicer than any other she'd ever seen. Though constructed of logs and rock, it was large and sprawling, a beautiful structure. Wyatt was inside, warm and cozy, while she . . .

"Damn you, Wyatt North!" she shrieked, which was so inane she almost giggled again. He could at least have the courtesy to come out and *try* to convince her to go inside. He had to know she was cold and uncomfortable.

Of course he knew, she thought with another onslaught of outrage. And he also knew it would be dark in a few hours. She noticed smoke rising from the chimney, and a picture took shape in her mind of a fireplace churning out heat and Wyatt sitting in a comfy chair soaking up the warmth.

For a few minutes she concentrated on loathing him. To think that she had once been starry-eyed in love with him. What a naive idiot she had been in those days.

She took another glance at her watch. She had been sitting in the truck for almost thirty minutes! Was he just going to leave her out here? There had to be a way to make him pay for his odious behavior today—there had to be. Melissa's eyes narrowed in vengeful speculation. What could she do to even the score?

Whatever it might be, it couldn't be accomplished with her in the truck and him in the cabin.

Clenching her jaw, she opened the door of the truck and got out. Marching to the cabin, she climbed the stairs, crossed the porch and brashly walked in. The front door opened directly onto an immense room that contained numerous chairs, two sofas, several bookcases and tables, and the largest fireplace she had ever seen.

Wyatt got to his feet. Just as she had imagined, he'd been sitting in a big chair near the fireplace. "Hi," he said with a friendly smile, as though this were an ordinary situation and she had just dropped in to pay a neighborly call.

His isn't-this-just-wonderful expression grated on her nerves. Ignoring his greeting, Melissa walked over to the fireplace. "I could have you arrested, you know," she said in a taut voice filled with anger.

Wyatt sank back into his chair. "Guess you could."

She turned to look at him. "You don't believe I would do it, do you?"

Wyatt smiled. "I don't know what to believe about you anymore, honey."

"Don't call me anything but my name. You don't have the right to use endearments with me."

"All right. If 'honey' bothers you so much, I won't use it."

"It doesn't just bother me," she said sharply. "It irritates the hell out of me. Just like you do."

After a beat Wyatt slowly nodded. "I see." His gaze moved over her form in the long raincoat. "I guess I didn't realize I irritated you so much. Are you irritated right now?"

She sent him a murderous look. "There aren't words to describe what I'm feeling right now. Just where do you get your gall? I should be on a plane this minute. Instead I'm—" she threw out a hand "—God knows where."

Wyatt held up a finger. "Which brings us to a question I've been thinking about. Is your mother expecting you?"

Adrenaline shot through Melissa. This could be her way out of this fiasco. "Yes," she said triumphantly. "And when I don't arrive as scheduled, she'll call my apartment. There won't be an answer, so she'll call the café. *Then* she'll hear how I got in your truck so you could drive me to the airport. She'll call in the law. She'll—"

"Hold it," Wyatt said, getting up and walking over to a telephone on a table, which Melissa hadn't noticed.

A telephone! She drew a rather smug breath. All Wyatt had to do was turn his back on her for three minutes, and she would call in the law herself.

But who was *he* calling? She saw him punch out a number from memory, and then it struck her: he was calling her mother!

She ran over and broke the connection before it was made. Pure venom poured from her eyes. "Mother isn't expecting me. Your call would only upset her."

"Oh, I see." Calmly Wyatt pulled the phone cable from the wall jack, then wound it around and around the instrument. "You won't find any other phones in the cabin, so don't waste your time searching for one."

Renewed fury radiated from Melissa's eyes. "What do you think you're going to get out of this?"

"Some conversation," he said evenly.

"Conversation! You kidnapped me for conversation? You really are crazy."

Wyatt smiled. "Crazy about you."

"Well, this is certainly the way to prove it," Melissa said with heavy sarcasm.

"You'll relax after a few days, and you might even let yourself like me again."

"Don't hold your breath."

Wyatt held up the phone. "I'm going to put this away. You might as well make yourself comfortable."

"Never!"

He left the room. Melissa stood there seething. Obviously he had gone to hide the phone, the jerk. Let herself like him? Absurd! He certainly had a warped sense of how a man went about earning a woman's affection.

Besides, nothing he could ever do would renew the affection she'd once had for him. She had been burned once by Wyatt North, and once was enough.

Pacing the room, Melissa fumed and fretted. Still, through the red haze in her brain, the furnishings and decor registered. Wyatt's affluence was everywhere she looked. Leather chairs. Bronze lamps. Leather-bound books. The books she bought were usually paperbacks, as hardcovers were too expensive for her budget. That was the trouble with Wyatt—he'd always had everything he wanted, the *best* of everything. Now he thought he wanted her again. Well, he'd had her once, but it wasn't going to happen again, not while there was breath in her body.

He came strolling in. "I'm going to bring in your luggage."

"Leave my luggage right where it is!"

"No, I don't think so." He walked out the front door, leaving it ajar.

Melissa ran across the room to peer out. "Who do you think you are, my keeper? I don't want my luggage brought into your—your damned den of iniquity."

Wyatt laughed with genuine amusement. "You sure are cute right now."

"You—you cretin. I loathe and despise you."

"Well, that's exactly what we're going to find out." He sent her a big grin.

Melissa advanced to stand on the porch. "I hope you know that kidnapping is a felony." Unperturbed, Wyatt bent into the camper shell to retrieve her suitcases. They had bounced forward during the drive and were closer to the cab than the tailgate. "Do you know what the police do to kidnappers?" Melissa yelled. "I hope they put you in the State of Montana's deepest, darkest dungeon."

Wyatt came out with a suitcase. "I don't think the State of Montana has any dungeons, dark or otherwise." His head disappeared as he crawled under the camper shell for another piece of luggage.

"There must be a dungeon somewhere in these United States, and now that I think about it, I believe that kidnapping is a federal charge. Maybe the FBI will send you to a dungeon in Alaska, where it's forty below zero and you have nothing to eat but stale bread and melted snow for water."

Wyatt succeeded in snagging the final suitcase. Slamming the tailgate in place and the shell door closed, he picked up Melissa's luggage and walked to the house.

"If you suggest it when you file your complaint, they might also periodically hang me by my thumbs," he said. Passing her, he carried the suitcases into the house.

Wearing a poisonous glare, Melissa followed. "You're not a bit funny, so you may as well stop trying to be." Wyatt kept going, leaving the main room and heading down a hall. Melissa stayed at his heels. It was *her* luggage, after all. "Where are you taking my things?"

"To your bedroom."

"Nothing in this ghastly place is mine, so what you're doing is taking my things to one of *your* bedrooms."

Wyatt set her suitcases down in the middle of a spacious bedroom. "Guess that's true. But while you're here, feel free to consider this room as yours."

"How generous of you," she sneered. "How munificent."

"Beats a dungeon, honey. Oops, sorry about that." Wyatt moved to the door. "Are you hungry? I could make an early dinner."

"If you think I'm going to eat anything *you* cook, think again."

Wyatt thought a moment. "That appears to leave you with two options. Either you cook for yourself or you don't eat." He walked out.

Never had Melissa felt such an overwhelming helplessness. But then, she'd never been "kidnapped" before, either. Muttering under her breath, she slumped onto a chair, her hands in the pockets of her raincoat. Walking out of here was impossible. Well, maybe it wasn't impossible if one knew in which direction to go. But it was impossible for her, so she wouldn't waste her time on that method of escape.

Wyatt had the truck keys in his jeans. Or had he already found a hiding spot for them, too? This was a big house—or cabin, as he called it—with probably a hundred places where one could hide a set of keys. On the other hand, telephones took up more space, and he had probably hidden several phones as he had the one he'd taken away. She would have better luck locating the phones than she would the truck keys.

Sighing, Melissa laid her head back against the chair and stretched out her legs. Her gaze went around the room. It was at least twice the size of her apartment bedroom and contained a huge bed—king-size—several bureaus, three chairs and numerous wall shelves, holding books and various trinkets. On either side of the bed was a stand with a lamp. The furniture was of good quality, and someone had brightened the room by adding red accessories. The curtains at the two windows were red burlap, and there was quite a lot of red in the bedspread and the chair fabrics. The room was appealing and homey, though it grated on Melissa's nerves to admit it.

Getting to her feet, she went to a window and looked out. It was still drizzling, still dark and gloomy outside. She heard a rap at the door. Wyatt called, "There's a fresh pot of coffee in the kitchen if you want some."

Melissa turned her head without answering. She was on to his game now. He was all sweetness and light, showing her what a wonderful human being he was. His intention was to wear her down with exaggerated kindness, to infiltrate her defenses.

It wasn't going to work. He could be as nice as pie for the entire week and she wouldn't give an inch. Inside, where it counted, he was a sneaky, manipulative bastard with criminal tendencies. Only someone with criminal tendencies would even think of kidnapping as a method of wooing a woman.

Staring out the window, she gnawed on a hangnail. To think that she was stuck out here for a week raised her blood pressure again, though not nearly as high as it had been a few minutes ago. It wasn't that she was accepting the situation, but what could she do about it, other than be surly and uncooperative?

Well, she couldn't be anything else, could she? she asked herself defiantly. She'd been kidnapped, for crying out loud.

That weird urge to giggle welled up again. There was something morbidly humorous about Wyatt kidnapping her.

But she couldn't let him get away with it. She must keep her guard up and remain angry. She had to remember constantly what he had done to her six years ago, and not fall into any traps of his making.

And he would set traps; she could bet on it.

Wyatt was sipping coffee in his chair near the fireplace. There was no sound coming from the bedroom he had assigned Melissa. Setting down his cup on the table, he thoughtfully rubbed his mouth. Her anger was only what he had expected, but how long would she stay mad? All of tonight, probably. Possibly all day tomorrow. Her pride wouldn't let her relent and relax too quickly. He had better be prepared for more fireworks from her.

Footsteps in the hall alerted him, but he stayed where he was. From sound alone he was able to track Melissa's route to the kitchen, then to the room where he was sitting. He glanced up as she strode to the other chair facing the fireplace and stiffly sat down. She was holding a cup of coffee and wearing slacks and a bulky sweater, when earlier she'd had on a skirt. He wouldn't let himself hope she was already adjusting to the situation, but her more-comfortable clothing and the coffee she was sipping did seem like a concession.

He said nothing, just retrieved his own coffee and took a swallow. Melissa was staring into the flames. Finally, she shot him a murderous look. "I want you to know that I fully understand what you're trying to accomplish with this ridiculous charade."

"You do? That's great, Melissa. Eases my mind a whole lot."

"Do you think I care if your mind is eased? That's not why I said what I did. I merely wanted you to know that I'm on to your childish game."

"You think this is a childish game? That's too bad. For a minute there I really believed you understood why I'd brought you here. It's not a game, Melissa. Would I risk spending the rest of my life in a freezing dungeon in Alaska with only stale bread and melted snow for food and drink for just a game?"

"You're laughing at me. Well, ha-ha to you, too, you jerk! It *is* a game, a demented perversion of normal behavior. Sane people do not kidnap other people. At least none that I've ever known."

Wyatt pointed a forefinger at her. "Do you know something? You lied to me."

"I most certainly did not!"

"Twice, as a matter of fact."

Her expression could have curdled milk. "What *are* you babbling about?"

"What I'm babbling about are the two times you told me that you'd forgiven me for what happened six years ago."

Melissa's chin rose haughtily. "That wasn't a lie."

"The hell it wasn't. Look at it this way. You said you'd forgiven me, but that you hadn't forgotten. It was a logical statement, because most people have a good memory and don't forget milestones in their lives. But you see, Melissa, if you had truly forgiven me, and everything that happened was nothing but a memory for you, you wouldn't still hate me for it. And you do hate me. You told me only a short time ago that you loathe and despise me. That doesn't add up to forgiveness in my book. Conclusion? You lied. Twice."

She sent him a saccharine smile. "Well, tell you what, Wyatt. When I file charges against you for kidnapping, you can file charges against me for lying. We'll see whose crime really matters, all right?"

"Would you really like to see me in a dungeon in Alaska?" he asked with a smile. "That stabs me to the quick."

"What I'd prefer is stabbing your black heart."

"You don't really mean that."

"No? Reverse roles with me for a minute and imagine yourself taken somewhere against your will. Imagine me holding the upper hand. How would you be feeling right now?"

"If you went to all that trouble to get me alone somewhere, I'd be thrilled beyond measure."

She smirked. "Well, since we've already established your recent loss of sanity, I believe you would be thrilled."

"Beyond measure," he reminded.

Melissa drew an exasperated breath. "This conversation is boring me to tears."

"Let's talk about forgiveness again," Wyatt suggested. "I have a feeling you really meant it when you said you had forgiven me."

"Oh, for crying out loud!" Melissa jumped to her feet. "I know what you're trying to lead up to, Wyatt. I am not going to discuss what happened six years ago, so you may as well forget it."

He shook his head. "Can't forget it. Too good a memory, I guess. Like you."

"Who cares about your wretched memory? I certainly don't." Standing near the fireplace, Melissa sipped her coffee, aware of his gaze on her. "Stop staring at me," she demanded.

"You're the prettiest thing in the room to look at."

"In that case, I'll go to another room." With that, she stomped out, paused in the hall for a moment to decide which room she wanted to sulk in and finally chose the kitchen. After topping up her coffee cup, she sat at the large, circular dining table.

The kitchen was a marvelous room, though she hated admitting it. All of the appliances were white. The cabinets and floor were a dark wood and the countertops were white. Again, whoever had decorated the place had used red as an accessory color. The rag rugs on the floor were red, the tablecloth was red and the curtains were white with a red floral design.

A thought occurred to her: someone was keeping this place in apple-pie order and she doubted Wyatt was the person. Did that mean they *weren't* alone out here? If there was a housekeeper or a caretaker, did he or she know about Wyatt's nefarious scheme to hold her prisoner for a week? Maybe her threats of arrest didn't bother Wyatt, but an employee of his might feel differently.

Melissa took a swallow of coffee with narrowed eyes. If there was another person on the place and he did nothing to help her, he would be considered an accomplice, which she would be only too happy to point out. Melissa's penchant for organization arose. She should find a notebook or something to write on, and document this entire episode. Yes, that's exactly what she would do. Then, when she walked into the sheriff's office, or maybe Tracy's—she wasn't all that certain about kidnapping coming under the FBI's jurisdiction—she would have a clear, concise complaint to file, written evidence of what she had been forced to endure against her will.

Wyatt came strolling in. He rinsed his cup and set it on the counter. "I'm getting hungry," he stated calmly, and went to the refrigerator to take out an amber casserole dish. Setting the oven dial, he placed the dish on the counter. "Preheating the oven," he said with a glance at Melissa.

"I prefer your not talking to me," she said coldly. "Do you think I give a damn if you're preheating your stupid oven?"

"Calling my oven stupid doesn't make it so, Melissa. Actually, this is a very intelligent oven."

"Oh, for Pete's sake," she muttered. "That oven is about as intelligent as you are, which is a pretty accurate indication of your IQ."

Wyatt leaned his hips against the counter and folded his arms across his chest. "You used to think I was intelligent."

"I used to think a lot of things that weren't even close to being true, which only proves how gullible I was. I'm not gullible now, Wyatt."

"Maybe a little bit gullible," Wyatt said with a hint of a smile.

Melissa's face grew crimson. Getting into his truck today couldn't be described as anything *but* gullible. "You tricked me," she accused. "You're probably not planning to sell me that lot at all, and I believed—"

"You're wrong. The lot is yours, just as I said. On your terms. Unlike some people, I *never* go back on my word."

"Oh, please," she drawled with obvious disgust. "Considering what happened today I readily admit to retaining some adolescent gullibility, but that's going too far."

Wyatt grinned. "Probably is." He glanced at the stove. "Oven's hot. I'll put the casserole in to heat."

"I couldn't be less interested in your activities, so please stop announcing your next move as though it were of great importance."

"Better use some pot holders," Wyatt said, completely ignoring her sullen, rude remarks. He pulled a set out of a drawer. "The casserole isn't hot, of course, but that oven sure is."

"Don't use the pot holders," Melissa advised churlishly. "Maybe you'll get the burn you so richly deserve." His grin made her want to leap out of her chair and slap it off his face. She realized then that she would like to goad him into a fight, a *real* fight, with name calling and yelling and the whole ball of wax. She had to get hold of herself, she thought. Her bad mood was accomplishing nothing.

Yet, if she wasn't in a bad mood right at the present, how would she feel? Certainly she couldn't pretend everything was peachy keen when she'd just been kidnapped.

Then there were a few other matters to consider. For one, she was getting hungry. Obviously she was going to have to eat Wyatt's food, however strongly she had sworn she wouldn't. She frowned suddenly. That casserole. Was he such a fast and capable cook that he'd been able to put together a casserole during one of their separations since their arrival? While she was in the bedroom, maybe? Or when she'd been sitting in the truck?

She cleared her throat. "Um...did you make that?"

Wyatt closed the oven door and laid the pot holders on the counter. "Nope. Brought it up here this morning, along with a lot of other food."

Melissa was stunned. "You planned this? It wasn't a spur-of-the-moment impulse?"

He laughed. "Melissa, I've been planning this since the night of the Ranchers' Association dinner-dance. I had a problem, though—when and how to get you to take a ride with me."

"Your telephone call this morning cleared that up, right?" she said sarcastically.

"You got it."

Groaning, Melissa put her elbows on the table and her face in her hands. The picture was complete now. From her own mouth during this morning's telephone conversation Wyatt had found the opportunity he had needed to implement his abominable plan to get her out here. He had tricked her into permitting him to drive her to the airport, using the lot as bait, and she had fallen into his scheme as though she'd been handed a script.

She dropped her hands. "You wanted to talk about forgiveness." Melissa got to her feet. "Well, put this in your pipe and smoke it. I will never forgive you for today. *Never!*" She swept from the kitchen.

"Dinner will be ready in about half an hour," Wyatt called cheerfully.

"Shove it up your nose!" she yelled over her shoulder.

Eight

Melissa stayed in the bedroom that Wyatt had told her to think of as hers through the dinner hour and on into the evening. In her own handbag she found several sheets of blank paper, upon which she began writing down the events of the day.

Wyatt North said plainly that he had kidnapped me, and that we would be staying here, at his mountain cabin, for a week, the time I had allotted myself a vacation in California.

She detailed his trickery in getting her into his pickup for the drive to the Billings airport, explaining their strange situation regarding the lot next to her building.

He has not been unkind, nor has he attempted anything that could be construed as sexual pressure. Yet I know...

Melissa frowned. She knew what? When she'd told him he was crazy, he had responded with, "Crazy about you." In retrospect she realized there'd been both a teasing and a serious tenor to his voice, as though he wanted her to figure out which it was for herself.

Ignoring the hunger pangs in her stomach, she tucked the papers back into her purse and dug out a nightgown from one of her suitcases. Upon returning to the room, she had discovered a private bathroom through a connecting door.

She had locked the door to the hallway, so she felt quite secure in her little domain.

After brushing her teeth, she turned off the lights and climbed into the huge bed. That was when she became aware of music. Apparently Wyatt was still up, probably sitting near the fireplace again and listening to music, which was tuned too low for her to make out clearly. Still, it provided a surprisingly pleasant backdrop for her troubled thoughts, going so far as to ease some of her tension.

She was certain she wouldn't sleep a wink, but when she awoke with a start and saw by the lighted clock on the nightstand that it was after midnight, she had to amend that opinion. Obviously she had slept for hours.

The house was completely silent, so Wyatt must have given up on her showing her face in any other part of the house and retired himself. Her hunger pangs were annoyingly persistent, and her mouth watered at the thought of a glass of milk. From experience she knew that a drink of milk would satisfy her hunger until morning, which she would worry about when the sun came up.

Stealthily she crept out of bed, found her bathrobe in a suitcase without turning on a light and tiptoed barefoot to the door. She listened for several moments, holding her breath so that she would pick up any sound in the house. There was none, so she slowly turned the knob and opened the door. A tiny night-light burned in the hall, sufficient light for her to make her way to the kitchen.

The bedroom area was far enough away from the kitchen that a light wouldn't alert Wyatt, Melissa decided, and she located the switch for the ceiling light and turned it on. The sudden infusion of light made her blink, but then she went directly to the refrigerator and pulled open the door.

Her eyes widened. The refrigerator was crammed with food, indisputable proof of Wyatt's insufferable plot to hold her prisoner for a week. And he had the unmitigated brass to talk about forgiveness. That would be the day.

Stiff with righteous indignation, Melissa took out a gallon of milk, opened cabinets until she found a glass, then filled it to the brim. Drinking a good third of the contents, she refilled her glass and returned the gallon jug to the refrigerator. Planning to take the glass of milk to her bedroom, she started for the light switch to darken the kitchen again.

Only Wyatt suddenly materialized in the doorway. Startled, Melissa stared. He was wearing a pair of gray sweatpants and nothing else.

"Having trouble sleeping?" he asked. "Your bed is comfortable, isn't it?" He knew her sleeplessness had nothing to do with the bed. Neither did his. But he would overlook no opportunity to make her talk to him, even if the subject matter was only bland and impersonal.

"I got up for a glass of milk," she said, which was completely obvious from what she was holding. He was filling the doorway, blocking her passage, and his partial nudity was unnerving. She tried to avoid looking at his naked chest, but involuntarily flicked it a glance. The mat of hair between his nipples gave her a start. He hadn't had any hair on his chest—or very little—before her move to California.

Nervous suddenly, she backed away and took refuge on a chair behind the table. Wyatt went on into the kitchen and opened the refrigerator door. "That milk looks good. Guess I'll have some, too." He took out not only a gallon of milk, but a plastic bottle of chocolate syrup.

"Don't tell me you still have to have chocolate in your milk," Melissa said in a scathing tone.

Wyatt sent her a grin. "Still just a kid at heart, I guess." He poured his milk into a glass and added a generous squirt of chocolate. Stirring the mixture with a spoon, he leaned against the counter and looked at her. "So you remember my preference for chocolate milk, hmm?"

"I didn't until now," Melissa said stonily.

"Do you remember the Whirl-In Drive-In? It isn't there anymore, a darned shame. We sure used to have some good times there, didn't we? All of our friends hung out at the Whirl-In. Do you remember their french fries? Made out of real potatoes. Best I've ever eaten.''

"*My* french fries are made out of real potatoes.''

"No kidding? I'll have to try them.''

"From jail?''

Wyatt looked a bit startled, but then he grinned. "You're not really going to have me arrested, are you?''

Melissa didn't answer, merely took several swallows from her glass. But she did ask herself the same question: was she *really* going to file charges when he took her back to town?

"Melissa?'' he said softly. "Are you?''

"I'm thinking,'' she said coolly. "It's only what you deserve, you know.'' She thought of the pages in her purse on which she had started documenting his crime.

"In my estimation this is the most romantic thing I've ever done,'' Wyatt said.

"Romantic, did you say?'' Her expression was incredulous. "You actually believe that kidnapping a woman is romantic?''

"Kidnapping you is. Forget other women. There are none to compare with you.''

She wasn't going to sit there and listen to his phony flattery. Melissa finished off her milk. "I'm going back to bed.''

"What can I say to change your attitude?'' Wyatt murmured. "How about this? You're the only woman I've ever loved.''

She got up quickly. "That's a line of bull and I don't want to hear it.'' She started around the table, but Wyatt stepped in front of her. "Don't you dare try anything,'' she warned.

"It's not a line, Melissa.''

The softness and texture of his voice alarmed her, not because of him but because of what it did to her. Deep inside she felt a curling heat, and any such response to Wyatt was ludicrous. Her eyes suddenly blazed. "Am I going to have to fight my way out of this room?''

His brown eyes drifted over her face. "Don't fight me over anything, Melissa. Let yourself relax and enjoy the place. You used to tell me on the telephone how much you disliked California. This could be a much better vacation than the one you had planned."

"I wasn't going to visit California," she retorted. "I was going to visit my mother. Now, move out of the way so I can leave."

He stood there for another few moments, then nodded and backed off. Melissa immediately dashed around him and to the door. "I hope you can sleep now," he called.

"Yeah, right," she muttered, hastening down the hall to her room. There were tears in her eyes, which infuriated her. She closed and locked the door, tossed her bathrobe on a chair and climbed into bed.

It was raining again. She could hear it on the roof. She had always liked the sound of rain at night, but tonight she had too much to think about to enjoy the pitter-patter of raindrops.

Her biggest worry now, she realized uneasily, was that Wyatt had a chance of succeeding with his nefarious scheme. Like it or not, she had been affected by his near nudity in the kitchen, by his tousled hair and good looks. Maybe that was understandable. He was an especially handsome man and she had once been mesmerized by his looks. But feeling something because he told her ridiculous lies, like her being the only woman he'd ever loved, was deeply disturbing. Was it possible for him to erode her determination to keep a wide chasm between them with an onslaught of flattery and charm? He wasn't going to suddenly jump on her, she felt, but subtlety always had worked with her much better than crudity or pushy machismo, and Wyatt wasn't stupid or dense.

God, if she succumbed in any way, if she permitted even one pass, she would never forgive herself.

She finally fell asleep, only to dream chaotic dreams that brought her awake several different times.

It was not a good night.

Melissa came awake slowly, stretched, glanced around the room and remembered where she was. Jerking upright, she checked the clock on the nightstand and was surprised to see that she had slept until almost nine.

She lay down again, as tense as she'd been last night. This was outrageous and something had to be done about it. How could a fact be so clear and so murky at the same time? Doing nothing about Wyatt's bloody gall in this fiasco was intolerable, and yet no way around it came to mind, no matter how intently she concentrated.

What that man deserved was a dose of his own medicine. But tit for tat in this instance meant *her* plotting to kidnap *him* someday, which was too ridiculous to consider.

Sighing dismally, Melissa forced herself out of bed. Pushing aside the curtain at a window, she glowered at the drizzling rain. A little sunshine wouldn't have solved her dilemma, but it might have lifted her sagging spirit a few notches.

After showering, she fixed her hair and put on makeup. Not for Wyatt North, God forbid, but she wasn't going to alter her own personal regime for him or anyone else. If he got any foolish ideas over the fact that she was wearing makeup, she would gladly and heartily set him straight. Her silly reaction to his naked torso in the middle of the night seemed a hundred years away this morning, and most definitely was not going to be repeated during her enforced confinement here.

Dressed in the same slacks and sweater she had changed into yesterday, Melissa made the bed and finally left the room. Her refusal to eat was foolish, she realized, tough as it had sounded when she had given Wyatt the word. She was ravenously hungry this morning and would eat whatever was available. She went directly to the kitchen.

To her annoyance, Wyatt was sitting at the table with a cup of coffee.

"Hi," he said cheerfully.

She shot him a dirty look and moved to the counter containing the coffeepot and a clean cup, obviously intended for her.

"Nasty day out there," Wyatt remarked. "I was hoping for sunshine today. There are some great hiking trails on this mountain and I've been thinking of showing you the area."

Melissa turned with her cup of coffee. "I'm not interested in being *shown* the area. Could I make myself some toast?"

"The refrigerator and the cupboards are full of food, Melissa. Make anything you want. I've already eaten, but if you'd like, I could fry up some bacon and—"

"I'll have some fruit and toast," she said coolly. The fruit was in plain sight, a large bowl of it on the counter—bananas, apples, oranges and pears. "Where will I find the bread?"

Wyatt got up and went to open a cabinet. "There's bread, doughnuts, sweet rolls and English muffins in here. Take your pick."

"What, no bagels?"

Reaching behind the bread, he pulled out a package of bagels. "Will these do?"

"You thought of everything, didn't you?" It wasn't said kindly, certainly not as a compliment. Resentment was in every line of her body as she waited until Wyatt had resumed his chair before helping herself to two slices of wheat bread, which she dropped into the toaster.

She stood like a sentinel watching that toaster, all too aware of Wyatt watching her in the same steadfast way. Her gaze briefly flicked his way. "Must you stare?"

"Just trying to figure you out," he said.

"Work on yourself, Wyatt. At least I'm not a criminal."

He couldn't help laughing. "I keep forgetting that."

"You have a convenient memory."

"Have you noticed how we keep returning to the subject of memory?" The toast popped up. "There's a plate in that cabinet to your right." Melissa found a small plate and put the toast on it. "As I was saying," Wyatt said, "our entire relationship revolves around memories."

"You were saying no such thing." Melissa plucked an orange from the bowl and brought it to the table, deftly balancing it, her plate of toast and cup of coffee. She sat down. "What you said was that we keep returning to the subject of memory. Let me add that you're the only one in this house even remotely concerned with the topic." She began peeling the orange. "There's only one phase of the past that interests me, and that's my father's murder. So you see, you can talk about the Whirl-In Drive-In, old friends and anything else that might flit through that mass in your head that passes for a brain, and I couldn't care less."

"Ouch," Wyatt said, though he grinned. "You're trying really hard to stay mad at me, aren't you?"

She gave him a disgusted glance. "Do you think I have to try? Believe me, it's the most natural feeling in the world right now."

"Real anger requires a certain level of adrenaline, which the human body can sustain for only so long," Wyatt said. "You're just clinging to remnants of yesterday's anger this morning."

"An analyst, too? There's just no end to your talents." Damn, she'd love to put him on the hot seat. Just once she'd like to see him squirm. Maybe she knew how to do it, too. "You certainly don't seem very broken up over your impending divorce."

"It's not pending anymore. I received the final decree in the mail a few days ago." Wyatt smiled. "You're looking at a free man, Melissa."

He hadn't squirmed in the least. Melissa pushed on. "Tell me about your wife."

His smile disappeared and his eyes narrowed slightly. "I'll be happy to, if you'll let me start at the beginning."

"You mean those days when you were sleeping around?" Melissa popped a section of orange into her mouth. "Why on earth would you think I'd be interested in your college love life?''

Wyatt wasn't even close to smiling now. "I didn't have a college love life, Melissa. I made one mistake and I paid for it for six years."

"Enough," she said, getting to her feet. "We're not going to start talking about poor you and judgmental me."

Wyatt got up, too. "How about talking about regret? Remorse? I've asked for your forgiveness, but do you think I've forgiven myself, or that I ever will? Melissa, sit with me, please. Talk to me."

She had brought her orange peelings to the sink. "Is the trash can under the sink?"

"Yes. Melissa, please come back to the table. We were just starting to make some headway."

She located the trash can and dropped in the orange peels. Straightening, she took a breath and looked at him. "You want me to ease your conscience. Why it's still bothering you after all these years I have no idea, but I'm not going to do it, Wyatt. I'm not going to tell you what you did was all right. Whatever price you paid for what you did wasn't nearly enough. That's the way I feel, and bringing me up here to brainwash me into thinking otherwise isn't going to work."

She returned to the table, but only to pick up her empty plate and coffee cup. Carrying them to the sink, fully aware of Wyatt standing there and watching her every movement, she rinsed the dishes and then slipped them into the dishwasher.

"I never thought you were so hard," he said quietly.

His comment hurt. She whirled around to face him. "Oh, get a grip, Wyatt. It takes a little hardness to even make it in this world. Don't ever expect timidity or meekness from me. I'm as far from the girl you knew in high school as any woman could be. And you want to know what makes people hard in the first place? It's other people steamrolling them."

"Like I did to you."

"The shoe does fit, doesn't it?"

He hesitated, then nodded. "It doesn't just fit, Melissa, it pinches like hell. Do you know that I would do anything to make it up to you? Are you able to grasp that concept? Wait, let me rephrase that. Would you please *let* yourself believe it?"

"My God, it doesn't matter if I believe it or not! Why won't *you* let yourself believe that?"

"You know why I can't."

"Because I'm the only woman you've ever loved," Melissa said scornfully.

"It happens to be the truth." Wyatt came around the table and stopped right in front of her. "I'll tell you what I believe, Melissa. Love isn't something one can turn on and off like a light bulb. Yes, you were hurt, with damned good reason. I would rather have cut off my own right arm than make that call six years ago. I knew what it would do to you, because it was doing the same thing to me. But I had no choice. I—"

"You made your choice several weeks *before* that call," Melissa said bitterly. She threw up her hands. "This is precisely the conversation I swore to avoid. I'm going to my room. Please don't follow me."

Wyatt's jaw clenched, and he caught her by her wrists before she could stalk off. "Damn you," she cried. "Let go of me!"

"Look at me." She kept her face turned away. "Melissa, when I walked into the Hip Hop and saw you, I nearly blacked out from shock. You were just as shocked—I could see it on your face. If all of your feelings for me had died, as you want me to believe, running into each other wouldn't have been such a shock. Don't you see? You're lying to me and you're lying to yourself."

Her eyes were wide with astonishment. "You couldn't possibly have the audacity to think I'm still in love with you. My God, Wyatt, get real. Your theory about love and light bulbs is utter hogwash. I didn't turn off my feelings, you jerk, you killed them! Now, let go of my wrists or so help me I'll kick you where it hurts the most."

He yanked her up against himself. "Kick me now," he mumbled into her hair. Touching her, holding her, was immediately arousing, quickening his heartbeat, thickening his voice. "You're so beautiful," he whispered.

And just like that, like a bolt from the blue, Melissa knew how to get even. She would have her revenge, and not only for the frustration of being brought here against her will. By the end of this wretched week Wyatt was going to suffer, damn him, suffer the way she had suffered in California after his phone call.

She became very still in his arms, though she laid her cheek on his chest. "I'm so very confused," she whispered.

Wyatt's pulse went crazy with wonder, with happiness. He had hoped, prayed even, that this would happen, that being together would create a chink in Melissa's armor of self-righteousness. This was a little sooner than he'd dared to envision it occurring, but she wasn't fighting his embrace. Rather, he sensed acceptance from her, and even a little response.

His lips moved in her hair while he inhaled its intoxicating scent. "I'm not trying to confuse you, Melissa. This is like coming out of a nightmare for me. Maybe the same thing is happening to you."

"Possibly," she murmured. *You snake in the grass. We'll see who has the last word.*

Dare he kiss her? He wanted to so badly he ached, but how far should he go in this first concession? He gently stroked her back, permitting himself that familiarity at least. She felt like the Melissa in his memory, but there was more of her to hold now. Her breasts were different, he realized. They were fuller, larger, and having them pressed into his chest was the most incredible sensation of his life. He was getting very hard, and as closely bonded as they were, she had to know it. Yet she didn't move away.

He brought his right hand around from her back, took her chin and tipped her face up to look into her eyes. They contained a misty quality, he saw, which nearly undid him. He *had* to kiss her.

His mouth descended to hers, very slowly. Regardless of her acquiescence thus far, he halfway expected her to pull back. But she stood there and let his lips meet hers. He kept the kiss tender and very gentle, a monumental effort when what he wanted to do was sweep her up in his arms and carry her to his bedroom. But his tongue remained in his own mouth, and it was a sweet kiss of lips upon lips.

Still, his heavy breathing related his intense desire, and Melissa was fully cognizant of what was going on in his nasty little mind. Oh yes, this was going to work beautifully, she thought. His kiss was just a kiss, she told herself. She could probably even make love with him and feel nothing.

Well, she might *feel* something. She was as human as the next woman. But he would never know her true feelings, the cad, not until she laid them on him at the end of the week.

Lifting his head, Wyatt attempted a smile that came off pretty weak. "You're a potent woman," he whispered hoarsely.

She licked her lips, slowly, seductively, noticing his almost hypnotic interest in the tip of her tongue. "We shouldn't be—be doing this," she said tremulously, as though she simply couldn't stop herself from responding to *his* potency.

His hands rose to cup her face. She could feel the tension in his body, his fingers, see it in his eyes. One rather trivial kiss and he was nearing the explosive stage. This was going to be easy.

"You have to know how much I want you," he whispered, his lips a mere fraction from hers.

He had learned boldness in the past six years, she thought resentfully. The Wyatt in her memory would never have said that to her. "I know," she whispered back. "But...let's give it a little time. I'll be here for a week. Let's not rush into anything."

With a labored breath, he closed his eyes and brought her head to his chest. "Whatever you say," he said raggedly. "If you only knew what this means to me...holding you... kissing you...how I've dreamed of having you in my arms." He gave a shaky laugh. "I'd like to hold on to you forever. Maybe I'm afraid if I let go of you, you'll disappear."

"I won't disappear. I'm very solid flesh and blood. Can't you tell?"

"Oh, God, Melissa," he groaned, and the utter agony in his voice brought a frown to her brow.

But she wanted him to suffer, didn't she? What had she thought he was going to do, go off into a closet somewhere and suffer where she wouldn't see it?

Okay, maybe her plan of revenge wasn't going to be as easy or simple as she'd thought. But it was a good plan and only what Wyatt deserved. Her own sensibilities would just have to tone themselves down some.

What *really* bothered her was how good he felt. That was her biggest concern, she realized. If he got to feeling too good, she could end up hurting as much as he was going to.

No, that wasn't going to happen. She was going to keep a lid on her own emotions and fan his into a frenzy. Then, at the end of the week, when he was completely starry-eyed, she would tell him she was going to marry another man. Yes, that would be the grand finale. He would demand to know who the man was, of course, and what would she say?

Well, she'd worry about that later. She snuggled closer to him for just a moment, then stepped back when she felt his arms begin to tighten around her. "Later," she said with her eyes full of promises.

Wyatt sucked in a ragged breath and repeated, "Whatever you say."

Nine

After Melissa went to her room, Wyatt walked the floor. There was a gladness within him—youthful in its flavor—that almost overwhelmed the desire, although he knew no other emotion would probably ever have the power to really accomplish that amazing fact. There wasn't one tiny part of his body that didn't ache for Melissa's. Although it was pure and utter torture, he couldn't stop his mind from devising erotic images, each of them depicting Melissa and himself in various stages of undress and crazed with passion.

He couldn't sit, though he tried to several times. He attempted reading, went outside and stood on the porch for a few minutes, then came back inside. His nerves were raw, standing on end, with his mind feeling as though he were teetering on the very edge of a precipice, shaky and uncertain of just when he was going to go hurtling over it.

Again and again he thought of the morning. She had let him kiss her. She had admitted confusion. She had stopped her sharp-tongued retorts and started being nice to him. She had said, "Later," and promised volumes with her beautiful blue eyes. It was too much too fast; it wasn't nearly enough and time was dragging.

He was standing near the fireplace, rocking back and forth on his boot heels when Melissa walked into the room. He looked at her with adoration, with longing, while his heart leapt around in his chest.

She was wearing her raincoat. "I'm going out for a breath of air," she said.

"I'll go with you."

"No, please. I need to do some thinking."

He nodded his understanding. "Don't go too far. The mountain can be treacherous if you don't know the trails."

"Don't worry. I'll stay in the clearing." She went through the front door.

Wyatt watched her from a window. She seemed to be deeply engrossed.

It was the truth. She was questioning her plan of revenge. Never had she considered herself a vengeful or vindictive person, and yet wasn't she admittedly obsessed with finding her father's murderer? Was that vengeance or justice? Maybe she didn't know herself as well as she'd thought.

She could ask the same question about Wyatt's sins. Did she want vengeance or justice? Justice was a reward or a penalty, as deserved. Vengeance was retribution for an offense. The definitions were worlds apart, and yet there were instances when either seemed appropriate.

Sighing, Melissa slowly circled the house. Behind it were several smaller buildings—a garage, she thought, and maybe a toolshed. There was also a long structure with a roof and only three sides. It contained a supply of neatly stacked firewood.

The air was damp with a light, misting rain. Melissa stopped, lifted her face and closed her eyes. The mist felt good on her feverish skin, which hadn't *been* feverish before that episode in the kitchen. Justice or revenge, revenge or justice. Which was it?

If only Wyatt hadn't moved back to his ranch. If only he hadn't dropped in at the café.

She had naturally thought of him when *she'd* moved back, but she hadn't dwelled on it because she knew he was married and living in Helena. He was right about her being shocked that day. She couldn't remember ever being more shocked about anything.

Except for the day Judd Hensley had called her about the remains of a body discovered on the Laughing Horse Reservation being identified through dental records as her father, Charlie Avery.

But had Wyatt's shock in the café been genuine or an exceptionally good act? Wasn't it just a little bit unbelievable that he'd happened to stop at the café completely ignorant of her ownership? Completely unaware of her return to Whitehorn?

Resuming her slow pace, Melissa heaved a troubled sigh. Why should she believe anything he said? And whether for vengeance or justice, didn't he deserve to be taken down a peg or two? It was within her power to do it. All it would take was being nice to him for six more days. He would expect kisses, to be sure, and would probably do his level best to get her into bed. But she could certainly sidestep sex. No other man had talked her into bed when she hadn't wanted to be there, and that was all Wyatt was to her, just a man. Not even a friend, to be honest. Not even someone she liked or respected.

Wyatt stepped away from the window when he saw her returning to the house. His stomach was tied in knots. The throbbing in his loins was more uncomfortable, though. They could have an incredible six days and nights up here, if she agreed.

She walked in with flushed cheeks and wispy curls around her face from the dampness outside.

Wyatt forced a casual tone in his voice. "I was just getting ready to build a fire." As though he needed to prove it, he began gathering paper and kindling from the rock alcove built into the wall of the fireplace.

Melissa took off her coat. "I'm going to hang this up."

He sent her a pleading look. "Come back."

She hadn't seen his look; she was on her way out of the room. "I will. A fire sounds great."

Wyatt realized that his hands weren't steady as he crushed sheets of newspaper and arranged them on the grate. He added kindling, then two small logs. Once the fire got going he would add more wood, but he always started a small fire first.

It was a routine he would be wise to remember with Melissa, he thought. Start small. Don't rush her. She was coming around, speaking civilly to him. And after this morning could he doubt the progress they had made in a very short span of time?

Melissa returned. The fact that she was smiling gave Wyatt's spirit wings. "The fire's starting to warm up. Sit here, next to it." He moved a chair closer to the fireplace.

"Thank you." She sank into the deep-seated, upholstered chair. "It's much cooler up here in the mountains than in town."

"At any given point of the year," Wyatt replied. "Because of the elevation. It's possible that this rain could turn to snow. I've seen snow up here at the end of August many times."

"Your father built this cabin?"

"He had it built, yes." The flames were ready for more fuel. Wyatt placed one large log in the center of the oversize grate. Then he moved his own chair closer to Melissa's and the fire. A peace, of sorts, settled upon him. He remembered his mother and father sitting in just this way, talking quietly, enjoying the warmth of the fire and each other.

"After Mother died, Dad didn't come up here for a long time," he said. "But then, when I was about fifteen, he started bringing me here again. To fish, mostly, but also to walk the trails. In his latter years he spent a lot of time up here. I think he felt closer to Mother here than at the ranch." Wyatt paused for a moment, then said quietly, "He never stopped missing her."

He turned his head to look at Melissa. "They had a very special relationship, the kind of marriage everyone should have."

"And few do," Melissa murmured, thinking of her own parents—her father gone, her mother bitter.

"Even one really good marriage gives the rest of us hope, though, don't you agree? If it's possible for one couple, it's possible for others."

"Possible, yes, but given today's divorce statistics, not very probable."

"Melissa?" Wyatt hesitated, but he had to ask. "Didn't you ever meet anyone important in California?"

Inwardly she stiffened. How candid could she be with him? How much of her private self could she expose to his scrutiny? He shouldn't be asking her questions like that. All she had to do to renew the pain of his perfidy was to recall his phone call. *"Melissa, I got a woman pregnant and I'm going to marry her."* She owed Wyatt nothing . . . except for maybe a little justice.

"No," she lied. There had been a few men whom she'd thought important, but the relationships had petered out for various reasons, none of which she was going to explain to him.

"But you must have dated. You're so beautiful, and men had to have noticed."

"I dated," she admitted. "But nothing came of it." She sent him a look. "And I'm not beautiful. I don't know why you keep saying that."

"Melissa, you're the most beautiful woman I've ever seen."

"That's silly." She got up in a hasty movement. "And I don't want to talk about it. How about some lunch? I'll fix it."

Wyatt slowly rose. He had offended her by talking about her looks, a fact he couldn't quite grasp. Didn't she know how beautiful she was? "I'll help," he offered.

"No, you stay here. I'm really very good in a kitchen."

"I'm sure you are," he said, but he wasn't positive she heard because she was already out of the room. Sighing, he sank back in his chair. Had this morning been a fluke? Had he read too much in the fact that she had permitted a kiss between them?

Despondent, he stared into the flames. Maybe he would never understand Melissa again. There had been a time when they had all but read each other's mind. God, it had been great. They had held hands whenever walking together, and everything had been funny. They had probably spent more time saying silly things and laughing than any other activity. And he had been so proud to be dating the prettiest girl in school, the prettiest, the nicest, the friendliest. Maybe even the smartest. Melissa had pulled straight *A*'s. He would have done as well if it hadn't been for science. He had never been able to get past a *B* in any of his science classes.

But he had excelled in math and sports. Though he had taken part in all the school had provided—basketball, baseball and track—football had been his favorite. Melissa had attended every game, and afterward they and a bunch of their friends would head for the Whirl-In. Those were wonderful memories.

Then had come college. He hadn't wanted to go, and had only done so at his father's insistence. He hadn't tried out for any of the sports teams, simply because he was merely biding his time until he could get out of school and back to the ranch. Melissa would return, too, and they would be married. It was what he lived for.

Everything had gone to hell the night he'd met Shannon Kiley.

Cursing under his breath, Wyatt got up to give the fire an unnecessarily vicious stir with a cast-iron poker. He *had* to make this week work. If he didn't, the future would be awfully damned bleak.

During lunch they talked about the weather, about Simon North, Wyatt's father, and about Nan Avery, Melissa's mother. Neither of them mentioned themselves, though their conversation was really just a cover-up for what they were each thinking.

Behind Wyatt's input was a vow—considered from many angles—to take it slow and easy with Melissa. Behind Melissa's was discord because of her wish for justice. That was how she was thinking of her plan to get even with Wyatt for abducting her now—as justice fair and square. It was a much more comfortable term than vengeance and, unquestionably, he had brought it on himself.

Still, she realized that she wasn't completely sold on the idea, fair or not. It depended, she decided while finishing her cup of tea, on how he replied to one crucial question.

She set down her cup and looked across the table directly into Wyatt's eyes. "If I asked you to take me back to town today, would you do it?"

Her question, coming without warning, startled Wyatt. "Uh..." Her stare was unrelenting. He could almost see the progress they had made flying away. And yet, even though advances had been made, they hadn't really resolved anything. He looked down at his plate and spoke in a low voice. "Not today."

"Tomorrow, Wyatt? The day after?"

Her calm tone surprised him. His gaze rose to hers. "I'd really like to stick to the original plan, Melissa."

She nodded. "I see." If anyone had ever asked for "justice," it was Wyatt. Melissa's feeling of guilt vanished completely. The hurt he'd inflicted six years ago had diminished with time—to a point—though she had been honest when she'd told him it would never be forgotten. But he had barged back into her life with all the subtlety of a water buffalo, and if she didn't do something about it, she would never be able to regard herself as anything but a coward for the rest of her days.

His expression was cautious. "You're not angry?"

She smiled sweetly. "I'm not going to get angry, Wyatt, I'm going to get even."

He blinked. "You're what? How?"

"I haven't quite figured that out yet," she lied. Standing, she began to clear the table. "You'll know when it happens."

"Well, hell," he muttered. How could she get even? What was percolating in the back of her mind? He had never thought of Melissa as capable of devious behavior, but then it had been a long time since they had spent any time together.

But wasn't that why he had brought her out here—so they could get to know each other again? She sure hadn't been letting it happen in town.

He got to his feet. "You made our lunch. Let me clean up."

Her smile was dazzling and definitely flirtatious. "How sweet. Sure, go ahead. I'll be in the living room."

Wyatt stood there after she was gone, feeling as though he'd just been stonewalled and not knowing exactly how it had happened. One minute she was talking about getting even and the next giving him a smile that raised his blood pressure.

Dismayed by it all, he slowly shook his head. Women were the most confusing of all God's creatures. Was there a man alive who truly understood them?

After the kitchen was in order, Wyatt put on a jacket and his hat and went outside to the woodpile. He carried in an armload of logs and deposited them in the fireplace alcove. Melissa was curled up in her chair, looking quite comfortable and relaxed. She smiled at him. "Taking care of chores?"

"Just bringing in some firewood." He left to get another armload.

Melissa's smile remained intact. She felt at peace with her plan now. She had given him every chance to elude justice and he had failed the test. So be it.

He made two more trips to the woodpile and the alcove was filled to the top. Before taking off his jacket, he added two small logs to the fire and stirred the coals to life. "We won't need a big fire until evening," he said.

"It's very pleasant," Melissa murmured, stretching lazily. "I love a fire."

After staring at that sexy stretch, he left for a minute to hang up his hat and jacket and then returned to sit in his chair. He didn't know which way to go with Melissa now. There was still a lot he wanted to tell her, but she would let him get only so close to certain subjects. A good five minutes passed with him staring broodingly into the flames.

Finally he couldn't bear the silence any longer. "Well," he said, "we've got all afternoon. Is there anything you'd like to do?"

Melissa made a snuggling movement. "I'm perfectly content, but maybe there's something *you'd* like to do."

He hesitated, then grinned slightly. "If I said what I'd like to do, you'd probably throw something at me. Maybe that lamp next to your chair."

She laughed. "Oh, I don't know. I just might surprise you."

"Melissa, you surprise me every minute of every hour."

She laughed again. "At least I'm not boring you."

"You could never bore me."

"Tell me what you'd like to do on this rainy afternoon," she urged. "Go on. Don't be shy."

"You're serious? You really want to hear it?"

"I'd love to hear it."

He looked away for a moment, then leaned forward in his chair, his forearms resting on his thighs, his gaze on the fire. "I think you already know."

"Do I?"

His head turned toward her. "Don't you?"

"Are we playing twenty questions? Is that what you're afraid to tell me?"

"Don't tease, Melissa. You know how I feel about you. What do you *suppose* I'd like to do this afternoon? And tonight, tomorrow, every day and night you're with me?"

Her pulse went wild, though she hid it well. "And where would you like this to take place? Here, in front of the fire?"

"Here would do just fine. So would a bed. For a fact, it could take place in any room of this cabin, in any section of any room."

Delicately she cleared her throat. "I see. This would include undressing, of course. You naked, me naked?"

"Sweet Jesus," he mumbled, closing his eyes at the sudden rush of blood to his groin. Was this how she intended to get even—by driving him crazy with desire and never doing more than talk about it? "Stop it," he whispered thickly. "Unless you mean it, don't say it."

"Oh. Then I guess I'd better figure out if I mean it," she said thoughtfully, deliberately sounding as though she were talking only to herself. "Maybe if you kissed me . . . ?" she added, speaking slowly and as if she were truly perplexed.

He didn't need a second invitation. In one fluid movement he left his chair and knelt in front of hers. Pushing her knees apart, he fit his hips between them and at the same time burrowed his hands behind her to bring her forward.

Melissa's eyes grew as big as saucers. That curling heat was in her belly again, and she *had* to ignore it, which, she was discovering, was no small achievement. Wyatt nuzzled his face into the curve of her throat. "You smell like no woman who ever lived," he whispered.

She was getting a little alarmed. "Wyatt, I said to kiss me, not—not this."

He raised his head to see her face. "When we made love before, I didn't know what I was doing. Neither did you."

"We . . . managed," she said weakly. "Besides, I really don't care to be reminded of how you got your—your experience."

"Didn't you get some experience?"

"That's really none of your business."

He took her face between his hands. His eyes were dark and burning with emotion. "You said you dated. You've

.nade love with someone other than me, haven't you? Tell me the truth, Melissa. Whatever else you do or don't do, tell me the truth about this."

She couldn't tear her eyes from his. There was so much passion in his eyes, so much emotion. "Wyatt..."

"Tell me!"

"All right, yes! I made love with other men. Why shouldn't I have?"

His hands dropped to her shoulders. "I never said you shouldn't have, did I?" But his voice was shaky and hoarse.

"Anything I did shouldn't bother you," she said, letting her resentment show. "*You* sure weren't sleeping alone."

He felt like the bottom had just dropped out of his stomach, and he had no right to feel that way. Love could bring the strongest man to his knees, he thought, which was right where he was, on his knees in front of Melissa, leaning into her, probably looking like a lovesick calf.

He didn't like that picture. Breaking all contact with her, he sat back on his heels. "That's one of the things I brought you up here to talk about."

Melissa's left eyebrow went up in utter astonishment. "You want to discuss you and your wife's sex life with me?"

"Ex-wife, and no, that's not what I meant. How crass do you think I am?"

"That's a loaded question, considering how you got me here."

He gave her a very long look, one that lasted until she became edgy about it and said, "What?" in a rather belligerent tone.

"I don't know how to take you. I have the feeling you want me to think you're not angry anymore about being here and it's not the truth. Melissa, why did you ask me what I wanted to do on this rainy afternoon?"

She shrugged. "Because you asked me."

"But you didn't leave it at that. You taunted me. You turned our discussion into something sexual. Then you pretended confusion and asked me to kiss you. Know what? I think we'll skip the conversation and the confusion and get to the kiss."

She hadn't quite kept up with his rapid accusations and ultimate conclusion, so she wasn't prepared for his touch. His hand snaked beneath her hair to cup the back of her neck. A thrill she wasn't anticipating shot through her with the speed and impact of a bolt of lightning. "Wait... Wyatt—"

Her objection was eliminated very effectively by his lips on hers. It was a kiss very much like this morning's had been, gentle and undemanding, which eased some of her tension. His mouth felt wonderful, in fact—soft and giving. She began kissing him back, moving her lips against his. It was a delightful kiss, sweetly unselfish and certainly nothing to cause alarm.

Then his mouth left hers to move over her face. She sighed, though she told herself her enjoyment was completely impersonal. She would feel the same if any attractive man kissed her so obligingly.

She could feel herself sinking into emotion, but that, too, didn't alarm her. She wasn't brain dead, after all, and Wyatt seemed perfectly contented with what she considered a rather innocent embrace. This time when he nuzzled her throat, she made no protest. She felt warmer than she had, but then the fire was putting out more heat than it had a few minutes ago.

He kissed her mouth again, and she felt a definite difference in style. His tongue slid along her lips, urging them apart. The strangest weakness was disabling her limbs, she realized, but the sensation wasn't only strange, it was quite delicious.

Then he really kissed her, with his tongue in her mouth and his body pressing hers deeper into the chair. Her mind was suddenly clouded, dazed. As if from a great distance she remembered that she wasn't going to get carried away by anything Wyatt did. But his weight against her and his

kisses, one after another, made reality and even justice seem
so trivial.

He backed away from the chair and pulled her down to
the floor. With both of them lying down, he leaned over her
and opened his lips around hers, taking her gasp of surprise into his own mouth. She wanted to say no. The thought
was suddenly crystal clear in her mind, the word in her
throat. But he kept kissing her and she couldn't get it out.
The only sounds she was able to manage were soft moans of
intense pleasure, which weren't at all a part of her plan.

This man was not the Wyatt of old. This man knew how
to kiss and arouse and make a woman lose sight of herself
and everything else. So dizzy the room seemed to be spin-
ning, she attempted to push him away. But even while her
hands were feebly pushing against his chest and shoulders,
she was sucking on his tongue. Obviously she had completely lost her mind, but she couldn't think of how to get it
back. In fact, she couldn't think at all, not about anything
but what he was making her feel. The floor beneath her felt
soft, when she knew it wasn't. Wyatt felt weightless on top
of her, when she knew he had to be at least a hundred and
ninety pounds. While the heat in her body rose to the feverish stage, her brain seemed to be floating and utterly use-
less.

She knew when he slid up her sweater and then pulled it
over her head. She knew when he undid her slacks and
worked them down her hips. But it was as if it was happening to someone else. Surely it couldn't be her, Melissa Avery,
lying on the floor with Wyatt North and permitting, even
encouraging each of his steps to seduction.

As though of their own accord, her fingers unbuttoned his
shirt and pushed it off of his shoulders. The intensity in his
eyes only added fuel to the fires searing her vital organs. His
hard breathing was no harder than her own. There was no
longer gentleness, or tenderness, and certainly no sweetness in their groping and grabbing at each other's clothing.
His shirt vanished. She registered him fumbling with his belt

buckle, with the button on his jeans, and with his zipper. His manhood sprang forth while he tore away her panties.

She croaked out two words. "Use protection."

He did it with all possible speed. Then he was there, at the heated, moist entry he needed so desperately. He thrust himself inside of her and groaned out loud. "Melissa...baby..."

Her hips rose to meet him halfway. Her eyes were closed for a long time and when she opened them she saw him watching her face. There was no levity on his, no light-heartedness, nothing remotely familiar or sweet. But she was too far gone to dissect expressions. He undid her bra and bared her breasts, then bent his head to suck on her nipples, all the time moving within her, moving, moving.

Her chest was heaving for air. Her brain wasn't floating anymore, it was being dashed about by intense emotions. The pleasure was overwhelming, but it wasn't enough. There was something she must reach, the ultimate high, and she closed her eyes to concentrate on attaining it.

Wyatt knew he was about to go over the edge. He gritted his teeth and clenched his jaw. If he failed Melissa now, there might never be a second chance. He was sweating, from the heat radiating from the fireplace and from his own exertions. But it had to be perfect for her or every gain he'd made since their arrival on the mountain could vanish in the blink of an eye.

He knew he'd make it when she began whimpering deep in her throat and tossing her head back and forth. Her legs went up around him, drawing him deeper inside her, clamping him tighter against her. Her fingernails raked his back, and she finally cried out, "Yes...oh, yes. *Yes!*"

Releasing his self-control with intense relief, he reached the pinnacle seconds behind her. "Melissa...*Melissa!*"

Ten

At first Melissa just lay there basking in the incredible afterglow of truly stupendous lovemaking. There were tears in her eyes, she realized when she turned her face toward the fireplace and the flames appeared blurred. Her heart was still pounding, but as reality began returning, she suspected her only alternative to an overfast heartbeat was none at all.

This was utterly insane. She had done exactly what she had vowed *not* to do—lose herself in Wyatt's arms. It wasn't making love with him that was so imprudent, it was her total immersion in the act, her amnesiac behavior. Every important aspect of her life had vanished from her foolish female brain, including Wyatt's betrayal six years ago, his trickery in getting her out here and her own plan to get even. How effective would a declaration of loving and marrying another man be after this?

Oh, how smug he must be feeling right now. So proud of his masculine power. So cocksure. If he dared to say something smug or condescending when he spoke, she wouldn't be able to keep her disgust for either of them to herself.

"Let me up," she said.

With a satisfied sigh Wyatt raised his head and looked at her. "I knew it would be like that for us, Melissa. I never stopped loving you. I—"

"Don't!" Wriggling, she pushed on his chest. "How can you say something like that?"

"Because it's true."

Tears filled her eyes again. Her plan was in shambles. How could she have behaved so outrageously? Other than

a complete fool, who was she these days? Before Wyatt re-
entered her life she had been a confident, reasonably contented woman with several important goals. Now she didn't
know herself at all, and it was all Wyatt's fault.

"Hey," he said softly, brushing away the moisture from
beneath her eyes with his thumb. "Please don't regret this."
Because she didn't know what else to do, she let him hold
her and actually wept on his shoulder.

Then something clicked in her head. Wasn't this exactly
what she had wanted to happen—him declaring eternal love
for her? He never needed to know how deeply she had been
affected by their lovemaking. Wasn't this really just an extremely influencing first step toward the moment when she
told him her trumped-up story of being in love with another man? A few days of heartache wouldn't kill her. She
had learned six years ago that one didn't die from a broken
heart, and even eventually got over it. More or less.

Enough of this maudlin self-pity in Wyatt's presence, she
thought, and twisted her head to see his face. She even
managed a tremulous smile. "I really do need to get up,"
she said. "I'd like to take a shower." She always did her best
crying in the shower.

Wyatt was concerned about her teary eyes. "Are you sure
you're all right?"

"Very sure." She saw the kiss coming and took a breath
and held it. His lips touched hers tenderly, then settled upon
them with a possessiveness she hadn't expected. Instantly
she felt her traitorous body responding. Jerking her head
sideways, she mumbled, "Sorry, but I couldn't breathe."

He smiled indulgently. "Go take your shower, sweetheart. I'll be waiting."

When he moved away from her she stared. He hadn't even
removed his jeans and undershorts, which were a tangled
mess from his knees to his boots.

Hastily she sprang up, gathered her clothes and ran from
the room. Wyatt chuckled deep in his throat. He had never
been happier than he was right this minute.

And it was only going to get better.

Melissa didn't cry in the shower. Instead, while soaping her body, she did some heavy-duty thinking. It seemed that more than ever Wyatt needed a dose of his own medicine. He had decided before ever bringing her here that he was going to seduce her, or at least make the attempt. She *did* have to accept some of the responsibility, but it never would have happened in Whitehorn, which he'd known all too well.

He kept talking about love, of never having stopped loving her, which was a crock. Did he think her a complete moron? Melissa grimaced. She *was* a moron, so why wouldn't he think so? How could she have melted into a whimpering lump of sexual clay for him? He was the last man on earth to whom she should respond so uninhibitedly. And why had she? Why, right now, did the mere act of recalling his lovemaking cause her blood to run faster?

She wasn't going to stand for any of it, she decided with a grim expression. He had committed a felony by abducting her and a crime of immorality by seducing her. Enough was enough. Not only was she going to go through with her plan of fair-and-square justice, but when he brought her back to town she was going to march into the sheriff's office and file a kidnapping charge against him.

In no hurry to return to Wyatt's company, Melissa dawdled while fixing her hair, applying her makeup and getting dressed. She had packed for a week in California, not for chilly, damp weather in the mountains, so her wardrobe wasn't very adequate. The cabin was comfortably warm, fortunately, so she was able to put on a summery dress. It was while she was giving her overall appearance a once-over in front of a large mirror that her decisions in the shower suddenly reversed themselves.

Startled at her own ambivalence, she frowned disapprovingly at her reflection. Could she really file a criminal complaint against Wyatt and send him to prison? Secondly, her seeking justice for Wyatt's *old* crimes was a dangerous undertaking. How much of his lethal chemistry could she take and come out of this unscathed?

Her chin lifted. The long and the short of it was that she had to convince Wyatt to take her back to town and then forget this whole awful episode. Planning retribution with the law and on her own was detrimental to her own future, and she would not think of it again.

Leaving her cosmetics strewn on the bathroom counter, she walked through her bedroom to the hall door. It was time for a showdown.

"Wow," Wyatt said softly when Melissa walked into the living room. "You look gorgeous in that dress."

The dress was one of several she owned in her favorite style—long, flowing and loosely structured. The fabric had a pale blue background that was barely discernible among the multitude of tiny flowers in shades of pink, green and lavender.

"And I love your hair down like this," Wyatt added, his eyes gleaming with admiration. It was also long and flowing, with just enough wave to give it shape. In their better days he had loved her glossy thick hair, loved touching it.

Melissa ignored his compliments and let her eyes flick over *his* clothing—pale gray slacks, a long-sleeved navy shirt and black loafers. He, too, had showered, and his jaw was shiny from a fresh shave.

"That outfit must be part of your Helena wardrobe," she said coolly.

Her tone, not at all what he'd been anticipating, sounded a warning bell in his head. "Do you prefer me in jeans?"

Melissa dismissed the topic with an indifferent wave of her hand. "We need to talk."

He almost laughed. "Talking" was the primary reason he'd brought her to the cabin, which he had told her in plain English, and precisely what she had been rebelling against since her arrival. Great, he thought. Maybe they would finally have a meeting of the minds. As fantastic as their lovemaking had been, their relationship could go only so far without some very crucial conversation.

But as anxious as he was to begin that discussion, he wasn't able to completely disregard his own plans for the evening. "I couldn't agree more," he said. "Wait here. I'll be back in a jiffy."

Frowning over his hasty exit, Melissa walked around the room. Wait for what? Damn it, she had come in all pumped up to lay into him, and waiting could undermine her determination.

But Wyatt was true to his word and returned almost immediately. Melissa's spine stiffened when she saw the bottle of very good red wine—already opened—and the two stemmed glasses he was carrying. He set about filling the glasses, then, wearing a smile, he walked over to her and held one out.

Melissa looked at it as though it were something poisonous. "Take it," he urged. "Please."

Slowly she inhaled and strove for rationality. A few sips of wine wouldn't befuddle her, and they might even reinforce her courage. "All right," she conceded, accepting the glass.

Wyatt held his up. "A toast. To you, to me and, most of all, to us."

Her eyebrow rose cynically. "I'd rather toast to freedom."

"Freedom of adventure? Freedom of speech?" There was a teasing twinkle in Wyatt's eyes.

"Just plain freedom." Her gaze challenged him.

He pondered that challenge for a moment, then nodded. "Sure, why not? Here's to just plain freedom."

They each took a sip from their glasses. "Would you like to sit down?" Wyatt asked.

Melissa's eyes narrowed on him. "What I'd like is for you to take me back to town. Not six days from now, not later tonight, not in the morning, but right now. I'm not asking, Wyatt, I'm demanding."

Disappointment streaked through him. "That's what you wanted to talk about?"

"Yes. Are you going to do it?"

He tried to make light of the topic. "You seduced me and now that you've had your fun, you want to leave? Is that it?"

"*I* seduced *you?*"

"Didn't you ask me to kiss you?"

"Oh, for God's sake," she muttered, tipping her glass for a healthy swallow. Lowering it, she glared at him. "I did not seduce you. You seduced me and we both know it. It was your only reason for bringing me out here. Well, you succeeded, so there's no point in keeping me here any longer. I want to go back to town, and I want to go now."

"You've got it all wrong. You see, that's why I can't take you back yet. You still have it all wrong," Wyatt said patiently.

"Don't you realize that you're going to force me to file kidnapping charges against you? I'll be honest. So far I've been going back and forth about it. I can't say that it would brighten my life any to see you behind bars, but you really should believe that I'll do it if you keep me out here much longer."

Watching her intently, he took a sip of his wine. Then, with a leisurely stride to his chair in front of the fireplace, he sat down.

His nonchalance raised Melissa's ire. She, too, strode to the same portion of the room, standing near the fireplace so she could see his face. Her own was as threatening as she could make it. "I strongly advise you to believe me," she said sharply.

Wyatt returned her stare. "I believe you."

"But you're still going to keep me captive for another six days."

He thought a moment. "Captive isn't a good word. Guest is much better. And it might not take six days. Depends."

Her anger erupted. "Guest! You almighty jerk! Do you think for one moment that I believe you're in love with me? You could say it a thousand times and it wouldn't make it true. People in love don't kidnap each other."

"Except in our case."

"There is no *our* case! There is no *us!* We do not have a relationship and we never will have!"

"We did about an hour and a half ago," Wyatt said calmly. "Or do you have a better term in mind for what happened between us?" He looked at his empty glass and got up for a refill. Holding the bottle, he asked, "Would you like some more wine?"

Melissa was seething and totally ignored his question. "God, I hate being the weaker sex. If I were as physically strong as you are, I'd get those truck keys away from you, one way or another."

"You don't need physical strength to get those keys."

"Oh, please. I suppose all I have to do is ask for them, right?"

"Wrong. You're a bright, intelligent person. I'm sure you'll figure it out sooner or later. I thought several times today that you were finally grasping my reason for bringing you here, but apparently not." He shrugged then and returned to his chair. "Actually, I've told you my reason several different times."

"For conversation," she sneered. "Which is why, of course, you took advantage of me this afternoon."

Wyatt let out a whoop of laughter. "That's one charge no court would convict me on, honey. But feel free to add it to my list of crimes when you file that kidnapping complaint. If nothing else, it sure would titillate the good citizens of Whitehorn."

Melissa was trying to remember what those people in the Old West who took justice into their own hands with cattle rustlers and horse thieves were called. Oh yes, she suddenly thought, they were called vigilantes. Just as Wyatt was going to force her to file kidnapping charges, he was forcing her into personal retribution.

"There was a time when nothing or no one could have made me believe you were capable of doing something like this," she said in a derisive tone. "You've changed, and not for the better."

"You've changed, too, Melissa. We both have."

"But I didn't turn into a criminal."

He couldn't help laughing. "No, I suppose not." He sobered. "But you're not as open-minded as you were, nor as pleasant. I remember a girl who laughed at everything."

"Well, *I* remember a boy, a young man, who was honest and decent and . . . and—"

"Loyal?" Wyatt said softly. "Faithful?"

She whirled around and stalked off to a window. It was almost dark outside. The forest was already dark, and only a pale, silvery light on the western horizon gave evidence of the setting sun.

"That's what you don't want to talk about, isn't it?" Wyatt said quietly, getting to his feet. "My disloyalty? My infidelity?"

Her shoulders twitched irately as she raised her glass to her lips and drank the last of her wine.

"Melissa?"

He had come up behind her. She shrank closer to the window. "Don't touch me."

"Why not touch you? Explain why I shouldn't touch you after what happened between us today. Are you afraid it will happen again?"

"Don't be absurd," she scoffed. "That was a—a fluke, a mistake. Believe me, it *won't* happen again."

"A fluke. Hmm. Well, I suppose it's possible. I've learned through the years that almost anything is. And everyone seems to see things in their own way, different from anyone else."

Arguing with Wyatt was getting tiresome. Was she going to go through with her little act of cooperation so she could pay him back, or wasn't she? In either case, she was tired of the dissension. Besides, she had tried everything within reason to persuade him to stop this ridiculous charade and he just kept right on begging for a symbolic kick in the shins.

She turned around, surprising him with an almost friendly smile. "I'll have some more of that wine now, if you don't mind."

Suspicion suddenly hit him. She had run hot and cold on him since she'd got here, one minute furious, the next as congenial as anyone he'd ever known. She had accused him of playing a game with her, but it appeared that she might be involved in some sort of game of her own.

He took the empty glass from her hand and walked over to the table where he had left the bottle of wine. "Getting hungry?" he asked while filling her glass. "Dinner will take only a few minutes to heat up."

"Another casserole? I noticed the covered dishes in the refrigerator when I made lunch. Did you have your cook at the ranch prepare food for this week?"

Handing her glass to her, he laughed lightly. "Guilty as charged."

"Indeed you are," she murmured, though the comment was tempered by a rather flirtatious look into his eyes.

Her ability to change moods amazed Wyatt. It also bolstered that spurt of suspicion he had noticed a minute ago.

But, he decided, he would go with the flow. "Come on," he said with a short laugh. "Let's go have some dinner."

The food was good, Melissa had to admit. "Your cook is way above average," she told Wyatt after they had eaten and were having a second cup of coffee. That is, Wyatt was drinking coffee. Melissa's beverage was tea.

"I'll tell her you said so. Coming from you, she'll appreciate the compliment." Wyatt set his cup down. "You've done well with the Hip Hop. Years ago I never would have guessed that your future lay in the restaurant business."

Melissa gave a small shrug. "It just sort of happened on its own. The only jobs I could hold and still stay in school were in fast-food establishments. After high school I found a full-time job in a regular restaurant."

"Waitressing?"

"No, in the kitchen. Cook's assistant. All it was was a gofer job, really. That cook was the grouchiest woman I'd ever known, but I learned a lot from her. She made marvelous bread and pastry. I started getting interested in cooking, and along with my night-school business courses, I took some cooking classes. I never did do any cooking for employment, although I do some in my own place. But the management end of the business was more appealing to me, which was what I aimed for."

"Apparently you hit the bull's-eye."

Melissa hesitated, then said quietly, "I was saving what I could to buy my own restaurant someday, but I was able to get a good deal on the café. I had a hefty mortgage at first, but I was determined to make it."

"And you chose Whitehorn for that start."

There was something intimate in his voice, which offended her. She looked him in the eye. "Don't ever think I came back to Whitehorn because of you. You were married and living in Helena, and I never dreamed you would move back to the ranch. I chose Whitehorn because of my father. I'd always hoped he'd come back, and now I want to find his killer."

Wyatt cocked a curious eyebrow. "Are you involved in the investigation?"

"No, but I'm going to be if Judd and the others don't make some headway very soon. What have they found? A few hairs, meaning what?"

"Maybe you're a little too impatient, Melissa. I'm sure Judd is doing everything humanly possible to uncover the murderer, who probably isn't even in the area anymore. Hasn't been for years, I'd be willing to bet.''

"Yes, Judd is trying," Melissa conceded. "So is Tracy, and Sterling. And maybe I am impatient, but I've had a missing father for most of my life. All that time his bones were lying on the reservation," she said with some bitterness. "Now I want to know why he was killed, and who did it, and I don't intend living through another twenty years *not* knowing."

"What could you do that Judd and Tracy aren't doing?"

"If I knew the answer to that question, I'd already be doing it."

Wyatt got up for the coffeepot. "I'd probably feel the same way if it were my father," he said while refilling his cup. He resumed his seat, thinking that they might not be discussing what was most important to him, their own past, but at least they were talking.

They had finished the bottle of wine with dinner, and unquestionably Melissa was more relaxed than when she had walked into the main room after her shower.

"Do you remember your father?"

Melissa nodded. "I have quite a few memories of him. Some aren't very clear, but yes, I remember him. And I have some old snapshots of him." Frowning, she studied her fingernails. "He worked as a ranch hand."

"Oh? Which ranch?"

Melissa drew an uncertain breath. "According to Mother he was restless and impulsive and changed jobs every few months. There's a chance that he was working on the Baxter place when he disappeared, but Mother is rather vague on that point. She told me that he might have been between jobs. She really doesn't like talking about it." Except for her immovable opinion about a woman being involved, Melissa could have added. "Anyway, from Mother's remarks I have the opinion that they weren't very happy together." Her gaze rose to Wyatt's. "Unlike your parents."

He nodded in mute understanding, murmuring, "More like my marriage."

Instantly Melissa recoiled. "I'm not going to discuss your marriage with you, Wyatt."

"We *have* to discuss it." He leaned forward. "How am I going to get you to forgive me if you won't talk about the past?"

"Are we back to that again?" Pushing out her chair, Melissa stood up. "I think the evening is over. I'm sure you can handle the dishes, so I'll say good-night." She walked out of the kitchen, leaving Wyatt agitated and staring after her.

"Damn," he mumbled, slumping back in his chair. He was beginning to think the only way Melissa was ever going to listen to him was if he tied her down.

But if she was so dead set against anything but animosity between them, why had she made love with him this afternoon? One thing was certain, he hadn't forced her. She had been as eager and hungry for him as he'd been for her. Just thinking of her passionate response was arousing.

It also changed the direction of this thoughts. For a few minutes in front of the fireplace she had been solely and wholly his. Was that the answer? To repeatedly seduce her until she finally admitted that she had special feelings for him? Would she forgive him then?

Eleven

The sky was clear the next morning, and sunshine beamed into Melissa's bedroom through an opening in the curtains. She sat up and realized that she had slept very well, though considering her restiveness the night before and yesterday's trials and tribulations, it was no wonder. The sun being out seemed like a gift after so many gloomy, gray days, she thought. At least today she could spend some time outdoors.

Melissa went through her normal morning routine and then, dressed in a denim skirt and white knit blouse with blue trim, she ambled rather desultorily to the kitchen. There was a pot of coffee on the counter, but Wyatt was obviously elsewhere. Pouring herself a cup, she wandered into the main room of the cabin and found it, too, vacant.

She stopped and listened. The cabin was as silent as a tomb and felt empty. Wyatt must be outside, taking advantage of that beautiful sunshine. Her pulse began racing. This could be her chance to look for those telephones, although she had better make sure that Wyatt really was outside. Setting her cup on a table, she returned to the bedroom area and began rapping on doors. "Wyatt?" No answer.

Cautiously she turned the knob and peered into a bedroom that appeared to be lived in. There were things on the bureaus and nightstands—books, magazines, a jackknife, some pads of paper and pens. Quickly she darted into the room and checked the closet, which, to her surprise, was filled with men's clothing. Not Wyatt's, though. By the size of the garments, whoever occupied this bedroom was a much smaller man. Instinct or intuition told her who occupied this room: a caretaker. Wyatt had undoubtedly told the man to take the time off. Melissa's lips thinned as she thought of Wyatt planning this week, seeing to food and total privacy.

Moving fast, she left the room and quietly closed the door, to try the next one. Rapping lightly, she called, "Wyatt?" No answer. But that door only opened onto a linen closet.

She finally located what she thought was Wyatt's bedroom, and it was as vacant as the rest of the house. Looking furtively down the hall to make sure he hadn't snuck up on her, she entered his room, which seemed like the most logical place for him to have secreted the phones.

First she glanced around the large space, noting that his bed had been carelessly made, with the covers pulled up to the pillows without benefit of a spread. There were three dressers of various sizes and two nightstands. Those phones could be anywhere, but intuition told her that she was on the right track.

She began opening doors and pulling out drawers in the furniture. Some contained clothing—underwear, sweaters and socks—but most were empty.

The closet! Whirling, she saw two doors and decided that one must lead to his closet and the other to his bathroom. The spacious bathroom, she discovered, was slightly steamy, indicating that Wyatt had showered not too long ago. Hurrying to the second door, she found that it was a walk-in closet with a multitude of built-in shelves and drawers, along with bars for hanging clothes.

She was down on her knees, in the process of sliding open a drawer that was about two feet above floor level when a voice behind her said casually, "Looking for something?"

Her heart nearly stopped. Red-faced, she turned her head to face Wyatt, who was leaning against the door frame with his arms folded. "I wasn't snooping through your things out of morbid curiosity," she said defiantly. "I was looking for the phones."

"They're not in here."

"Well, they're somewhere in this house!"

"Maybe they are and maybe they aren't," Wyatt said, giving her a maddening grin.

Embarrassed at getting caught and angry that he would grin at her in that smugly masculine fashion, Melissa jumped to her feet. She did it negligently, however, because she banged her knee into the edge of the drawer. "Ow," she yelped, and without thinking, raised the hem of her skirt to inspect the damage to her knee, which hurt like the very devil.

Wyatt walked in. "Let me see what you did."

She dropped her skirt. "It's nothing. Just a bruise."

"Did you break the skin?"

"No," she lied. It wasn't *very* broken, she told herself, just enough to show a dotted line of blood. The closet felt cramped with two people in it and she tried to slip past Wyatt to leave.

But he had other ideas. Taking her by the arm, he demanded, "Let me see that bruise."

"My bruise is none of your affair." She tried to jerk her arm free of his grip. "Wyatt, damn it, let go!"

"Okay, fine, have it your way." Without another word, he bent over and scooped her off the floor and into his arms.

She started yelling. "Put me down, damn you! What do you think you're doing?"

She was put down, all right—tossed rather unceremoniously to the middle of his bed. He followed her descent before she could get off the bed and lay over her, easily holding her in place. His face was no more than an inch from hers. "Now," he said. "Am I going to see that bruise the easy way or the tough way? You choose." Clamping her lips shut, she turned her face to the side. "Don't make the mistake of thinking I'm not serious," Wyatt warned.

She turned angrily flashing eyes on him. "It's only a bruise and none of your business. Let me up. I don't like being on your bed." Then she saw the heat of desire developing in his eyes. She licked her suddenly dry lips. Her own body was working against her. His weight, his scent, the configuration of his torso and thighs were overwhelming weapons to combat.

"Don't," she whispered, all but reading his mind.

"Close your eyes," he said huskily. "Think about yesterday in front of the fireplace." Lowering his head, he began kissing her cheeks, her forehead, the tip of her nose.

Her breath caught in her throat. "I—I don't want to do this again." It was a lie. She *did* want it. Deep inside of her, the wanting was developing at an alarming rate. The bed beneath her was soft and yielding; the man over her was hard and sexually persuasive. Her normal strength was deserting her muscles and limbs, and her brain seemed to be dissolving into witless mush.

"Melissa," he whispered, seeking her lips. He loved her. He had always loved her, and he knew she wouldn't melt in his arms if she didn't love him, too. Maybe he would never succeed in getting her to admit it, to face the truth, but he recognized her feelings even if she did not.

Weakly she tried to elude his kiss, but she gave up very quickly and parted her lips for his mouth and tongue. About two seconds into the kiss, their passion exploded. They tore at each other's clothing, undoing buttons, pushing aside her blouse and his shirt, all the while kissing and gasping for air.

"Oh, Melissa, what you do to me," Wyatt whispered thickly between kisses.

She could have said the same, but not only was his mouth on hers preventing speech, she wasn't certain of the wisdom of such revealing comments.

But then wisdom had little to do with what was happening on his bed. Adrift in her bedazzled mind were questions and doubts about her own morality. How could she be so untrue to herself? Why didn't she escape his arms, his mouth, his hands? No one was forcing her to stay where she was. No one was forcing her to writhe at his touch, or to moan when he caressed her breasts.

He unbuttoned her skirt and pulled it down, then her panties. Breathing erratically, she watched his eyes, his beautiful, expressive eyes, while he undressed her.

"Me, too," he whispered, twisting around to get rid of his boots and jeans. Naked, he sat up to look at her, adoringly running his hands over her silky skin. Dipping his head, he wet her nipple with his tongue, then sucked gently.

"Oh," she cried as a delicious thrill shot through her body.

His head came up. "Am I hurting you?"

"No...no." She reached up to his neck and urged his head down for a kiss on the mouth. He moved on top of her and the kiss became rough and needful. Reaching down, she guided his engorged manhood to the unbearable ache between her thighs. He slid into her at once, unable to do anything else.

Their lovemaking was tempestuous, almost savage. He thrust into her as deeply as possible, again and again, and in the back of his mind was last night's conclusion that in this, at least, she was his.

"Wyatt," she moaned, begging for release.

He gave it to her, taking her to the stars, going with her. Their climaxes were a fraction off simultaneous, and so strong and overwhelming they all but blacked out.

Wyatt was the first to stir by raising his head to look at Melissa. Afraid of saying the wrong thing, he said nothing. But he searched her eyes, and she lay there and let him, honestly not knowing what he might see. This time she felt no shock over her behavior. Rather, confusion held her almost frozen in place. Was she destined to become Wyatt's pawn, his plaything? Disappointment in herself inserted itself into the confusion.

"Say something," he said softly, gently brushing a lock of hair from her cheek.

"Say what, Wyatt?" Her voice was neither strong nor steady.

"I don't know. Say it was great. Say you love me. Say..." He stopped himself. Even hinting at the word *marriage* might make her angry and resentful again.

"It was great," she said dully.

"And?"

"That's as far as I can go."

"But you do love me, I know you do."

"Then you know far more than I."

"I know you don't respond to other men like you do to me."

"Oh? You know that? How?"

"I feel it. In here." He tapped his chest.

Her plan of retribution flashed into her mind. Maybe she would go through with it and maybe she wouldn't, but paving the way, at least, seemed sensible.

It also seemed slightly demented. Sighing, she broke eye contact. "I don't know what I feel just now. Please don't pressure me about it." And then a horrifying thought struck her. Panicked, she pushed on his chest. "You didn't use protection. Let me up!"

"Aw, hell," he mumbled, angry at himself for getting so carried away that he'd forgotten protection. It would be too ironic for words, given his history with Shannon, if he had gotten Melissa pregnant this morning.

His eyes narrowed on her stricken face. It might be ironic, but it would sure make her sit up and take notice of him. He felt a quickening of blood and tissue at the thought of Melissa having his baby, and suddenly wasn't sorry at all that he had neglected protection. What if it really had happened? What if Melissa had conceived and was pregnant this very minute?

"Wyatt," she said sharply, wriggling to escape his weight. "Get off of me!" She felt like smacking him one, and herself, too. Never had she done anything so foolhardy before.

Even inexperienced with this sort of risk taking, she felt she shouldn't just lie there.

But the look of profound tenderness in his eyes brought her squirming and wriggling to a startled halt. "What are you thinking?" she asked, her voice laden with suspicion.

"About a baby. I'd love to have a daughter with you." Why should he lie about it? he thought. He couldn't think of anything better than Melissa having his baby.

She grew weak, too weak to do more than whisper, "Let me get up. Please."

He looked at her, studying the perfect features of her beautiful face, and felt his love for her compounding. "Melissa, let's start over. Let's pretend the past never happened."

Closing her eyes, she drew in a long-suffering breath. "That's not only an absurd idea, it would be impossible to do." Her lids lifted and she glared directly into his eyes. "I want you to take me back to town. Do you have the slightest idea of what you're doing to me?"

He smiled. "I know what I was doing to you a few minutes ago. Is that what you're referring to? Incidentally, I could do it to you again, in case you haven't noticed."

She groaned out loud, because while she hadn't noticed his remarkable recovery from utter repletion, she was doing so now. "Not again, Wyatt. I'm saying no. Does no mean anything to you, or are you one of those Neanderthals who think a woman means yes when she says no?"

Her sarcasm registered, but he simply couldn't contain the truth in his own soul. "I want to make you pregnant," he whispered. His hips moved, causing a slow slide of his manhood inside her.

"No," she moaned, tossing her head on the pillow. "No...no...no." But now the no was for herself. She shouldn't be feeling anything and she was. She shouldn't be responding, and she was. Tears of desperation filled her eyes. How did he have so much power over her senses? She couldn't fall for him again, she just couldn't.

But this was nothing like their youthful romance, when he had been the sweetest guy in her world. The one time they had made love, she had been extremely emotional, but hadn't even remotely felt what he was able to draw from her now. Maybe he was right in spite of her distaste for the idea: maybe they had already started over. It was clear she wasn't dealing with the Wyatt she remembered.

Strangely, that progression of thoughts completely demolished her responsiveness. Her body stiffened and Wyatt felt it. One second she had been with him, albeit reluctantly, and the next she was lying under him like a rock.

Frowning, he became very still and probed the depths of her eyes. "What happened?"

"No more, Wyatt. If you want me to ever speak to you again, you'll let me get off of this bed."

There was a steely quality in her voice he had never heard before, she meant what she'd said. Instead of another step forward, they were regressing.

Saying nothing, he released her and moved to one side. She got up immediately, gathered her clothes and left him lying there questioning the last few minutes with a knot in his gut.

Melissa straightened the clothing in her suitcases and carried the luggage out to the cabin's front door, passing Wyatt, who was slumped in his chair by the fireplace. He stood up slowly.

"Melissa, I'm not taking you back yet," he said soberly, eyeing her luggage.

"Yes, you are!" she said, her voice set in a strident pitch.

"Please, just calm down and talk to me."

"So you can throw me on another bed?" Her glare was murderous. "How dare you talk about wanting to get me pregnant? Do you actually have the gall to think you can restructure my entire life? My plans, which obviously mean nothing to you, do not include becoming a single parent."

"My God, Melissa, do you think I would let you have the baby alone?"

"If you dare mention the word *marriage,* I swear I'll *walk* back to town!"

"Don't be ridiculous."

"So now I'm ridiculous? Let me tell you who's ridiculous, Wyatt. A man who thinks he can get away with kidnapping, that's who." Melissa advanced on him as she yelled, "What, really, did you hope to accomplish by your disgusting tactics? And don't say conversation again, because we've talked plenty."

"Never about the right things."

"Oh, you mean because I won't listen to lies about how you were trapped into marrying Shannon that we haven't talked about the right things?"

A muscle began jumping in Wyatt's jaw. "Don't accuse me of lying, Melissa. I've *never* lied to you."

"What do you call your story about driving me to the airport, if not a lie?"

"Except for that, I've never told you anything but the truth."

"You have a real knack, do you know that? I'll bet there isn't a person alive who could corner you on any subject known to mankind!"

Grimacing, Wyatt put his hands over his ears. "Are you trying to deafen me? Stop that infernal screeching."

Melissa drew herself up indignantly, but inside she felt about two inches high. Screeching had not been her intention when she had brought out her luggage. He was just so damned infuriating.

Stonily she sat on her largest suitcase. "I'm not moving from this spot until you take me back to town. I mean it, Wyatt. I'll sit here for three days if I have to."

In a final, determined rebellion, she had dug in her heels, Wyatt realized. Thinking hard, he rubbed the back of his neck. He could walk out and do something, maybe take a good long hike, and see if she was still parked on her suitcase when he returned.

But he had never intended any discomfort for her while planning the week, and sitting on a suitcase for "three days" couldn't be anything but discomfiting. Her stubbornness just might work in his favor, he thought then. Hadn't he figured that the only way he would ever get her to listen to him would be to tie her down? In essence, she had tied herself to one small portion of the room.

"You're not serious," he said, testing the degree of her determination.

"I'm deadly serious," she said coldly. "The only thing that will get me off this suitcase is a ride to town."

"And nothing I say or do will change your mind?"

"For Pete's sake, how many times do you have to hear it?" Disgusted, Melissa looked away. It was only a second before she caught movement from Wyatt in her peripheral vision, and she couldn't stop herself from looking to see what he was up to. Her eyes widened when she saw him carrying a chair over to her and her luggage. "I'm not using that chair, so you might as well put it back where it belongs."

"It's not for you," Wyatt said calmly. "It's for me." Placing the chair within inches of her knees, he sat on it.

Quickly she moved her knees so they wouldn't touch his. "You are the most irritating person I've ever had the misfortune of knowing," she said in a distinctly irritated tone. "If you're not going to take me home, why don't you just leave me alone?"

"Because I can't." Wyatt sat back, reasonably comfortable on his straight-backed chair. "Leaving you alone, ignoring you, just isn't possible."

"It's a nice day. Go for a walk or something," she said peevishly.

"I thought of that, but a better idea came up."

"Sitting and staring at me is a better idea?" She sneered.

"Staring at you is pure pleasure, Melissa, but it's not my better idea. No, this is the perfect opportunity for some serious conversation."

"Well, it's going to be one-sided," she snapped with self-directed anger for putting herself in this ludicrous situation.

"Fine, if that's the way you want it."

"What I want obviously doesn't mean two hoots to you, so why don't you just cut the bull, Wyatt? You're an arrogant SOB, and we both know it. You've had everything your way for so long, you can't function on any other level. You know, I kept thinking of you as the Wyatt I used to know, but that was a dire mistake. You're so far from the nice guy you once were it's like you became a whole other person."

"You're right. Not a hundred percent right, but you're pretty close. What do you suppose caused so much change?"

"I don't know and I don't *want* to know."

Wyatt leaned forward. His eyes contained an intense light. "You *do* know. You just won't admit it."

Her lip curled. "Your marriage. Well, pardon me if I don't get all soppy and wet-eyed with sympathy over something you caused yourself."

"I did cause it myself. I know that better than anyone else. It's what I've lived with for six years, but I wouldn't welcome your or anyone else's sympathy. Understanding, yes, but not sympathy."

Melissa folded her arms and gave him a cold look. "I understand perfectly. I understand that you couldn't keep your pants zipped six years ago and you had to pay the penalty. Well, poor you. While you're commiserating with your own past, please take note of the fact that *I* kept my clothes on and never had to pay any penalties."

His eyes narrowed on her. "You can't compare you and me. You're a woman. *You're* the one who could trap a man into marriage by getting pregnant. Men don't have that dubious advantage."

Disdainfully, Melissa turned her head. "I find this conversation repugnant. Next you'll be telling me that Shannon seduced you against your will." She gave a short, sardonic laugh. "Or that she raped you. I sincerely doubt that she got pregnant because she wanted to." Despite her derisive attitude, the topic was painful for Melissa. Wyatt hadn't only shattered her heart six years ago, he had badly damaged her trust in all of mankind. But it wasn't all of mankind sitting there with a hurtful, pleading look in his eyes, it was Wyatt, and discussing his unfaithfulness was bringing back the terrible months after his telephone call much too clearly.

Her chin lifted, a monumental effort when she really felt like sinking into tears. "Talk about something else if you *must* talk, or go away and let me be."

"I'm not going anywhere, Melissa. What I am going to do is tell you exactly what happened six years ago."

"No," she gasped. "I won't listen."

"Then get up off of that damned suitcase and leave the room," he said harshly.

They glared at each other, an unnerving standoff that had Melissa wishing she hadn't been so adamant about sitting right where she was until he agreed to take her back to town.

"Say any damned thing you want," she finally said sullenly. "It won't change anything."

"Maybe not, but to me it's worth a shot." Wyatt took a deep breath. "You were in California, I was in college in Missoula. We wrote dozens of letters. We talked on the phone at least three times a week, discussing our plans to get married. The only time you weren't occupying my mind was when I was studying, and even then I'd be reading along and suddenly see your face. I loved you so much and I wanted us to be together. You kept delaying your move back to Montana."

Melissa couldn't let that remark pass. "I had no choice," she said angrily. "Could I leave my mother when she wasn't making enough money to support herself let alone my younger brother? She needed my earnings to pay the rent and eat. Maybe those are minor considerations for a North, but at that time they weren't minor for the Averys."

"I understood what you were doing. I accepted it, Melissa. I kept telling myself it wouldn't be forever. Several times I thought of going to California and begging your mother to move to the ranch so you and I could be married. We could have all lived there. Dad wouldn't have minded."

"She never would have come. I can't even get her to come back to Montana for a visit."

"I know that now, but there were moments when I missed you so much I would have done anything to solve our dilemma."

"So you consoled yourself with other women," Melissa said bitterly.

"No, I did not," he said sharply. "You were the only woman I had ever made love with, and that was the way I intended to keep it. I took a lot of ribbing from my classmates because I didn't date or pay attention to the girls on campus. And let me say right here, Melissa, that there were more than a few very attractive, intelligent women who let me know they were interested."

"There were attractive, intelligent men interested in me, too," she retorted. "But unlike you, I remained faithful."

"So did I. Until one night, when my roommate talked me into going to a party with him. It was a semiformal affair, which in itself was enough reason to avoid it, but Jason—you must remember my mentioning his name—kept at me until I agreed. It was a private party thrown by a wealthy Missoula family with political connections.

"Anyway, I went. There must have been a hundred people milling around in that big house, and the quantity and quality of the food and drink was staggering. For the first time in ages I let go and relaxed. It was fun, entertaining, and I began enjoying myself. Someone was forever pushing a drink into my hand, and after the first few, I stopped counting."

Melissa wasn't looking at him, but she was listening. He took another deep breath and braced himself for the tough part of his story. "I was introduced to so many people I didn't even try to remember their names. And then this girl, this young woman, walked up to me. She introduced herself."

"Shannon," Melissa whispered. She was fighting tears, fighting them hard. Crying over Wyatt's story right in front of him might destroy her.

"Yes, Shannon. I'm not going to gloss this over, Melissa. She was beautiful and vivacious and I was just drunk enough to notice." Wyatt paused, then said quietly, "I barely remember it, but I went to her motel room with her after the party. She lived in Helena and had gone to Missoula expressly to attend the affair. I woke up the next morning in her bed with a killer hangover that got worse when I realized what I had done."

Though Melissa's face was turned away from him, he was positive he saw the sparkle of tears in her eye. He felt like crying himself, but got past the moment by clearing his throat. "I got up and dressed immediately. Shannon asked what was wrong. I explained that I was in love with you and that we were engaged to be married. I left.

"The next few days were a nightmare. I wanted to call you and confess, but knowing how hurt you'd be, I decided that I couldn't appease my conscience at your expense. A month went by, and then I got a call from Shannon. She said she had something important to discuss with me and demanded I go to Helena. Maybe I suspected what it was. I don't know. But I went, and she said she was pregnant, and because she hadn't slept with any other man for months, it was my baby. Before I could say anything, she said that abortion wasn't an option and she wouldn't damage her father's reputation by bearing a child out of wedlock. Wilbur Kiley was and still is a state senator. She wanted a ring on her finger and would settle for nothing less."

Wyatt fell silent and stared down at the floor for a long time. "I called you in California to tell you about it myself. That's the story, Melissa. I didn't sleep around during our separation, except for that one time. And if this sounds self-pitying, I can't help it, but I paid for that one night, paid in spades."

Twelve

Wyatt raised his eyes. "Melissa, look at me."

Her head turned slowly and their eyes met. In his were misery, remorse and a plea for understanding. In hers were tears.

Wyatt spoke so quietly his words were barely audible. "I know this is hurting you, but you have to hear it."

There was resentment in Melissa's wet eyes. "And so you were married."

"Yeah."

"Why didn't you live happily ever after?" The question was posed bitterly.

"Because we didn't love each other. No marriage can succeed without love, Melissa. I have a theory, which could be right, wrong or somewhere in the middle, but I think Shannon knew what she was doing the night we met."

"She *deliberately* got pregnant? That's ridiculous. Women can only conceive at certain times of the month. It's highly unlikely her fertile time coincided with meeting you and that she immediately came up with a plan to land you. Your theory is hogwash."

"Is it? I think she wanted a wealthy husband. Not that her family was in need. The Kileys have been well off for generations. But there were signs after we were married that she'd been thinking of something like that the night we met. Why else would she want me, if not for the money?"

Melissa stared at him through the mist in her eyes. Didn't he know how incredibly handsome he was? How he looked to a woman—strong and straight and startlingly masculine? If his theory had any credibility at all, it was probably because Shannon Kiley had taken one look and decided she wanted him.

"If you were so unhappy with your marriage, why did you stay in it so long? I know you said it was because of your son, but that hasn't changed and you finally got a divorce," she said huskily, almost accusingly. There must have been something between him and Shannon for him to stay so long. There had to have been, however much he denied it.

Wyatt sighed softly. "I didn't have you anymore, and I did have Timmy. He's a great kid, Melissa, and I love him a lot. Too, the institution of marriage had always seemed sacred to me. Because of my parents, I suppose. When Dad was still alive I didn't want to appear dishonorable in his eyes. I don't know, Melissa. Now it seems like a terrible waste, but at the time I thought I should try and make it work."

"For six years," Melissa said dully.

"Until I discovered she was having an affair."

"An affair? Were you hurt by that?"

"Hurt?" Wyatt gave a brief, cynical laugh. "I was so relieved I couldn't see straight. I had her dead to rights and she knew it. When I told her I had proof of her infidelity, she didn't fight me on the divorce. Status means everything to her, Melissa. She didn't want the publicity of a court battle, which I promised would be the case if she didn't agree."

They sat without speaking for a long time. Wyatt kept watching her, waiting for some sort of reaction. When it came, it wasn't what he'd hoped for.

"Do you feel better now?" she asked in an accusing tone. "Unloading your conscience on me was what you wanted all along, but did it really make you feel any better about yourself? Maybe it obliterated your guilt, assuming you've been living with guilt. One question, Wyatt. Now that you've bared your soul, if that's what you really did, what do you expect from me?"

"I'd be happy to start with belief," he said.

"Belief." Melissa chewed on her bottom lip for a moment. "You mean believe that you made only one mistake, that everything changed in both of our lives because of one night at a motel? And if I believe you, what comes next?"

Wyatt inhaled a long breath and then slowly released it. "Trust, affection, love and marriage." There, he had said it, and if she clobbered him over it, he would take it like a man.

If she wasn't so torn up, she would laugh, Melissa realized as the strength drained out of her. "I can see you don't want much."

His eyes and voice were suddenly intense. "I want you. I want the rest of your life. I want your thoughts, your love and your time." He leaned forward. "I want you to have my babies, and I want the kind of marriage my folks had. With you as my wife, Melissa, only you."

"In other words, you're proposing."

"No, not yet. Not until you're with me a hundred percent. Not until you believe every word of what I just told you and forgive me—*really* forgive me—for making a bad mistake. Not until you realize it *was* a mistake and only that."

"A mistake," she echoed in a near whisper. Was that what had caused so much unhappiness for her, a mistake? Caused so many tears and sleepless, agony-filled nights? Wyatt had stubbed his toe and she had taken the fall. A mistake. What an innocent-sounding word for so much heartache.

He tried to take her hands, but she withdrew them. "No," she said.

His mouth tightened, but could he blame her? "Will you think about what I told you?"

"I... hope not." But she knew she would think of little else. Maybe if they hadn't made love up here on the mountain she could forget his tale of woe and get on with her life. Would she ever forget now? She sighed wearily.

"I never set out to hurt you," he said with a down-hearted expression. "At least believe that."

Her head had started aching, and she lifted her hands to massage her temples. "Will you take me back to town now?"

"Melissa, please stay. Stay because you want to."

"Stay?" she repeated, visibly astonished. "And do what?" Her expression became closed. "No, Wyatt, I need to go home. I need to be alone."

He tried another tack. "You haven't had breakfast. At least stay long enough to eat."

"I'm not hungry." It was the truth. Her stomach felt as empty as the Grand Canyon, but it wasn't caused by hunger. So this was why he had abducted her, to tell her that all he had done six years ago was make a mistake. It was how he saw it, she realized, how he felt about it. Maybe he was right, but her side of the coin had been so badly bruised she could hardly take seriously his declarations of love and hope for a future together.

At least she couldn't right now. The one factor that she couldn't ignore was her response to Wyatt's lovemaking, even though it had absolutely no connection to his story. Her behavior must have immeasurably increased his hopes, she thought uneasily. In fact, the stage was set perfectly at this moment for her to put her plan of justice into motion.

But her heart just wasn't in it. Lying to him about there being another man in her life no longer seemed like justice, but rather an adolescent method of reaping revenge. There had been enough pain between them, and she wasn't going to deliberately cause more.

She got up from her perch on the suitcase. "I'm ready to leave," she informed him, speaking firmly, leaving him no room for further argument.

After a brief hesitation, Wyatt stood also. "I'll get the truck keys." He walked away, leaving her alone with her suitcases.

A great weakness overtook Melissa, and she leaned against the front door for some necessary support. That had been the conversation she hadn't wanted to have. Anyone could rationalize a sin or a crime, and Wyatt was smart enough to devise a story of entrapment that would affect any woman's emotions. Hers were in shreds right now, and she prayed that she could get through the drive to Whitehorn without breaking down. Her urge to cry had to be stifled at any cost. She could do her crying when she was alone in her apartment.

Wyatt carried her luggage out to the truck, then opened the passenger door for her to get in. "Thank you," she murmured, albeit stiffly.

"You're welcome." Shutting the door, he walked around the front of the truck and climbed into the driver's seat. After inserting the key into the ignition, he turned his head and looked at her. "I wish you would change your mind and stay. I swear I wouldn't pressure you, Melissa, not about anything. You can see how the weather has changed. We could take a hike. The mountain has trails leading to scenic sites that I know you'd enjoy seeing."

She gave her head a shake. "No. I couldn't pretend that everything is all right between us. Hiking and looking at scenery should be done when people at least feel friendly toward each other. It would be nothing but a farce, and I can't do it. Not today."

"You don't feel friendly toward me? Not at all?"

She looked at him. "No, I don't. Do you think I should?"

Sighing, he turned the key and started the motor. "I was hoping."

"The world doesn't revolve around your hopes," she said, managing to speak civilly in spite of the turmoil she felt.

He turned the truck around and began driving. "You don't believe my story, do you?"

"I believe that *you* believe it," she said, staring out the side window at the dense forest they were passing through.

"Do you think I made it up?" She didn't answer. "Do you think I was sleeping with every woman I ran across while I was calling you and planning our marriage? Damn," he muttered under his breath, wounded that she might consider his narration untrue. Even part of it. He had been scrupulously honest, omitting only those segments that lent nothing to the story and would only hurt Melissa to hear them.

But it was also true that he had slept with his ex-wife for the better part of six years, and that fact had to be somewhere in Melissa's mind along with everything he had told her.

"I'm sorry," he said then, his voice husky with emotion. "I'm so damned sorry. I'd do anything to make it up to you, anything."

"No one can change the past," she said, still staring out the side window.

"No, but you can sure as hell change the present," he shot back. "And what about the future? Melissa, we're still young. We could have it all—children, a long and happy marriage. Don't throw it out without giving us a chance. That's all I'm asking for, a chance. I knew if I didn't get you alone somewhere you'd never listen to me. That's the only reason I took you to the cabin."

Cocking a dubious eyebrow, she slowly brought her head around. "The *only* reason?"

Color crept into his face and neck, but he gave her a steady, though brief, eye-to-eye look. "I didn't take you up there to seduce you, however it turned out. That's something else you have to believe." Frustration got the better of him, and he slapped the steering wheel. "I know I'm asking a hell of a lot, but I've got to try. If I lose you a second time..." The tears in his eyes shocked him, but he suddenly couldn't see very well.

Pulling the truck to the side of the road, he put his head down on the steering wheel. Surprised by it all, Melissa frowned at him. What on earth was happening?

And then she realized what he was doing. But she had never seen a grown man cry before and wasn't sure if she should say something consoling or pretend not to notice. Making matters worse was the huge lump in her own throat. Nervously she smoothed the hair back from her face and tried not to look at the man bent over the steering wheel. Her inherent kindness wouldn't let her ignore his misery for long, however, and she took a breath and extended a hand to lay it on his arm.

"Wyatt?"

Turning his face away from her, he got out of the truck and walked off, leaving the door hanging open. When he disappeared into the trees, Melissa stared at the spot with a horrible sinking sensation. How had things come to this—him crying, her on the verge?

He wanted too much, she told herself defensively. At the same time she still felt somehow to blame for his unhappiness. But she wasn't to blame, he was, her common sense argued, so why did she feel as though she had committed some unpardonable sin? He couldn't possibly shed as many tears as she had six years ago, not if he stayed in the woods for a week.

She checked her watch and kept an eye on the trees. Should she just sit here and wait, or what? They were not an ordinary couple, and she couldn't go running after him as though they were. But she should do *something*.

After another few minutes she got out and called, "Wyatt?"

To her surprise, he answered. "I'll be there in a minute."

The huskiness of his voice gave Melissa a pang. His last words before stopping the truck had been, *"If I lose you again..."* She remembered how his voice had cracked.

With a groan of utter despair, she returned to her seat in the truck and laid her head against the passenger-door window. He loved her and wanted her to completely forget the past. Okay, that was his side of this awful situation. But what was hers? Why, if she felt nothing but disdain for him, had she permitted such abandoned lovemaking between them? Without question, she had a lot of soul searching to do. Did she believe the story he'd told her or didn't she? Had Shannon really been the only woman he'd slept with all the time they had been apart? Not that even one misstep was acceptable behavior for an engaged man who swore undying love on the telephone at least three times a week. But was it understandable? Hadn't she had her desperate moments in California? Not that she had sought the comfort of another man, but Wyatt had been at the peak of his sexual drive and living a celibate life, while she hadn't even yet experienced a climax. Her thoughts had been focused on romance, not on sex. There was no comparison between the two of them, she realized unhappily.

"Oh, God," Melissa whispered, feeling like the dregs at the bottom of a barrel.

When Wyatt returned to the truck and got in, he immediately took his sunglasses from the visor and put them on. "Sorry about that," he said to her. Adjusting the shifting lever to Drive, he started the truck moving.

Melissa didn't know how to respond to his apology, so she said nothing. They rode in uncomfortable silence. At least Melissa was uncomfortable; she couldn't tell what Wyatt was feeling because he stared straight ahead, keeping his eyes on the road.

The trip out of the mountains took much less time than the trip in, which verified Melissa's suspicion that Wyatt had done a lot more driving than was necessary the day he'd brought her out there. Today he made only two turns before reaching the highway, when before he had driven at least a half-dozen different roads.

Spotting Whitehorn in the distance, Melissa heaved a sigh containing some very peculiar ambiguities. Ostensibly it was over; she would soon be home again. But what would Wyatt do next, if anything? He'd taken his best shot, and how did he view the results?

Even more disturbing, how did *she* view the results?

Approaching the town limits, Wyatt finally spoke. "Would you like me to drive you to the sheriff's office so you can file those kidnapping charges?"

She gave him a look. "That would be handy for Judd, I suppose. He wouldn't have to drive clear out to your ranch to arrest you." After a moment of silence, she added with a sigh of weary resignation, "Don't worry about it. I'm not going to file charges."

A slightly cynical smile touched Wyatt's lips. "Why not? I committed a crime. Shouldn't I have to pay for it? One always pays for sins or crimes in one way or another. If I've learned anything in my lifetime, it's that."

Melissa also produced a cynical smile. "I think I'll let the big guy upstairs make the decision on whether or not you deserve to pay a penalty. I'm not going to do it."

"What's stopping you? Cowardice, disinterest or love?"

"I'm not a coward," she said sharply.

"No, you're not a coward," he agreed. "Guess that leaves disinterest or love." He sent her a glance.

"Those are not the only options, Wyatt, so stop being so damned smug."

"Smug I'm not," he mumbled, then spoke with more clarity. "What in hell do I have to be smug about?"

"Nothing, which is exactly my point." That wasn't entirely true, Melissa thought uneasily. He had seduced her with a kiss—twice, to be accurate. He wouldn't be human if he didn't feel a little smugness over his own potency.

Wyatt took the shortest route through town to reach Melissa's building. He parked behind her car, just as he had the day he had talked her into letting him drive her to Billings. Melissa got out immediately, but so did Wyatt. "I'll carry your luggage up those stairs," he announced.

"I can do it."

"I'm sure you can. But *I'm* going to do it." Opening the door of the camper shell and dropping the tailgate, he fished out her suitcases. "Lead the way and unlock your door."

"You do enjoy giving orders, don't you?"

"Don't get mad again. I'm not in the mood for another argument."

Doing a slow burn, Melissa preceded him up the stairs and unlocked the door of her apartment. "Just set them down right here," she said when they were no more than two steps into her laundry room.

"Fine." Wyatt lowered the suitcases to the floor. Straightening, he gave her a long look. Melissa couldn't see his eyes through the dark lenses of his glasses, but she didn't need to see them to feel their intensity.

"Well . . ." she said hesitantly, wishing he would leave without further dissension.

"About that lot," he said. "Have your lawyer draw up the contract, or do it yourself if you know how. Keep it simple. It doesn't have to be pages and pages of legal mumbo jumbo. I'm selling, you're buying. List your terms. When it's ready, let me know and I'll come to town and sign it."

"Oh, the lot. Yes, I'll do that. I'll call when it's ready." The lot had completely slipped her mind. During the last few days she had lost track not only of her plans but of her own self. All because of this man, who was a disturbing combination of the Wyatt in her memory and a sexy stranger who would make any woman's heart beat faster. Emotions were running wild in her system, but they were so jumbled and tangled she wasn't able to act on any one of them.

"Well, I'm sure you'd like me to leave." Wyatt turned to go, then turned back to her. "I probably should apologize for ruining your vacation plans, but I'm not really sorry for what I did. At least we talked, which never would have happened if I hadn't brought you to the cabin."

"I'm not looking for an apology," Melissa said. "It's over and I only want to forget it."

"Forget it? Is that what you intend to do?" It hurt that the only thing she had gotten out of their time together was a wish to forget it. He suddenly felt drained, sapped. He had tried everything he knew how to atone for the past. There were no more ideas cooking in his brain that might bring them emotionally closer. This, then, was the end of the line. Frustration and sorrow burned in his gut.

He took the two steps that separated them and slid his hand beneath Melissa's hair to clasp the back of her neck. Her eyes widened in stunned surprise, but what the hell? he thought. At this point he had nothing to lose.

Lowering his head, he pressed his mouth to hers in a rough, emotional kiss. He felt her hands move to push against his chest, and she tried to turn her head to break free of the kiss. But he held her head steady by the strong grip he had on her neck, and he kissed her until his own legs felt shaky.

When he needed air, he raised his head and looked into her eyes. "Just remember one thing, Melissa. You could go to the ends of the earth and you would never find a man who loves you more than I do."

Her mind searched for a retort, something that would cut him down, put him in his place. But his stinging kiss was still on her lips and her brain felt numb. *You could go to the ends of the earth, and you would never find a man who loves you more than I do.* The tears she'd been battling for hours suddenly erupted.

"Go," she whispered hoarsely. "Just...go."

He looked at the tears streaming down her face. "You're not going to forget. Don't even try." Releasing her, he walked to the door. "Call me when the contract is ready." He walked out.

Melissa all but collapsed on the dryer, bending over it to sob uncontrollably with her head on her arms. Gradually her sobs subsided, and finally she was able to straighten up, pick up her suitcases and carry them to her bedroom.

She was about to throw herself across her bed when the phone rang. Clearing her throat and wiping her eyes, she answered on the fourth ring.

"Melissa? I saw you getting out of Mr. North's truck. You're home so early. Are you all right?"

It was Wanda from downstairs. She couldn't face anyone today, Melissa thought. Not today. "Um...I caught a— a bug or something, so I came home. I'm going to stay in bed today and hope I feel better tomorrow."

"Oh, that's the pits, hon. Is there anything I can do? Are you able to eat? I could bring you up something."

She hadn't had anything but a few swallows of coffee all day, Melissa remembered, and while she didn't feel hungry, she really should eat something. "An omelet, Wanda. Plain. No cheese. And some wheat toast."

"A pot of tea?"

"Yes, that would be great."

"I'll be up in ten minutes."

"Thanks, Wanda."

Wyatt drove with a grim, brooding expression. At the edge of town he debated about going to the ranch or returning to the cabin. Did he prefer being alone for a while or getting back to work? He had five hired hands at the ranch and the house help, which pretty much eliminated the possibility for any solitary thinking.

But maybe he had done enough thinking. It was really up to Melissa now. She knew how he felt about her—he couldn't have said it any plainer—and she knew the facts of the past as he had lived it. What more could he do?

Sighing roughly, he turned the pickup toward the ranch. When he got there he would call Helena and talk to Timmy. Talking to his son always gave him a lift. Then he'd try to reach Joe Lott, the man who lived and worked at the cabin as caretaker. He had told Joe to take some time off and that he would let him know when to return. Joe might as well get back to work, too.

Thirteen

By the end of the day Melissa felt more like her normal self. For hours she had alternately walked the floor, cussed, wept and laid in her bed staring at the ceiling. By that evening her emotions had apparently worn themselves down and she was able to think about Wyatt and the last few days without experiencing another explosion of one sort or another.

One thing was abundantly clear: Wyatt was bitter about his marriage. But his theory about Shannon getting pregnant on purpose was ridiculous. An accidental meeting? One night together? No, Melissa couldn't swallow that portion of his story. The rest of it? Well...she just didn't know.

When Wanda had delivered the food from the café she'd exclaimed, "Lordy, hon, you look terrible. You really are ill."

Well, she wasn't ill, but Wanda was right about her looking terrible; a glance in a mirror at her pasty face and puffy eyes had stunned Melissa.

Her eyes were still a little puffy that evening, but the color had returned to her skin and her nerves were no longer screamingly raw. Wearing a nightgown and bathrobe, she curled up in her favorite chair in her living room. Not once since opening the Hip Hop Café had she done what she had today—feigned illness to avoid going downstairs and seeing to her business.

But she had a much bigger problem to deal with than her taking an unnecessary day off—Wyatt, of course. She might have doubts about portions of his history lesson, but he had finally convinced her that he still loved her. Yet should his feelings influence hers? It was ironic that justice had been served without any lies from her about there being another man in her life. Wyatt was suffering as she had suffered six years ago, and what bothered her most about it was her own lack of satisfaction. His unhappiness added nothing to her happiness, she realized sadly. In fact, his misery could almost persuade her to truly forgive and forget.

That wasn't all he wanted, though. His intention of proposing marriage one day was astounding. If she had been the least bit kind today, if she had even pretended to understand and accept his story, he would have already proposed.

The thought sent a tingling thrill up Melissa's spine, which didn't please her. Getting tingly over Wyatt when he wasn't even in the vicinity was merely a delayed reaction to the great sex between them at the cabin, she told herself. And yes, it had been great. The best. She had never gotten so lost in a man's arms before, nor experienced so much pleasure from making love. But that didn't mean she was *in* love, did it?

Her feelings for him were different now, though, she had to admit. If they had just met and had no shared past to remember and ache over, she would have no reason not to fall very hard for Wyatt.

Melissa drew a deeply troubled breath. Facing her own feelings was extremely difficult. If she succeeded in overcoming the past and permitted herself to trust Wyatt again, and then he did something else to hurt her, she would probably end up a mental case. Could she take such a risk?

On the other hand, could she *not* take the risk? He would be back, she was certain of it. If nothing else, they had to see each other to complete their transaction on the lot. Maybe she should bend a little and give him the chance he had begged for. They were *both* different people today than they'd been six years ago. And the honest-to-God's truth was that there was the most persistent ache in her body that she knew only Wyatt could pacify. Maybe that was no more than chemistry or raging hormones, but shouldn't she at least make the attempt to find out if it meant more?

It was shortly after noon hour the next day when Melissa looked up the phone number of the North Ranch in the Whitehorn directory. Dialing the number, she all but held her breath in nervous anticipation. A woman answered.

"North Ranch."

"Hello. This is Melissa Avery. Does Wyatt happen to be around?"

"He's not in the house, Ms. Avery, but I can have someone locate him and ask him to return your call."

"Would you do that, please? I need to talk to him about a business transaction we're working on. My number at work is 555-3707. I would appreciate hearing from him as soon as possible."

"I'll pass on the message. Goodbye."

"Thank you." Putting down the phone, Melissa sat back in her chair with an unsettled sigh. She was in the café's awful little windowless office, as that was where she kept her typewriter. For the last hour she had been putting together the contract on the vacant lot for her and Wyatt's signatures, and it was now completed except for one essential ingredient: the legal description of the property. She could get the information by going to the assessor's office at the courthouse, but since she needed to tell Wyatt that he could come by this evening and sign the document, she had decided to get it from him.

Sitting straighter, she read the contract in the typewriter again, checking it for typos and content. It was, as Wyatt had suggested, simply structured and only one page long. She was buying, he was selling, her terms were succinctly stated and that was that. There were no superfluous phrases or, as Wyatt had put it, any legal mumbo jumbo. If that suited him, it suited her, and once the legal description was typed into the space she had left between paragraphs, it would be ready for signatures.

Her phone rang. Thinking that someone had located Wyatt very quickly, she drew a nervous breath and picked it up. "Hip Hop Café. Melissa speaking."

"You're back. I was hoping you would be."

"Pardon?" Melissa frowned. The masculine voice was familiar, but not so familiar that she was able to put it with a face.

"This is Paul."

"Paul?"

"Paul Rodell."

"Oh, Paul. I'm sorry I didn't recognize your voice, but my mind was a million miles away. How are you?"

"Just fine. I stopped in for coffee and was told by one of your waitresses that you were on vacation."

"I . . . was." She gathered her wits. "Actually, I planned to be gone for a week, but . . ." That lie about catching a bug got stuck in her throat. "I decided to come home early."

Paul chuckled in her ear. "You just can't stay away from your business, can you?"

Melissa smiled wanly. "Something like that."

"Well, the reason I called—*one* of the reasons—I was wondering if you had secured the land next to your building."

"It's almost mine, Paul. To tell you the truth, the purchase should be completed very soon now. But I won't own it free and clear for some time, possibly six or seven months." Her terms in the document included a monthly payment of one thousand dollars, but she planned to pay as much on the balance due Wyatt as she could scrape together each month.

"That long, hmm? Well, that means you won't be looking for that expansion loan until February or March of next year."

"I think that's about right," Melissa confirmed.

"Well, fine. You know where to come when you're ready for the loan. Melissa, about the other reason I called. Let's

drive to Billings and having dinner tonight. We could catch
a movie and be back around midnight.''

"Uh...I can't, Paul. Not tonight." It occurred to her
rather suddenly that she really didn't want to date Paul on
any night. He was a nice guy and she liked him, but going
out with him again would only encourage his interest, and
she didn't want his interest encouraged. Frowning, she bit
down on her bottom lip, wishing ardently that she hadn't
caused this unlikely liaison in the first place. It was her fault,
not Paul's, and now she had to let him know how she really
felt.

"Paul, I'm going to be up-front with you. I've been seeing someone else." *Oh, yeah? Who? Wyatt?* When had she
learned to lie so well? But there *was* something between her
and Wyatt, and even if there wasn't, Paul Rodell was not the
man for her.

"Oh, I see."

The sudden chill in his voice couldn't possibly be missed.
"I'm sorry, Paul," she said gently.

His voice took on a macho quality that Melissa saw
through at once. Like most men in this situation, he wasn't
going to let her know that she had just injured his pride.
"No problem, Melissa. Don't give it a thought."

"Still friends?" she asked quietly.

"Of course. I'll see you around. Goodbye."

Sighing heavily, Melissa put down the phone. Now he
would probably find reasons to refuse her that bank loan
when the time came, she thought regretfully. Hopefully he
was professional enough about his job to keep it separate
from his private life, but she really didn't know him well
enough to foretell the outcome of this conversation.

Frowning, she dropped her gaze to the contract in the
typewriter, and Wyatt's image appeared in her mind. She
could only deal with one man at a time, and right now he
was first in line. Paul wouldn't want her anyway if he knew
what had taken place at Wyatt's cabin.

* * *

"Melissa? Wyatt here. Marion said you called."

He didn't sound angry or upset because of yesterday, she thought, greatly relieved. "Yes. I've been working on the contract and I need the legal description of the lot. Do you have it handy?"

"Hold on."

Melissa doodled on a yellow pad while she waited, though her thoughts were on Wyatt. *"You'll never find a man who loves you more than I do."* She swallowed hard, aware of just how influencing that declaration had been.

"Melissa? Got something to write with?"

"Yes, go ahead."

He read off the description listed on his deed. "That's it. How are you doing?"

Melissa cleared her throat. "I'm fine. Once I type this in, the contract will be finished. Would this evening be all right for you to come to town and sign it?"

"Yes. What time?"

She had been thinking of something all morning, but now that the moment was at hand, she became a little queasy with dread. Yet the ball was in her court where Wyatt was concerned, and somehow she had to let him know that there possibly *was* a chance for them.

"I—I was wondering if you'd like to come for dinner."

"In the café?"

"That's what I had in mind, yes."

"I'll come for dinner if we eat in your apartment."

Melissa's heart skipped a beat. "Oh. Well, that wasn't exactly..." Wyatt was silent, apparently to give her time to rethink her invitation. "I guess that would be all right," she finally said.

"Great. What time do you want me?"

Wanting him was precisely the problem she'd been struggling with. She didn't know if she loved him, she didn't know if she could ever love him again, but she had learned one thing at Wyatt's cabin: a woman could want a man without calling it love.

"Around seven," she said.

"Seven it is. See you then."

Wyatt climbed the outside stairs of Melissa's building and rapped on her apartment door at seven sharp. He was afraid to hope that she had softened toward him, but why else would she invite him to dinner?

The door opened. "Hello," she said, hiding her nervousness behind a smile.

"Hi." He drank in the sight of her. Her dress was an exquisite lavender-gray color and draped enticingly over her body. What he liked best, though, was that her hair was loose, framing her beautiful face, caressing her shoulders.

"Come in." Melissa stepped back. Wyatt was wearing dark slacks and a white shirt, unbuttoned at the collar, probably more clothes from his "Helena" wardrobe. She took a breath, annoyed with herself for immediately dredging up the past.

Wyatt walked in and closed the door. "Something smells good in here."

"Beef Stroganoff." Melissa led him past the kitchen to the living room. "We'll have dinner in a few minutes. Would you like a drink? I have some hard liquor—vodka and scotch—or beer and soft drinks."

"I'll have a scotch and water, thanks." Being offered a drink was a surprise. "Make it light."

"It's in the kitchen. Have a seat. I'll only be a minute."

Melissa's mood was so vastly different from any he had witnessed since their reunion that Wyatt's hopes became renewed tenfold. Too on edge to sit, he wandered around her living room with his hands in the pockets of his slacks.

She returned with two glasses, one of which she passed to him. Here was his second surprise—Melissa, too, was having a cocktail. How many other surprises did she have in store for him this evening? An internal excitement made him feel youthful and almost giddy.

"Cheers," he said while lifting his glass in a toast.

"Cheers," she repeated. They sipped. "Wyatt, I have a few things to say. Let's sit down." She went to a chair and he sat on the sofa. Next to her chair was a small, round table, and she reached for two sheets of paper lying on it. "This is the contract I drew up. It's only one page, but I made a copy. Before we get to it, I'd like to thank you for allowing me to buy the lot. When I first learned you had bought it, I thought you had done so to...well, I don't know...but I guess I thought you bought it because I wanted it."

"I didn't know you wanted it."

"I know that now." Her eyes met his. "I hope you understand why I couldn't accept it as a gift."

He sat back. "Probably because you didn't want to feel indebted to me."

Melissa frowned slightly. "That was part of it, yes, but I couldn't take a gift of that nature from anyone."

"Melissa," he said softly, "I'm not just 'anyone.' Someday I'm going to give you the world."

Her breath caught. "Please don't count on it, Wyatt. I've thought a great deal about our past and what's happened since we met again, and I can't deny anymore that there is something between us. But I need time, maybe a lot of time, maybe much more time than you're willing to give me."

"I want you now," he said quietly. "But if you need some time..." His voice trailed off and after a moment he smiled. "I'll be satisfied with whatever you're willing to give me. Will that work? Melissa, just being here with you like this...you can't know what it means to me."

Melissa's heart was pounding. Wyatt exuded sex appeal. He was so handsome it hurt to look at him. And for the first time it occurred to her that she just might be the most stupid woman alive. A handsome, sexy, generous man was madly in love with her, and she kept saying no because of some ancient history?

She was suddenly too emotional to maintain that particular conversation. Taking a breath, she held up the contract. "I hope this isn't *too* simple." Rising, she walked over to the sofa and held it out. "Please read it and tell me what you think. I'll be in the kitchen."

Taking her drink with her, she hurried from the room and into the kitchen, where she weakly leaned against the counter and swallowed half the contents of her glass in one gulp. Though mixed with water, the scotch burned going down and hit her stomach hard. She shivered at the sensation, then set the glass on the counter.

Wyatt walked in. "It looks fine to me. Got a pen?"

"Uh...yes, by the phone." Nervously she dashed to the phone, picked up the pen and turned around to give it to him. She didn't have far to reach; he was right behind her.

Their gazes locked. Instead of taking the pen, Wyatt took her hand. She couldn't tear her eyes from his, nor could she breathe normally. Her heart was hammering, her pulse racing. He loved her, and dear God, did she love him, too?

She felt his thumb gently moving on her wrist. "You look especially beautiful tonight," he said huskily.

"So—so do you," she whispered.

Slowly he pulled her forward until they were standing only inches apart. His right hand rose to her hair. "I'm so glad it's still long. I always loved your hair." A shadow entered his eyes. "Oh, Melissa, if only—"

She pressed her fingertips to his lips. "Don't. I'm trying very hard to forget the past."

His eyes probed hers. "You really are?"

"If we had no past, if there was only the present..."

"Then you would love me." He said it sadly because he knew it was true. But she didn't want to talk about the past again, and neither did he. "Melissa..." He pulled her into his arms, holding her tightly against himself.

A sigh whispered from her as she laid her cheek on his chest. His solid, warm body felt so good, and she couldn't help nestling even closer.

He tipped her chin and looked into her eyes. Seeing acquiescence, he tenderly pressed his lips to hers. He hadn't come here for this—at least he'd told himself during the drive from the ranch to keep his hands to himself—but neither had he expected Melissa's incredible change of heart. Though not apparent until now, the abduction had worked. His spirit soared in a direct ratio to his rising blood pressure.

The kiss deepened. He felt her drop the pen to the floor and lift her arms to curl around his neck. Her mouth opened for his tongue, and suddenly their embrace was no longer in the soothing, comforting category, which was how it had started.

His eyes opened, burning into hers. "Melissa?" It was a question of how far she would let him go. He needed her, almost desperately, but it was her decision to make.

"It's all right," she whispered throatily. "Give me a minute." Slipping from his arms, she turned off the oven and then, with pot holders, opened its door to remove a covered pan and place it on a trivet on the counter.

Wyatt watched the procedure through slightly narrowed eyes, uncertain of her intent. But his uncertainty vanished when she laid the pot holders aside and walked over to him to take his hand with a softly stated, "Come."

This was truly incredible, a miracle, he thought as she led him to her bedroom. Apparently she needed some time to sort out her emotions where a permanent commitment was concerned, but she was an honest-enough woman to admit their powerful physical attraction.

So be it. Someday she would be his wife. He knew that as surely as he knew anything, but he would bide his time and give her plenty of space to come to that decision on her own.

Besides, how could a man be unhappy when the woman he loved was in his arms? Her bedroom was decorated in deep rose and lavender, but he saw none of the pretty, imaginative touches Melissa had used to make this room hers, not the wallpaper, not the matching drapes and bedspread, not the scatter rugs. All he could see was her, and all he wanted was her.

His hands started at her wrists and slowly moved up her arms, drifting across her shoulders to her throat and then caressing their way to her face, which he cupped while he kissed her lips with all of the love and ardor in his soul.

"I didn't plan to do this," she whispered breathily when she could speak.

"Nor did I." But Wyatt wondered if either of them really knew what had been in the back of their minds since their telephone conversation regarding the contract and Melissa's surprising dinner invitation.

It didn't matter, he thought then. Their kisses were becoming urgent, and each began unbuttoning the other's clothing. Melissa pushed his shirt from his shoulders. He finally got the bodice of her dress unbuttoned and open, and her bra unfastened. They moved with more haste then, shedding their clothes, throwing back the bedspread, then lying down together, arms and legs tangling erotically.

"Oh, Wyatt." Her hands slid around his neck, then upward to twine into his hair. "I—I don't understand myself at all anymore."

He became very still and slowly lifted his head to search her eyes. "As much as I want you right now, as painful as it would be to get off of this bed and leave this room, I would do it if my being here makes you unhappy."

Her head moved back and forth on the pillow. "No, no, it's not that." Her eyes slid from his. "I—I'm afraid."

"Of me?" When she didn't answer, he gave her a slight shake with his hands on her shoulders. There was no anger in the gesture, only a profound affection and some dismay. "Melissa, I'll never hurt you again. How many ways can I say it? How can I prove it to you?" Lowering his head, he kissed her with great tenderness. Then he looked at her once more. "Tell me what you want me to do."

She looked into his beautiful brown eyes and saw only love. Her fears were her own, and she would have to get past them on her own. "Stay," she whispered. "I want you to stay."

"My love," he said softly, and took her lips in another tender kiss.

That was how they made love—slowly, compassionately, with rougher emotions contained. Melissa fell into a dreamy state and marveled at this side of him, marveled that he could be so gentle and giving and patient. He kissed every inch of her, and his mouth on her skin was like nothing she had ever felt before.

When every nerve in her body was sensitized to his touch and she could bear no more, she moaned raggedly, "Now, Wyatt, now."

He took a moment for protection, then entered her with the same unselfish gentleness with which he had brought her to this passionate peak. Clinging to him, she felt the beginning of her climb to completion, the swirling heat in her lower body, the urgency that was both delicious and torturous.

Her hips rose off the bed to meet his thrusts. Her eyes were closed, her head back. "Harder," she groaned. "Harder."

That was all he needed to hear. Pulling out all the stops, he set free the wildness within himself and rode her hard and fast. In seconds she cried out. "Wyatt... Wyatt..."

He was with her, and his voice mingled with hers. "Melissa... sweetheart... oh, baby."

Silence descended upon the room as their breathing returned to normal. Neither moved. Neither spoke.

At long last Melissa took a deep breath and exhaled it slowly. "I hope you like dried-out beef Stroganoff."

Raising his head, he looked at her and laughed. She laughed, too, and it was the first time in six years that they had laughed together. It felt wonderful, and when they stopped laughing they were still smiling.

Wyatt shook his head, openly displaying his amazement. "You are the most fantastic woman who ever drew breath. Do you know that?"

She lifted her head and kissed his lips. "Never was, never will be. But thanks for saying so. Let's get up and see if we can salvage dinner."

He was grinning. "You're the boss."

She gave him a playful pinch on the shoulder. "I'll remember you said that."

"Until we're old and gray, I hope."

Laughing again, they got off the bed.

Fourteen

They sat at the table long after they were done eating and talked. Not about the two of them, but about high school pranks, dances, football games and old friends. "Do you remember...?" preceded numerous stories that made them laugh, almost hysterically a few times. It was a wonderful evening, one of the most pleasant in Melissa's memory. And underlying the camaraderie Melissa felt with Wyatt was the excitement of sexual awareness.

Again and again she found herself admiring Wyatt's handsome face, the unique way his head cocked to one side at times, his perfect smile and white teeth, his hair and the twinkle in his marvelous brown eyes. She knew he was doing the same with her. Sometimes his gaze burned her with its intensity, as if he was absorbing every nuance of her every expression.

Finally they had finished the small bottle of dinner wine, a pot of tea and another of coffee. Wyatt got up and stretched; they had been sitting there for hours. He gave her a smile that was slightly teasing. "I could be easily talked into staying the night."

Laughing lightly, Melissa got to her feet. "Not a good idea, Wyatt. My employees arrive early and I don't relish gossip."

He walked around the table to be near her. His hand rose to caress her hair and his smile became pensive. "How about tomorrow night? May I come by again?" he asked.

Melissa gave it some thought, then shook her head. "I can't goof off through every dinner hour, Wyatt. It's the busiest time of day in the café."

"*After* the dinner hour?"

"Um . . . let's wait a few days."

"But a few days takes in the weekend."

"Yes, I know. But I still need a little time. And Mondays are generally a little quieter in the café. Come by on Monday night."

"Instead of you cooking, let me take you to dinner. We'll drive to Billings or Butte or somewhere in between. Just to get out of town."

"Sure . . . why not?"

He bent his head and kissed her. It was a low-pressure, lovely kiss that seemed in tune with their lengthy table talk. "Monday seems a long way off," he murmured.

The warmth of his kiss remained on her lips and in her system. Monday *did* seem a long way off, but she couldn't ignore her weekend business.

The thought of business gave her a start. "We forgot to sign the contract," she exclaimed, and slipped away from him to retrieve the document from the top of the refrigerator, where she had laid it for safekeeping while putting the finishing touches on dinner. After they had each signed, Melissa handed him the original.

"You can keep this," Wyatt said.

"No, *I* owe *you* the money. You should have it."

He shrugged. "Whatever suits you."

She felt his gaze on her mouth and decided that she would be the one to instigate a good-night kiss. Stepping closer to him, she raised up on her toes and kissed his lips. Immediately his arms clamped around her, and the kiss felt a lot more like a hello than a goodbye.

"Damn, you're something," he whispered when they came up for air. He didn't want to leave, but it was growing late and he knew Melissa got up early in the morning to open the café. Reluctantly, he took a backward step. "This was a great evening, Melissa, the best."

"I think so too."

"I'll see you on Monday. Can you get away around five?" She nodded. "Five will be fine."

They walked through the laundry room to the outside door. Wyatt looked at her, then caught her around the waist and brought her close. "Until Monday," he whispered, kissing her soundly and very thoroughly. Then he left.

Breathlessly she closed and locked the door. An elation she had never before felt made her step light and almost dancelike. Returning to the kitchen, she began cleaning up. Talking had seemed so much more important than doing the dishes, and she knew it would take her only a few minutes to accomplish the task.

But her mind was in a dreamy state, she realized when she caught herself working in slow motion. A smile tipped the corners of her lips. She was not going to rush into a commitment with Wyatt, but things were definitely moving in that direction, and surprise of all surprises, she felt good about it. Very good. "Leave the past in the past," she murmured to herself, thinking it good advice. At least it was good advice where Wyatt was concerned. There were aspects of the past that she would never permit herself to lose sight of, specifically her father's murder.

A frown created a tiny wrinkle between her eyes. She was doing nothing to help find Charlie Avery's killer other than hounding Whitehorn's law-enforcement agencies. Maybe there was something she *could* do, like hire a private investigator. How would Judd and Tracy view such a step from her? Would they label it interference and be uncooperative, or would they be willing to share what information they did have with a PI?

It was something to think about, Melissa decided. For one thing, since there were no private investigators in Whitehorn, she would have to locate someone from another area.

Sighing about that subject, she let her thoughts return to the evening and Wyatt, which eliminated her frown and brought another smile.

The truth was, she felt happy. Joyful. And she wasn't going to think about old hurts anymore. That phase of her life was over.

Wyatt had good, honest, industrious men working on the ranch, which had been proven time and again during his residency in Helena. During those years he had made as many trips to the ranch as he could work in around Shannon's demands that he attend every political function and play the role of a proper son-in-law to State Senator Wilbur Kiley. Wyatt didn't dislike Wilbur. In fact, he and Wilbur had gotten along quite well. It was Shannon who had her nose in the air because her father was an important, influential figure in Helena.

In retrospect, Wyatt wondered how he had endured it for so long. His body might have been in Helena, but his soul had been at the ranch. It was all behind him now and he was home where he belonged, but at moments he was struck so hard with that incredible fact that he would actually get light-headed.

He was happy, he realized. Really happy for the first time in years. Next weekend he would have Timmy—his first visit, as stated in the custody decree—and he'd have him every second weekend after that. He could hardly wait to show his small son the ranch, to teach him to ride as his own father had taught him, to introduce him to Melissa. She would love him—how could she not? He had no misgivings on that subject.

On Saturday he talked to his men for a few minutes, ascertaining what chores or tasks were lined up for the day, then saddled a horse for a ride. The sun was bright enough that he wore dark glasses, and riding his own land in the sunshine and thinking of his freedom and Melissa made him feel like shouting in childlike glee.

Instead, he kept his dignity intact and rode along grinning. Deliberately he headed for a section of the ranch opposite to where the men would be working. He wanted nothing to intrude on his own euphoric thoughts today other than his horse's hooves on the ground, bird calls and an occasional honeybee.

Time was all Melissa had requested of him, which he would give her, gladly. He visualized the day when she needed no more time, when she was certain of her feelings for him and they would plan their wedding. His heart skipped an impassioned beat. He loved her so much, and he would never hurt her again, not even in the smallest way with some thoughtless remark.

His thoughts went back in time to when his mother had been alive, and how kindly she and his father had spoken to each other. To his knowledge there had never been a cross word between Simon and Sheila North. That was how he wanted his and Melissa's marriage to be, how he swore it would be. The future looked so great he couldn't stop smiling: he and Melissa and Timmy together...their own babies...Christmases...birthdays...weekends at the cabin. Maybe before they started having babies they would do a little traveling. A honeymoon in Paris, or whatever appealed to Melissa.

He sighed contentedly.

It was late afternoon when Wyatt rode into the compound and unsaddled his horse. Feeling sweaty, and with dust on his clothes, he walked to the house contemplating a shower. Entering through the back door, he saw Marion, who'd apparently been waiting for him.

"Wyatt..." She stopped to clear her throat. "Shannon is here."

"Without Timmy?" When Marion nodded, his mouth tightened. Why would Shannon make a trip to the ranch now when she never would during their marriage? "Where is she?"

"In the den . . . for more than two hours."

His eyes narrowed to mere slits. In their six years of marriage Shannon had consented to come to the ranch only one time, and during the drive back to Helena she had complained incessantly about the isolation and boredom of the place. "Don't ever ask me to go back. I cannot imagine anyone—especially an educated man like your father—living such an incidental, limited existence."

Wyatt hadn't tried to argue her out of her attitude. It was fine with him if she didn't like the ranch. In fact, he'd found her narrow-mindedness rather amusing. If anyone he knew was living an "incidental, limited" life, it was Shannon, who had no personal ambitions or goals of her own and whose only claim to fame was her father's career.

Once Wyatt had pointed out that while she should be justifiably proud of Wilbur's accomplishments, he was still only a *state* senator, and if he had any real political ambitions he would have risen to the federal level of government. Shannon had become furious and they had traded insults for a while, until Wyatt had tired of the argument and left the house.

Her coming to the ranch now—especially without Timmy—boded no good. If she had enjoyed the place and felt some nostalgia for it in spite of their divorce, he would not feel so wary. But he knew how Shannon's mind worked, and she hadn't made the long drive from Helena without some devious plan in the mill.

"Thanks, Marion," he mumbled. Taking a deep breath, he strode through the house to the den. The wide double doors were open, and he stood in the doorframe for a moment. Shannon's back was to him, as she was standing at a window looking out, one hand holding a cigarette, the other a drink.

"Shannon?" He walked into the room and watched her turn around. As usual, she was dressed expensively and stylishly. Today's outfit was a stunning off-white dress and matching jacket. She was smiling.

"Hello, Wyatt. How are you?" She laughed lightly. "Been out on the range, I see." Her green eyes drifted over his dusty hat, jeans and shirt.

Wyatt's expression remained guarded. "Where's Timmy?"

"At home. I needed to speak to you alone."

"What about?"

"So abrupt," she exclaimed in a teasingly scolding manner.

Moving with rigid precision, Wyatt took off his hat and walked over to the desk to lay it down. Turning, he sat on the edge of the desk with his arms folded and a hard, unsmiling expression on his face. "Why are you here?"

Shannon took a long drag on her cigarette, then went to a table containing an ashtray to snuff it out. Looking at Wyatt, she took a sip from her glass. Finally she answered, "Where else would I find you?"

"Okay, so you need to talk to me. What about?" He couldn't imagine a topic that would connect the two of them in any way, shape or form. Their divorce was final, financial settlement and all. There were no loose ends to tie up, and there was no sensible reason for her to be here that he could think of. "We don't have anything to talk about," he added gruffly.

"Oh, but we do." Shannon studied her nearly empty glass for a second, then walked over to the liquor cabinet, where she dropped a couple of ice cubes into the glass before adding bourbon. "I asked Marion for the ice. Hope you don't mind." She turned to face Wyatt.

"Get to the point," Wyatt said brusquely. He didn't like her being here, nor did he like the feeling in his gut that she was up to no good.

"Well, it's like this." She took a swallow from her glass, then held Wyatt with a steady look. "I'm pregnant."

He stared at her as though struck dumb. Those two words brought back the evening six years before when she had made the exact same announcement.

But this time he wasn't the naive young man he'd been then. He spoke coldly. "If that should happen to be true, it's not my baby."

Without a word Shannon went to her purse and extracted a piece of paper. "I knew you would think I was lying, which is why I asked my doctor for this." Crossing the room, she held out the paper to Wyatt. "Go on, take it."

With visible reluctance he took and read it. His heart began to beat faster and his mouth went dry. He read it again, merely to take a moment to digest the information, then his eyes lifted. "This letter is probably a phony, but even if it's not and you really are pregnant, what does it have to do with me?"

She spoke quite casually. "You could be the father."

His mouth twisted angrily. "What in hell are you trying to pull?"

Her eyes widened. "Pull? Why would I be pulling anything? Facts are facts, Wyatt. I'm pregnant and I feel certain that you're the father."

"We both know how skilled you are at lying," he said harshly. "And why in hell would I believe the child is mine when you were having an affair right under my nose? Do you think I'm completely stupid?"

"I never thought you were stupid while we were married and I don't think so now. I am not trying to *pull* anything, as you so cruelly accused. Wyatt, this child could be yours. Doesn't that mean anything to you?"

"This child is Rick's!" Rick Malone was the man with whom Shannon had been having the affair. "Why come to me? Why aren't you badgering him?"

"Well, I would hardly categorize a discussion of one's unborn child as badgering." Shannon walked over to the liquor cabinet and poured herself yet another drink.

"Prove it's mine," Wyatt challenged. "Prove it's mine and I'll do everything humanly possible to help you with its upbringing."

Turning, Shannon's eyebrow lifted. "With money? No, Wyatt, I'm not here because of money. I want your name on our child's birth certificate."

"Then prove it's mine!" he shouted. "There are tests—"

"Which I will not permit until after the baby's birth. You owe me this, Wyatt. I didn't get pregnant all by myself. You were there, and enjoying yourself in the bargain."

Wyatt was becoming so enraged he feared he might do something violent. To put space between them, he walked around the desk. Then he leaned forward with his fists on the desktop. "You will never convince me without medical proof that this baby is mine. What did you hope to accomplish by coming here?"

"I hoped you would do the honorable thing, as you did before."

He was dumbfounded. "You thought I would marry you again? Have you lost what little mind you did have? Go to Rick. Tell him your lies, or tell him the damned truth, but get *him* to marry you. It's not going to work with me, Shannon, not this time."

Sipping her drink, she looked away. "Rick...is gone."

"Gone where?"

She went to her purse for another cigarette, which she promptly lit, deeply inhaling the first drag. "I don't know where he went, but he left Helena."

"In other words, he had his fun and left you flat. Incidentally, if you care so much for that baby you're carrying, how come you're smoking and drinking?"

"Stop criticizing everything I do!"

"Well, think of the baby, at least," he retorted disgustedly. Was there a chance the child was his? Frantically his mind raced, trying to remember the last time they had slept together. He had always been so diligent with protection, but he had also heard that there wasn't a birth control product on the market that was one-hundred-percent foolproof.

Shannon gulped the contents of her glass and immediately went for a refill. Scowling, Wyatt watched. With a fresh drink, she moved to a chair and sat down. "I'd like to make a deal with you. Please hear me out. Marry me and we'll get another divorce after the baby is born. I wouldn't ask you to live in Helena, nor would I make any demands regarding financial support. You know how I feel about scandal, and I merely want it to appear as though we decided to try again."

Wyatt shook his head. "No, absolutely not. Let me tell you something, Shannon. I'm happy, or I was until a few minutes ago. Melissa and I are going to be married—"

"Melissa?" Shannon jumped to her feet. "You contacted her in California? Already? Or maybe the two of you *stayed* in contact during our marriage. And you had the nerve to—"

"Just hold on a minute. I was *not* in contact with Melissa during our marriage. Unlike you, I tried to make it work. But in my absence Melissa moved back to Whitehorn, *without* my knowledge, I might add. It was pure accident that I walked into her café one day."

"Her café? She owns a business?" Shannon said with a sneer. "So, the marvelous Melissa—"

"Damn it, don't you dare demean her! You know nothing about her, and you have no right—"

"I know nothing about her? What about all the schoolboy babbling you did the morning you woke up in my bed in that motel in Missoula?"

"And I suppose you remember every word."

"You bet your sweet bippy I do." Shannon's expression changed from angry to placating in the blink of an eye. "Look, I didn't come here to fight with you. Wyatt, I'm in an awful jam. You could help me out of it. It would only be a temporary measure and I would be grateful for the rest of my life. Please reconsider."

Wyatt became very still. His emotions were in shambles and he could barely form a complete thought. But Shannon's desperation was her own doing and he had given her enough of his life. If the baby was his—proven by medical tests—he would do everything he could for the child, the same as he was doing for Timmy. But that was as far as he was going.

He took in a long breath. "I'm not going to marry you."

She started crying and moaning. "Oh, God, what am I going to do?"

"I think you're asking the right person. At any rate, it's your problem, not mine. Right now I'm going to go and have a shower. You know your way out."

Wiping her eyes, she followed him to the doorway of the den. "How can you be so cold and unfeeling? I *know* this is your baby, whatever you might think."

Wyatt stopped. "No, you don't know. That's what you'd like to convince me of, but I'm not falling for it, no matter how many tears you shed."

"You're an unsympathetic bastard."

He laughed grimly. "There are a few unflattering names I could lay on you, so don't go too far in that direction." He started through the doorway.

"You loved me once, I know you did."

Wyatt's steps slowed, but he could be only so cruel, so he ignored her frantic cry and continued down the hall.

In his bedroom he tore off his dusty clothes and walked nude into the attached bathroom. Turning on the shower, he stepped into the stall and lifted his face to the spray. That was when the pain struck. What if the baby *was* his? He couldn't remember when they had last made love. There had been so much trouble and dissension for a while that dates and timing totally eluded his desperate attempts at recall.

Laying his forehead against the wall tile, he groaned out loud. Shannon's plea for a second marriage was ludicrous and he would never agree, but what if the baby was his? Utter misery gripped him. He wanted more children, but not this way. He wanted *Melissa's* children.

After drying off, Wyatt pulled on a pair of sweatpants and stretched out on his bed. With his hands locked beneath his head, he stared at the ceiling. Odds were that Rick was the baby's father. He would wait, Wyatt decided, wait until the child was born and then demand a test to prove parentage. By then he would undoubtedly have to go through legal channels to force Shannon's cooperation, but that wouldn't stop him. In the meantime, he would tell Melissa what had occurred here today. In fact, he would like to call her right now and tell her.

Turning his head, he eyed the phone. But relating today's events on the phone went against his grain, and would probably go against Melissa's, as well. This was something he had to do in person, face-to-face. Melissa would understand, wouldn't she?

He closed his eyes in abject misery. If something happened to destroy the gains he and Melissa had made in their relationship, he wouldn't be able to deal with it. It wasn't fair. They had come so far since their first shocking meeting in the Hip Hop, when neither had been prepared for seeing the other.

A knock on his door brought him to a sitting position. "Yes?" Getting off the bed, he strode to the door and pulled it open. It was Marion.

"Wyatt, dinner is almost ready. Shall I set a place for Shannon?"

His entire body went rigid. "I thought she left."

"She's still in the den, Wyatt, and..." Marion hesitated, then continued "...she's been drinking steadily."

"I'll handle this, Marion," he told her. "Thanks." She left and Wyatt closed the door. With his lips in a thin, grim line, he found a sweatshirt and pulled it on, then stuck his feet into a pair of old moccasins. Why was Shannon hanging around? He'd thought he had made his position clear enough, and he didn't relish the prospect of another bout of pleas from her and refusals from him. "Damn," he muttered, leaving his bedroom and heading for the den.

The scene there stunned him. Beside the chair Shannon was occupying was an ashtray overflowing with cigarette butts, and the bottle of bourbon, all but empty. Her head was slumped forward on her chest and he got the picture: she had drunk herself into a stupor.

Cursing under his breath, he walked over to her and shook her shoulder. "Shannon?" She barely stirred. He shook her again and spoke louder. "Shannon?"

It was apparent that she wasn't going to come around, and a feeling of angry helplessness hardened Wyatt's eyes. Even if she came to and tried to leave now, he couldn't let her drive.

He went to the den doorway and called, "Marion?"

The woman appeared in the hall. "Yes?"

"I'm going to put Shannon to bed and I need your assistance."

"Certainly," she agreed.

What he needed more than assistance, Wyatt thought wryly, was a witness. No way was Shannon going to be able to say that he'd put her to bed and then taken advantage of her, even to an accusation as trivial as removing some of her clothes.

Maneuvering his arms under her legs and back, he picked her up. "I'm going to take her to the blue guest room, Marion. Then I would appreciate your removing enough of her clothing to make her comfortable."

"Yes, I can do that." Marion preceded Wyatt down the hall and opened the door to the blue guest room.

"Turn down the bed," Wyatt requested, which she did. He laid Shannon on the clean blue sheets, then stepped away. Looking at the woman lying there, he realized that he didn't like her in the least. There had been times in their marriage when they had gotten along and he had thought it was working. But Shannon's innate dishonesty and determination to maintain the upper hand had again and again destroyed what little hope there had been for their hapless relationship.

He felt no guilt at all for refusing her absurd "deal." This time it appeared that *she'd* been the one caught in the snares she set for other people. Wyatt would bet anything that Rick Malone had left Helena after Shannon had announced her pregnancy. Rick hadn't struck him as the marrying kind of man, and from what Wyatt had learned about him upon discovering his and Shannon's liaison, he didn't have an honorable bone in his body. He flitted from woman to woman, usually married ones, and lived off a family trust fund. He was smooth, suave, a roamer, and not about to be tied to a wife and kid.

Either that, Wyatt thought, or Shannon had simply decided she didn't like being single and had come up with this plan to get him to marry her again. She wasn't above talking a doctor friend into writing that letter, and maybe her story of pregnancy was nothing but a lie. Wyatt ardently prayed that was the case.

Disgusted with the whole thing, he shook his head. "Undress her, Marion. We'll let her sleep it off." He walked out.

Fifteen

The Hip Hop Café was crowded with customers. Melissa, coming out of the kitchen carrying a huge tray loaded with dinners, passed Wanda going in. "Thank goodness you cut your vacation short," Wanda said for at least the third time in as many hours.

Melissa continued on to the table of six she was presently serving and began distributing the meals. The phone behind the counter started ringing, and she shot it a brief, harassed look. Smiling at her patrons, she finished passing out the plates containing their entrées.

Out of the corner of her eye she saw Wanda answering the phone, catching it on the run. Wanda said a few words, then laid the instrument on the counter. Melissa glanced at her and the waitress mouthed, "It's for you."

"Could we have another basket of those delicious rolls?"

Melissa nodded at the lady making the request. "Certainly. I'll get them right away." All but running to the kitchen and back, she deposited the basket on the table. "May I get you anything else?"

"I think we're fine for now. This chicken looks wonderful. Oh, maybe a little more coffee."

Once Melissa had the coffeepot in her hand, she made the rounds and topped off a dozen cups at different tables. Finally, she dashed behind the counter and picked up the phone. "This is Melissa. Sorry to keep you waiting."

"Sounds like things are a little hectic there."

"Oh, hello, Wyatt. Things are so hectic you wouldn't believe it. Two people called in sick and Wanda and I have been trying to keep up. Was there something . . . ?'' She was watching four more people come through the door and look around for a table.

"I need to talk to you."

She could feel the silent pressure of the newcomers. "I really can't talk now, Wyatt. Call me tomorrow. No, wait. Sundays are always busy and I still might be shorthanded. Please, let's just keep our date for Monday evening. We can talk for hours then."

He hesitated. Shannon showing up at all was unnerving enough news to pass on to Melissa, but his ex-wife sleeping in the guest room could be so easily misunderstood.

Still, he had vowed not to pressure Melissa and it was obvious she was on the run tonight. Besides, it was probably best to have this conversation face-to-face.

"All right," he agreed. "We'll talk on Monday. See you then."

"Thanks, Wyatt. Bye." Melissa hurriedly put down the phone and went to greet the newcomers. "Good evening. Table for four?"

Wyatt went to bed at eleven, though worry kept him awake for another hour. He didn't like Shannon being at the ranch; he especially didn't like her spending the night in his guest room. What he probably should have done was load her into her own car and drive her back to Helena.

Then, for a while, he stopped thinking about himself and worried about Shannon. Although it was certain he had never loved her and could barely tolerate her now, she had been his wife for six years and was possibly desperate at present. If she was telling him the truth, that is. Knowing her as he did, he also knew it wasn't wise to believe anything she said without tangible proof. All right, maybe the doctor's letter was genuine. If he gave her the benefit of the doubt on that score, she was pregnant and looking for a scapegoat. But did she really think he was stupid enough to believe the child was his?

Muttering a curse, Wyatt turned over in bed and punched his pillow into a more comfortable shape. Regardless of common sense arguments, he couldn't ignore the extremely slim chance that the baby might be his. As Melissa had so succinctly pointed out, he hadn't been sleeping alone during his marriage. But his memory told him that the last time he and Shannon had shared a bed had been too long ago for her to be holding him responsible for her pregnancy.

Whatever the truth was, it was a hell of a mess and he hated having to tell Melissa about it. But tell her he would. She had to know, and she had to hear it from him.

He finally fell asleep visualizing various ways in which to relate the news.

Wyatt's dreams were erratic and disturbing. People appeared and disappeared. He was in one place and then another. His body moved restlessly in the bed. Then, suddenly, a scene became very clear. He was in a huge barn. It was supposedly his, but it wasn't the barn on the ranch and it was full of junk and clutter. He was trying to clean it, working hard and making no headway. It was as though he couldn't focus on any one object, and he kept moving among the litter with a frantic feeling, driven by an inner force that urged him on, because for some earthshaking but unclarified reason it was utterly crucial that he get the barn in good order.

The tenor of the dream changed and he was no longer alone, though he couldn't see the woman who was touching him, as everything had become dark and shadowed. He felt her hands on his bare chest—where had his shirt gone?—and then her mouth. He sighed in his sleep, picturing the woman as Melissa as his insides became warm and languid. He touched Melissa and discovered bare skin. Groaning softly, he sought her lips with his. They kissed.

Something was wrong. He pulled himself from sleep. Melissa neither smoked cigarettes nor drank bourbon, and he could taste both. Jerking away from the female body in his bed, he sat up and switched on the lamp. "Shannon!"

She was stark naked and blinking in the sudden infusion of light. "What're you doing? Turn off the damn light."

Her words were slurred; she was still drunk. Wyatt slid off the bed and stood up. "Get yourself out of my bed and back to the guest room. Do it now!" He couldn't remember ever being so disgusted with another human being. Would she stop at nothing?

"You used to be a lot more receptive to making love," she said sullenly.

"I used to be married," he retorted sharply. "Get out of here, Shannon."

She slowly dragged herself from the bed, picked up the sheet she had obviously covered herself with for the trip from the guest room and haphazardly wrapped it around herself. Then she looked at him with a venomous expression. "You're going to pay for this insult, Wyatt."

"Take your best shot, lady."

She started from the room. "Oh, I will. Believe me, I will." She stumbled out and left the door open.

Wyatt hurried around the bed, shut the door and locked it. Raking his hair in aggravation, he looked at the bed and knew he would never go back to sleep after this. He started dressing, pulling on jeans, shirt, socks and boots.

Tiptoeing through the house, he left by the back door, got in his pickup and headed for the mountains. He'd been trying to reach Joe Lott, his caretaker for the cabin, but apparently Joe had left the area for the week he'd been told to take off. That was okay, Wyatt thought. He would just as soon be alone out there tonight and tomorrow. It sure as hell was certain that he wasn't going to show his face at the ranch any time tomorrow. No telling when Shannon would come to, realize her little game hadn't worked and finally leave.

He wasn't going to be around to see it.

Thankfully, Melissa wasn't shorthanded on Sunday. She had slept well and greeted her early morning customers with a warm, welcoming smile. Thinking back to when she had bought the old café and nervously hoped for success, she had to marvel at just how successful the place had become. Expansion wasn't merely an ego trip for Melissa; more space and tables were becoming a dire necessity. Nothing bothered her more than having people waiting when every table and booth were already occupied.

As the morning progressed, Melissa became aware of a nagging voice in the back of her mind. It had to do with Wyatt's phone call the night before. Had she been too short with him? She'd been on the run, granted, but hadn't he said that he *needed* to talk to her?

The morning passed with the before-church breakfasters coming in, then those who ate after church. Immediately behind them the lunch crowd began arriving, and on Sunday, lunchtime went on for hours. Melissa knew what to expect from the afternoon. First the early dinner crowd would show up, followed by the normal dinner-hour diners and, finally, those who preferred a late meal.

It was around two when Melissa could no longer ignore that voice in her head. She *had* been short with Wyatt. Maybe the reason he'd called was important. She should call him back and ... No, she didn't want to call. She wanted to see him, to apologize for cutting him off last night, to explain how really busy she had been. If her and Wyatt's present relationship was going to flourish, which she now hoped would be the case, she shouldn't put business before him.

"Wanda?" Melissa walked up to her waitress. "I need to be gone for about two hours." Two hours should do it, she figured. A half-hour drive to the ranch, an hour with Wyatt and a half-hour drive back to town. "It's important."

"Well, sure, Melissa." Wanda studied the concern on her employer's face. "I hope nothing's wrong."

She shook her head. "It's only an errand, but I really have to see to it. Keep things going while I'm gone, okay?"

"You can count on me."

"Thanks, Wanda."

Melissa ran up the inside stairs for her purse and then down the outside staircase to her car.

Wyatt's pickup was absent, Melissa noted with a frown as she parked next to an expensive and unfamiliar red sports car. It was a beautiful vehicle, low slung and sleek, and Melissa gave it a long, curious look while walking up to the front door.

She expected Marion to open the door, but instead a strange woman stood there. She was wearing a stunning sea green dress and matching accessories. Her blond hair was attractively arranged and her makeup was perfect. All in all, she was one of the most striking women Melissa had ever seen.

Melissa knew she was staring, but the woman was such a surprise. "Hello."

"Hello." The woman spoke coolly, openly sizing her up.

Melissa drummed up a smile, though she had an awful, unexplainable feeling of dread. "Is Wyatt at home? His truck isn't here, but—"

"I don't know where Wyatt is. But don't tell me, let me guess. You're Melissa Avery."

"Uh . . . yes."

The woman smiled, though Melissa couldn't find a dram of warmth in the expression. "And you're calling on Wyatt. How sweet."

Melissa's face flamed, but then she found her backbone. "And you're . . . ?"

"Shannon North."

Melissa's color changed again, becoming paler by degrees. "I see." Her heart was pounding like a tom-tom. Questions about Shannon's presence at the ranch bombarded her stunned brain. Only by supreme effort was she able to stand there.

Their eyes met, Shannon's deep and green, Melissa's deep and blue. Melissa found herself wondering how she measured up in this elegant woman's opinion. She was wearing a long, flowing, sky blue skirt and a blouse with a mauve background and tiny blue flowers sprinkled through it in a pretty pattern. Her hair was arranged in her preferred working style, a thick French braid, and there was lipstick on her lips and blusher on her cheeks.

But she felt dowdy compared to Shannon North. Wyatt had mentioned something about Shannon being beautiful—the statement being connected to the night they had met at that fateful party—but that wasn't like seeing the woman's beauty and style with her own eyes.

"Well . . . I may as well be running along," Melissa said, praying she sounded as though meeting Wyatt's ex-wife like this really didn't bother her.

"Let me walk you to your car."

Melissa's eyes widened. "If you wish."

Shannon closed the door behind her and walked beside Melissa to her car.

Melissa faced her. "Will you tell Wyatt I dropped by?"

Shannon smiled. "Of course."

This woman's smiles gave her cold chills, Melissa thought, opening the door of her car, eager to leave. She was doubting Wyatt again, she realized unhappily—doubting his story of lies and deceit from Shannon and six years of misery for himself. Maybe that was unfair, but why was his ex-wife here at the ranch? There could be a perfectly logical explanation. Maybe that was the reason Wyatt had called her last night.

But that "perfectly logical explanation" might be one she wouldn't like, Melissa thought, feeling a renewal of the pain she had lived with for so many years.

"Well . . . goodbye," she said numbly.

"Please wait a moment. Maybe we should talk."

"Talk? What about, Mrs. North?"

Shannon took a deep breath. "Please call me Shannon. There's no reason we should stand on formality."

Melissa merely looked at her, questioning her own sanity and Wyatt's. Questioning Shannon's presence again, and why she would want to talk to her.

She felt an enormous shock when Shannon wiped away a tear. "I'm sorry. I promised myself just a minute ago that I wouldn't get emotional."

"Emotional about what?" Melissa asked quietly, though her pulse was running wild. Something was horribly wrong—at least where she was concerned. Wyatt's divorce *was* a fact and final, wasn't it? He hadn't lied to her about that, had he? *Please God, no.*

Shannon was looking the other way, as though uncomfortably lost in thought. "Is this about Wyatt?" Melissa asked.

"I would have no other reason to talk to you, would I? You see..." Again she dabbed at her eyes. "This is much more difficult than I thought it would be."

"Is this about Wyatt and...me?" Melissa asked in a distraught whisper.

Shannon took another long breath, which sounded terribly troubled to Melissa. "Primarily it's about Wyatt and me. Melissa, I'm pregnant with Wyatt's child. Neither of us knew about the baby when we agreed on the divorce." Shannon paused and looked pensive and saddened for a moment. "If we had, I'm sure we'd still be married. We had our problems, as most married couples do, but I never dreamed he would demand a divorce. I guess...we just gradually lost track of our love for each other."

The life went out of Melissa. This was the other side of the coin, she thought dully, feeling as though something huge and powerful was squeezing the breath out of her. She had heard Wyatt's side and now she was hearing Shannon's.

But she was hearing more than ancient history. Shannon was pregnant *now*. Melissa's mouth was so dry she had trouble speaking. "You've told Wyatt?"

"Just last night."

Melissa withered inside. Shannon had stayed here last night. Had she and Wyatt used the same bed? Oh, God, she thought in a silent cry of agony. Just when she was starting to trust him again, and fall in love with him again, she had to deal with this. How could she? She didn't have the strength to relive the same nightmare she had barely survived six years ago.

He had called, Melissa remembered again, and she'd been too busy to talk. Was this what he had been going to tell her—that his ex-wife was carrying his child and...and what? What were their plans? They must have made some. Had he been going to tell her their plans, as well as the rest of it?

Melissa suddenly frowned at the dramatically beautiful woman standing so close to her. As shocking as her story was to Melissa's nervous system, nothing Shannon had said explained her reason for bringing her into this.

"Why did you feel it necessary to talk to me?" Melissa hated her own thoughts. Wyatt had lived with this woman for six years. *And* slept with her. How could he not have loved her? She was beautiful, conscious of fashion and obviously intelligent.

"When—when I told Wyatt about the baby, he became very angry." Shannon stopped to bite her lip, as though on the verge of tears. "I couldn't believe his reaction in view of how much he dotes on Timmy. Then he began talking about you. I asked him if you had become important to him and he evaded the question. I told him I would understand if he had found another woman, but he said that wasn't it. He explained about knowing you for a long time...something about the two of you dating in high school...but he was so casual about it that I dropped the subject.

"Anyway, when we went to bed I asked him why he had gotten so upset over hearing about the baby. He—"

Melissa broke in, speaking stiffly, numbly. "You...went to bed...together?"

Shannon looked crestfallen. "I'm sorry. I shouldn't have mentioned that to you." She sighed poignantly. "Looking back, I really don't know why we got a divorce. He had heard some rumors about me and another man, completely untrue gossip. Rick was a friend, his as well as mine. Wyatt was always so jealous of me. That was one of our problems, I know."

Melissa was fighting nausea. They had slept together just last night. Shannon had given him an opportunity to explain about his being in love with *her,* and he hadn't done so.

"Did—did he ever tell you why your pregnancy upset him?" she asked in a weak, hoarse voice.

"He—he finally said—just before we went to sleep—that he owes you."

"He *owes* me? What does he owe me?" That word rang a bell and created resentment and anger. He had used it right to her face, after all, telling her that he owed her for what he had done to her six years before. But that was before they had become close again. Melissa's head spun from so many disorienting aspects of this unpleasant situation.

"Melissa, I didn't intend to hurt you, but—" Shannon looked helpless "—I have to think of the baby. He said he had jilted you when he met me. Is that true? Were you two planning to be married when Wyatt and I first met?"

Melissa licked her dry lips. Every cell in her body was screaming in agony. "Yes," she whispered.

Shannon's eyes sparked with anger. "Then why did he seduce me the very night we met?" The anger remained in her expression. "He was engaged to you and making love to me. Oh, this is worse than I thought. Now he has this notion of owing you, and he's *still* making love to me. If I had known this last night, I would not have permitted what happened between us, believe me."

Melissa couldn't bear to hear another word. "I—I really must be going."

"I understand," Shannon murmured sympathetically. "Melissa, I think Wyatt would marry me again and give our second child his name if you would release him from that old debt. He made me promise to stop smoking and take care of myself, which I fully intend doing. I *know* he will return to me and his children, Melissa, if you release him.''

Melissa sucked in a long, slow, disheartened breath. ''There's nothing to release him from, but consider it done, Shannon.''

Shannon smiled tremulously. ''I'll never be able to thank you enough.'' Her expression became shy. ''Melissa, I really like you. Maybe you and I can see each other again sometime.''

Battling tears, Melissa shook her head. ''No, I don't think so. It would be better for all of us if we stay away from each other.''

Shannon sighed. ''I suppose you're right.'' She paused. ''Do you have any idea when you'll tell Wyatt how you feel?''

''We have plans for tomorrow night. If he keeps the date, I'll tell him then.''

''Would you do me an enormous favor and not mention my talking to you? He has *so* much pride, and it's so easily damaged.'' Shannon gave a short, rather breathless laugh. ''I don't want him to end up hating both of us. Just tell him…'' She waved her free hand. ''Oh, I can't tell you what to say. You'll handle it tactfully, I know you will.''

''Considering what you've told me, I'm sure he'll be relieved. It should be a simple matter.'' Melissa climbed behind the wheel of her car.

To her chagrin, Shannon reached into the car, took her hand and squeezed it. ''You're a very special person, Melissa. I wish we *could* be friends. Goodbye.''

Closing the door, Melissa started the car, backed up to turn around and drove away. When the ranch was behind her, well out of sight, she pulled over to the side of the road and wept until there were no more tears to shed.

Sixteen

Melissa managed to stumble through the rest of Sunday, but though she tried, she couldn't fall asleep that night. She forced herself to lie in bed until she felt like tearing out her hair, then, admitting defeat, she got up to drink hot tea and prowl the apartment through the dark hours.

Sad and despondent, she watched the sun come up from her kitchen window, then did something she had never so much as thought of doing before: she called each of her employees and told them the café was not going to be open that day. They would be paid as usual, but they were not to come in. Once that chore was behind her, she threw on a sweat suit and took a long, early morning jog.

Exhausted, she returned to the apartment and fell across her bed. She was asleep almost immediately and didn't wake up until three in the afternoon. Blinking bleary-eyed at the digital clock on her bedstand, she groaned and then forced herself off the bed and into the shower.

She was dressed and waiting for Wyatt at quarter to five.

Wyatt parked at the curb directly in front of the café and looked around in surprise. The only other vehicle in sight was Melissa's, when normally the street was lined with cars and pickups during business hours. Peering at the café, he saw the Closed sign on the front door. "What the hell?" he mumbled, instantly concerned about Melissa. With the time and dedication she gave her business, it wouldn't be closed without a significant reason. Something was seriously wrong.

Hurrying to get out of his pickup, he ran to the stairs and took them two at a time. Reaching Melissa's door, he pounded on it. "Melissa?"

She opened the door. "Hello."

Wyatt stared. There was no smile on her pale face, no sign of welcome or friendliness. His heart sank. "Sweetheart, are you ill?"

"No."

"But the café is closed."

"That doesn't mean I'm ill. Come in." She moved away from the door, leaving it for him to close.

"Well, something's wrong. What is it?" he questioned, following on her heels to the living room. It had to be something especially bad for her to close the café and look like she did, Wyatt thought worriedly. There were dark smudges under her eyes and a pinched, tragic line to her lips. His voice grew gentle as a truly unhappy possibility occurred to him. "Honey, is it your mother?"

"My mother?" It took Melissa a second to grasp his meaning. "My mother is fine. Sit down, Wyatt. This shouldn't take long, but you may as well be comfortable."

A painful premonition began gathering in the pit of Wyatt's stomach—whatever it was that "shouldn't take long" had to do with their relationship. Uneasily he sank to the edge of a sofa cushion, but there was nothing relaxed about his posture.

"So, what's going on?" he asked.

Melissa was sitting with her back straight and her head high. Her hands were folded in her lap. "I've decided not to see you again."

Had he heard her right? "You've decided what?"

She cleared her throat. "I'm sure you heard me. I've been doing a lot of thinking, and you and I are not even close to being compatible. I don't visualize us as enemies, certainly nothing like that. In fact, there's no good reason why we can't say a civil hello should we run into each other. But...I don't want to see you again, as in going to dinner . . . and such."

He slumped back against the sofa, too stunned to speak, and stared at her as though she had just announced the precise date of the end of the world. He finally got one word out. "Why?"

"I just explained why. Weren't you listening?"

"What did you mean when you said we're not compatible?"

"Wyatt, I don't intend to get into any sort of debate with you about this. My mind is made up."

His eyes narrowed. "What happened between Friday night and tonight? Why is the café closed? Why do you look as though you haven't slept in days?"

"Don't grill me," she said sharply.

He got to his feet, every line of his body exuding anger and frustration. "Don't grill you? Did you think you could calmly announce what you did and I would accept it without some questions? A *lot* of questions? When I left here Friday night everything was great between us. You were as sweet and loving as anyone could be, and now this?" Pacing in a circle right in front of her, he muttered a vicious curse and stopped with his hands on his hips and his feet apart, a belligerent stance. Melissa watched him uneasily. "At least give me the courtesy of an honest explanation," he said with some sarcasm.

"I already did."

"Like hell you did!" he shouted. "Why is the café closed?" For some reason that Closed sign on the door of her business felt like the key to this mess.

"I needed a day off."

"You could have taken a day off without shutting down the whole works," he pointed out.

"Put it this way, if it makes you feel better. I *wanted* to close the café."

"Why? You said you weren't ill. Melissa, this isn't like you."

She jumped to her feet. "That's enough. I said I wasn't going to get into a long debate with you and I'm not. I'd like you to leave now." Why was he arguing with her? Considering his present situation with Shannon, he should be relieved. Unless...he wanted both Shannon and her. Melissa's spine stiffened.

"So it's over for us, just like that," Wyatt said.

"Exactly," she said, looking everywhere but into his eyes.

He stood there and stared at her, studying, searching, probing for some clue, some sign as to why she had so abruptly reversed herself on the subject of their burgeoning relationship. Had he been moving too fast? Had she thought about the abduction and again become angry over it?

But she didn't seem angry. Rather, she seemed broken, spiritless, almost robotlike. Something had happened that she wasn't talking about.

"And I have nothing to say about it," he said in a choked voice, a voice that conveyed his shattered hopes and dreams as well as intolerable pain. "It doesn't matter that I love you and always will."

Melissa kept her head high. "It might, if I believed you."

The blood drained from Wyatt's face, leaving a pallor to his skin that Melissa didn't miss. "When was the exact moment between Friday night and now that you stopped believing?" he asked.

"Don't be absurd," she retorted. "There was no exact moment." But there was, she thought weakly, and she turned away from him so he couldn't see her face, just in case a glimmer of her inner misery was visible. How could he stand there and tell her he loved her and always would when he had spent Saturday night making love to his ex-wife? He was the worst kind of man there was, the kind who cheated and lied, and did it to more than one woman at the same time. For all she knew there could be other women besides Shannon and herself. He could be using the same line on all of them. Fretfully, Melissa raised her hands to her aching temples. God, how many times did he think he could put her through this?

Dropping her hands to her sides, she swung around. "Please go."

He felt so helpless, so mystified. "Melissa . . . don't do this."

She saw the tears in his eyes and steeled her heart against them. He had used tears before to influence her, and she wasn't going to fall for that phony act again.

Melissa started for the living room doorway. "I'll wait in my bedroom until you leave. You know your way out."

Everything had turned upside down so fast, and without warning. Wyatt stared at the empty doorway long after Melissa had gone. Something in what she'd said kept nagging at him: *"You know your way out."* He had said those same words to Shannon on Saturday night, but she hadn't gone. When, exactly, *had* she left? He hadn't been at the ranch to see her departure for himself, nor had he thought to ask anyone about it when he returned around three today. Shannon had been notably absent, and that had been enough.

His blood started pumping furiously as his mind took off on a wild tack. Was it possible that Shannon had something to do with Melissa's turnabout? Hell yes, it was possible, he thought disgustedly. Anything was possible with that woman. But why wouldn't Melissa have said so, if Shannon had paid her a visit?

"Aw, hell," he muttered, sinking into the nearest chair. Just thinking of the lies and distorted truths that Shannon might have told Melissa made him feel as weak and vulnerable as a newborn kitten. How did a man defend himself against an unscrupulous woman like her?

He had to try. Pushing himself out of the chair, he headed for Melissa's bedroom. The door was ajar and he pushed it open. She was sitting on the edge of her bed. Seeing him, her eyes became wide and startled. "Don't come in here, Wyatt. I asked you to leave."

Leaning against the woodwork, he folded his arms across his chest and hit her with a hard look. "Did my ex-wife come here?"

"Don't be absurd."

Wyatt frowned. He'd been so positive of his conclusion. But he still wasn't convinced that he was on the wrong track. "Have you ever met my ex-wife?"

From the stricken expression on Melissa's face, he had his answer. "Lord," he mumbled, closing his eyes as waves of dread, fear and panic rippled through his system. He and Melissa were back to square one, all because of Shannon's lies.

No, that wasn't true. They were back to square one because Melissa *believed* Shannon's lies. It was still a matter of trust with them, and she was never going to really forget the past, no matter what he did to atone for it.

He opened his eyes, taking in Melissa's discomfiture, her inability to look him in the face. He had no more taste for this, he realized with an empty sigh. No more taste for bickering and apologizing and begging for forgiveness for doing what he'd had to do.

"You met her sometime this weekend, apparently, but where?" he asked.

She had promised Shannon to say nothing about their little talk, but Wyatt had figured it out for himself. "At your ranch. I drove out there yesterday."

"I see. Instead of seeing me, you met her. That's really great." He kept looking at Melissa, feeling both empathetic toward her and lifeless within himself. "I know what she told you," he said in a flat, dull voice. "At least I know the basics of what she said. The embellishments I can only imagine. I'm sure you're sitting there expecting me to start tripping over my own words with anxious explanations and apologies, Melissa, but that's not going to happen. I'll say one thing again. I love you, I always have, I always will. The rest is up to you. Believe what you have to. Believe Shannon or believe in me. You know where to find me."

He walked out. The sound of his footsteps painted a picture in her mind of his traversing the apartment and leaving by the laundry-room door. He was gone.

Melissa couldn't move. Move? She couldn't even think. Her mind swirled aimlessly, dredging up bits and pieces of events and conversations that had happened since she'd met Wyatt again. Who was the liar, Wyatt or Shannon? *"Believe Shannon or believe in me."*

Moaning deep in her throat, she covered her face with her hands.

Admittedly, Melissa's mind wasn't on her business in the next few days. She found herself staring into space too many times when there was work to do, and looking for excuses to climb in her car and get away by herself. She drove to the reservation several times, but other days had no destination, and traveled some roads she had never been on before and many that were only vaguely familiar.

One afternoon she turned onto Route 17, which she knew led to the No Bull Ranch owned by Maris and Luke Rivers. They sometimes ate at the Hip Hop, and Melissa had come to like them both. But she wasn't planning on stopping for a visit; Route 17 was really just another road to her.

After about fifteen to twenty miles of open country, Maris blinked and stared, then pulled her car to the side of the road. Never had she seen such a messy yard as that surrounding Winona Cobbs's Stop 'N Swap establishment. There were goats, chickens, dogs and cats wandering among the junk, and several faded signs proclaiming eggs and honey for sale. Melissa knew Winona, though not well, but couldn't resist saying hello, probably because she had never before seen a place quite like hers.

Turning off the ignition, she got out and began picking her way through the clutter to the door of Winona's shop. She was stopped by a cheerful, "Hello, there!"

Whirling, Melissa saw Winona coming from an outbuilding of doubtful usage. "Hello, Winona."

"Well, as I live and breathe, Melissa Avery." The woman walked up, her round face beaming. "What a pretty thing you are today. And how nice of you to drop in. How about a glass of iced sun tea?"

"That sounds wonderful. Thank you."

"I'll be right back. We'll sit under that big tree over there."

Smiling, Melissa nodded. But instead of heading for the huddle of chairs she could see under the large tree, she wandered over to a table crowded with glassware. Everything was dusty, but Melissa picked up several different pieces and looked them over. One, a red bowl, was especially appealing.

Winona appeared with two tall glasses. "How much for this bowl?" Melissa asked.

"Oh, you don't want that old thing. It's supposed to be carnival glass, but it's only a cheap copy. If you're interested in the genuine article, I have some fine pieces in the shop."

"I'm not a collector, Winona, and I wouldn't know genuine from fake. I like this bowl just fine. How much do you want for it?"

"Well ... two dollars should do it."

Melissa dug out the money from her purse, then laughed because Winona's hands were full and she couldn't take it. "Just tuck it in my pocket," the older woman told her.

She complied. "I'll run and put the bowl in my car."

"I'll be under the tree," Winona said.

Melissa put the bowl on the front seat of her car and left her purse there, as well. Then she hurried over to the tree, where Winona was seated. Accepting a glass of tea, she took a nearby chair. "This is very pleasant. Thank you," she said, tasting the tea.

Winona sipped and swallowed. "Now, suppose you tell me what brought you way out here."

Melissa sighed. "I was just driving around and decided to take Route 17. No reason, really."

Winona smiled. "No reason that you know of, but there could be a reason all the same."

Melissa gave her a curious look. "Are you talking about predestination?"

"Do you believe in predestination?"

"I'm not sure. Frankly, I haven't given it a lot of thought."

"You're not deeply religious?"

"Well . . . Mother always sent me to Sunday school as a child, and we attended church services pretty regularly as I grew up. But there are a lot of sensible arguments against predestination, aren't there?"

"When one considers the tragedies in life and believes in a benevolent God, yes, there are many sensible arguments against predestination."

Melissa looked off into the distance and spoke thoughtfully. "I find it difficult to believe that, before he was even born, my father was destined to be murdered at a young age."

They were silent for several long moments, then Winona said softly, "You're not happy, are you, Melissa?"

She jerked her head around to look at her hostess. "Is it that obvious?"

"It is to me. Give me your hand, child."

Everyone knew of Winona's psychic power, or rather, everyone *talked* about it. Whether it was true or not, Melissa felt a strange prickling on the back of her neck when she put her hand in Winona's.

The older woman closed her eyes. Melissa stared at her a little alarmed at this unexpected event. Yet something kept her silent. Winona's hand was warm, and comforting in an eerie way.

"Your father's murderer will be found," Winona murmured, adding after a moment, "in time. You think of him often, but he is not the cause of your unhappiness. The cause is a man, though, and a woman." Winona frowned. "How odd. Another woman with two faces."

Her eyes opened. "I had a vision with Tracy Roper regarding her investigation of your father's death. Do you know Tracy? FBI agent married to the sheriff? I suppose I should be calling her Tracy Hensley."

"Yes, I know her. I talk to her often. What kind of vision did you have with her, Winona?"

"It was about a woman with two faces." The frown was still creasing Winona's forehead. "Now I see something very similar with you."

"It must be the same woman."

"But it's not. That's what's so odd."

"Did you actually see a woman with two faces? I mean, graphically? Can you describe her?"

Winona smiled. "Symbolically, my dear. It's impossible to explain."

"And how do you interpret such a vision?"

Winona let go of Melissa's hand and reached for her glass of tea, which she had set on the ground next to her chair. "It could mean many things, Melissa—from a woman taking on a whole new persona to one who merely pretends to be what she's not."

"And you saw this, just now while you were holding my hand? You actually saw a man making me unhappy and a woman with two faces?"

Winona nodded. "Does that make any sense to you?"

Melissa sat back. "It might."

It was Thursday before Wyatt got hold of his temper enough to call Shannon in Helena.

"Wyatt!" she exclaimed in his ear. "What a marvelous surprise. I've been so hoping to hear from you."

"Have you?" He spoke coldly, because when dealing with Shannon he felt either red-hot rage or icy pragmatism. "I understand you talked to Melissa before you left the ranch."

"Oh, she told you. She promised she wouldn't. I guess you can't trust anyone, can you?"

"That seems to be the general consensus of opinion these days," he replied grimly. "But just so you know, she *didn't* tell me. I figured it out for myself. The reason I'm calling is to tell *you* something. After your baby is born, I'm going through legal channels to find out who fathered the child."

"You're what?"

"You heard me. If the child is mine, I'll be going to court to demand equal custody. Naturally, I will accept financial responsibility."

"You son of a bitch."

"I thought you might say something like that. So long, Shannon. See you in about six months."

He hung up.

Since talking to Winona Cobbs, Melissa was in constant torment. She tried to go over the architect's drawings for the addition to her building and couldn't concentrate enough to grasp the layout. Her menu planning for the café was virtually in the ash can, because she just couldn't muster up any enthusiasm for food.

She cried a lot. The slightest reference by anyone to anything even remotely sad had her blubbering like a baby. She wasn't sleeping well and usually spent more time walking the floor at night than she did in bed.

In a daze most of the time, she passed friends on the street without seeing them. The worst of it all was an internal, ongoing argument between her common sense and a fantasylike side of herself she hadn't been aware of possessing. "Psychic power is a lot of hooey," one voice told her.

"Oh, yeah? If someone like Tracy takes Winona seriously, why shouldn't you?" another voice argued.

The problem was that Winona had hit the nail so squarely. Melissa *was* unhappy—horribly unhappy—and the condition was definitely caused by a man and a woman. It was the part about the woman having two faces that gave Melissa cold chills, because she had believed every word

Shannon had said without once considering that she might be lying or even slanting the truth in her favor. And if that were true, she, Melissa, who had always rated her intelligence quotient as higher than average, had been taken to the cleaners by a woman who was clever, unscrupulous and a damned fine actress.

The final straw, of course, was the awful way she had treated Wyatt that night.

On second thought, the final, *final* straw was that she had fallen in love with Wyatt. Again.

"Oh, Lord," she moaned when that irrevocable fact wormed its way through the mishmash in her brain. It was what she had fought against since the day he had walked into the Hip Hop; obviously she had lost the battle.

So... was she going to do something about it, or was she going to live out her life in torment? *"Believe Shannon or believe in me."*

It was too simple a statement to create so much turmoil in a person. Why couldn't she do one or the other and then act upon it?

By the beginning of the following week Melissa's choices had narrowed. She knew she couldn't go on in the same addled state of mind in which she had stumbled through this week. There was only one sensible course of action to take, and that was to see Wyatt and have it out with him.

With her hands shaking, she picked up the phone and dialed the number of his ranch.

"North Ranch."

It was Marion, the housekeeper, and Melissa felt a perverse relief that Wyatt himself hadn't answered. "This is Melissa Avery. I—I need to talk to Wyatt."

"He isn't here, Ms. Avery. He said he would be at the cabin for a few days. That was yesterday afternoon. You could call him there."

"Oh." Melissa took a breath. "I don't have that number. Could you give it to me, please?"

"Certainly. It's 555-8828."

Melissa jotted the number on a piece of paper. "Thank you." She put down the phone, looked at the number and realized that she was glad Wyatt hadn't been readily available.

Rising, she walked around the room with a feeling of utter despair. What would she have said to him if he had come on the line? Winona's "vision" wasn't proof that Shannon had talked to her solely to cause trouble for her and Wyatt, nor that she had lied about anything. Had she spent the night at the ranch or hadn't she?

Maybe that was what she really needed to know, Melissa thought uneasily. Maybe if she heard from Wyatt's own mouth that Shannon had *not* shared his bed, she would be able to apologize for her rudeness that night and take it from there.

The more she pondered that theory, the more sense it made. But she couldn't ask him about it on the phone. Somehow she had to gear up her courage and talk to him in person. She had to see his face when he gave her an answer, see his eyes. He never had been able to prevent his emotions from reaching his eyes.

He was at the cabin. Fine, she would go out there and... She stopped with her fingertips on her lips in a questioning pose. Could she find the cabin on her own? The trip out there had been confusing, but the trip back had been much shorter and had involved only a few turns and a few different roads. Thinking hard about the route, Melissa decided she could do it.

In fact, she would do it now, before her courage deserted her.

Without taking the time to change from her dress into something more appropriate for a trip to the mountains, she grabbed her purse and car keys, stopped to speak to Wanda for a second and raced from the building to her car.

Though her heart was beating a mile a minute, she felt like she was doing the right thing. At least she was doing *some-*

thing, which was a heck of a lot better than moping around like a lost soul. Whatever happened at Wyatt's cabin, however their confrontation turned out, her moping had to come to a screeching halt.

Seventeen

Wyatt and Joe Lott had been cutting wood all day. They were stacking split logs in the three-sided woodshed when they heard the noise of an engine. As quiet as the mountain was, vehicles were often heard from miles away. This one, however, was getting close to the North property line.

"Someone's coming," Joe commented.

"Sounds like it," Wyatt agreed, fitting his armload onto the growing pile of fireplace fuel. The road, which ended abruptly at the clearing, couldn't be seen from the woodshed, so Wyatt walked to the back left corner of the cabin to get a look at whoever was driving in. At the sight of Melissa's car, he became very still for a moment, then walked back to Joe.

"Joe, would you mind taking off for a couple of hours?"

A teasing twinkle appeared in the man's pale blue eyes. "Need some privacy?"

"Yeah, I do. Call before you come back, okay?"

"Sure. I'll go and do some visiting."

Wyatt slapped his old friend and caretaker on the back. "Thanks."

Joe took off his gloves and laid them on a block of wood. "See ya later." He headed for his pickup.

Admitting nervousness, though he swore Melissa wasn't going to see it, Wyatt sucked in a lungful of air, then removed his own gloves and used them to knock some of the bits of bark and wood chips from his jeans. He heard Melissa's car drive up and stop just as Joe's pickup drove away. Perfect timing, he thought, and walked around the cabin to the parking area.

Melissa got out. "Hi."

Wyatt walked up, noting that she wasn't quite meeting his eyes. "Hi. Have any trouble finding the place?"

"A little. I took a few wrong turns, but—" her smile wobbled slightly "—here I am."

Yes, here she was. He wanted to ask why in the worst way, but he had a feeling she planned to tell him. It would be best if he let her do it in her own good time.

"Come inside," he invited with a pointed glance at her short sleeves. As usual, she wasn't dressed for the weather. The day was sunny but the mountain air was crisply cool. He'd worked up a sweat cutting and chopping logs, but standing still he could feel the coolness penetrating his long-sleeved flannel shirt.

"Thanks," Melissa murmured. What did she sense from him? she asked herself. He appeared rugged and outdoorsy right now, so handsome her legs felt unsteady from her just looking at him. But was he glad to see her? She couldn't tell. His eyes, normally so expressive, contained no expression at all.

They started for the cabin. "Who's the old gentleman who just drove away?" she asked.

"Joe Lott. He stays up here to keep an eye on the place. Been with us for over twenty years, first at the ranch, then here." Wyatt opened the front door and stood back so Melissa could go in first.

"I hope my arrival didn't chase him off," she said.

Wyatt shut the door behind him. "If you knew Joe, you'd know that a pretty woman would be the last thing to chase him off. He had some things to do. I'm going to put on a pot of coffee and take a shower. Make yourself to home. I won't be long."

Melissa, who had walked to the middle of the room, turned to look at him. "Why don't I put on the coffee and let you go directly to the shower?"

Her offer surprised Wyatt, though not nearly as much as her being here did. "Good idea. Thanks." He left her alone.

Drawing an uneasy breath, she went to the kitchen. It took only a few minutes to prepare the coffeemaker, then she stood at a window that provided a view of the clearing behind the cabin. From the chainsaw, axes and array of logs and wood outside, it was obvious what Wyatt had been doing before she got there. It was also fairly evident that he had sent Joe Lott away, for which she was grateful. The things she needed to say to Wyatt couldn't be said in the presence of a third party.

Then she realized something. A large part of her nervousness had abated. In fact, she felt calmer and more like her normal self than she had since... She swallowed, thinking of that meeting with Shannon. Stewing and worrying and walking the floor because of that destructive incident had to stop, and it never would if she didn't clear the air with Wyatt. Maybe "clearing the air" wasn't the best term for what was haunting her. Wasn't "hearing it from his own lips" much more accurate?

Ten minutes later, when Wyatt walked in, Melissa was seated at the table with a cup of coffee. "I set out a cup next to the coffeepot for you," she said. He was wearing clean jeans and a shirt, and his hair was damp from the shower. He looked handsome and manly, and Melissa felt like she could look at him forever. She drew a breath, thinking hopefully that "forever" just might be the outcome of her visit.

"Thanks," he said, walking over to the counter holding the coffeemaker. Pouring himself a cup, he turned around to look at her. "Would you be more comfortable in the living room?"

"I'd just as soon stay in here, if you don't mind. I like this kitchen."

He nodded. "I like it, too." Moving to the table, he pulled out a chair and sat down.

There was tension in the air; they both felt it. But they each sipped from their cups and remained silent for several moments.

Wyatt spoke first, looking at her across the table. "It's good seeing you. I wondered if you..." He stopped, reminding himself not to pressure her. "Did you go to the ranch first, before coming here?"

"I called. Marion told me you had come up here for a few days. She gave me the telephone number, but . . . I decided to come and talk to you in person instead of calling."

"I'm glad."

Their eyes met and held, stirring emotions in each of them. Melissa swallowed hard. "Wyatt..." She set down her cup. "I . . . don't know how to begin." She paused and frowned. "No, that's not true. I know exactly where to start. I treated you unfairly the night you came by to take me to dinner, and I'd like to apologize."

"Apology accepted," he said quietly, but that was all he said. Melissa coming here was a dream come true and his hopes were running wild. Right now, though, anything he said would be like putting words in her mouth, and he wanted to hear her own words, not an echo of his.

Eyes cast downward, Melissa ran her forefinger around the rim of her cup. "You said for me to believe Shannon or believe in you. It's not quite that simple, Wyatt. Shannon said some things..." Pausing for a breath, she lifted her eyes. "She's very beautiful, isn't she?"

"She thinks so."

Melissa frowned slightly, again studying her cup. "I think so, too. Wyatt...what you said about her trapping you into marriage six years ago...you don't really believe that, do you?"

Wyatt leaned back in his chair, regarding Melissa with a steady gaze. A few moments passed, as though he was making up his mind about something. Finally, he spoke. "I'm going to tell you something I've never said to another living soul. I wouldn't tell you, either, but I want you to know my innermost thoughts. I'm not positive Timmy is my son. Oh, he's my son," he added quickly. "He'll *always* be my son, but I'm not positive that I'm his biological father. The night she announced her pregnancy, Shannon lied about my being the only man she had slept with in months. I found that out after we were married. She had been dating several different men, and knowing Shannon, I'm sure they weren't just holding hands.''

Melissa looked stricken. Wyatt rushed to reassure her. ''I couldn't love Timmy more if things had been perfect for Shannon and me. But to answer your question, yes, I believe she tricked me into marriage. I believe she knew exactly what she was doing the night of the party—finding herself a husband because she was *already* pregnant.''

''Oh, Wyatt,'' Melissa said sadly. ''She—she told me she's pregnant now.''

''She told me the same thing.''

''Is it true?''

''She showed me a letter from a doctor that says it's true.'' He saw the startled look in Melissa's eyes. ''She didn't show you the letter?''

''No.'' Melissa was suddenly so unnerved she didn't know what to do. Why had she come? Why was she putting herself and Wyatt, too, through this? Her eyes darted around the kitchen, as though she were looking for an easy escape. ''Maybe I don't have any more questions.''

Wyatt saw the panic in her eyes and realized she was on the verge of bolting. They had only started talking, and he couldn't let her stop now. ''Yes, you do, Melissa. How about this one: Wyatt, do you believe the letter is authentic?''

Melissa stared at him. ''Don't you?''

''Not all doctors are ethical, Melissa. Maybe I shouldn't make such an inference when I have no proof. But Shannon has a lot of friends and she might have talked one into writing the letter. She's very good at—'' he paused, watching Melissa very closely ''—manipulating people.'' He paused again. ''Deep down, though, I think I do believe it.''

''Is . . . it your child?'' she asked, her voice cracking.

''She says it is. I say it isn't. I told you about her affair with Rick Malone.''

''You never mentioned the man's name, but it's immaterial.'' Pushing back her chair, Melissa got up and went to look out the window. Literally, she was wringing her hands. "Could—could it be your child?"

He looked at her straight back, her slender waist, the thick braid of her hair and the pretty dress she was wearing. He loved her, deeply and forever, but how would it help her or their relationship to discuss his and Shannon's sex life? Still, if she was driven to know everything, he would tell her. Before answering he slowly inhaled and exhaled. "We were married, Melissa. We shared the same bedroom. Do you want to hear details? Particulars? If you do, just say so. I'll tell you anything you're up to hearing."

She turned to look at him. "No. No details, please, but *could* the child be yours?"

"There's a slim chance, yes. A *very* slim chance. I intend to find out once the child is born, which I informed Shannon of the other day."

"You saw her again?"

"No, I called her. Specifically to tell her that I intend going through legal channels to demand medical tests to prove paternity when the baby is born. If it's mine, I want full parental rights."

Melissa's fingertips rose to massage her temples. "Shannon—Shannon talked about your marrying her again."

"Melissa, if you really believe that, why are you here?" He studied her. "You don't believe it, do you?"

"I did, but then..." Her voice trailed off and, rather than stand there and look helpless, she went for the coffeepot and returned to the table. After topping off her cup, she looked at Wyatt. "More coffee?"

"Just put the pot on the table and sit down." She complied, not because he had demanded it but because she needed to sit again. Wyatt leaned forward. "Shannon is accustomed to getting whatever she wants, Melissa, and when she told her lover about her condition and he left Helena— she told me that herself—she thought of me. She came to the ranch actually believing she could talk me into marrying her again. I know how her mind works, and I'm sure she thought a few tears and a poor-little-me attitude would get her what she needs again—a husband. It didn't work. 'Not this time,' I told her. Then I made a bad mistake. I told her about you.''

"What did you tell her about me?"

"That I intended to marry you."

Melissa sucked in a sharp breath and looked away from the intensity in Wyatt's eyes. "Oh, God," she whispered. "I feel like I'm breaking up a family. I wondered, you know. I wondered when you told me about your divorce if you were cutting your ties with Shannon because of me."

"You had nothing to do with it," he said sharply. "Look, it was a bad marriage from the start, but I tried to make it work. I lived in Helena, when I hated the place and every day I spent there. She refused to even visit the ranch, let alone live on it. Melissa, when I found out about Rick Malone, I felt like a ten-ton burden had suddenly disappeared. *That's* what ended our fiasco of a marriage, not your return to Whitehorn. I didn't even know you were back until I walked into your café.

"Let me say this. Even if you weren't in the picture, I wouldn't marry Shannon again even if the baby *was* mine."

Melissa was still avoiding direct eye contact. "She told it so differently."

"Well, like I said, either you believe her or you believe me."

There was one more question nearly killing Melissa, and she figured that since she had gone this far, she might as well go for broke. "Did she sleep with you when she was at the ranch? Did you make love to her?"

Wyatt laughed bitterly. "I can see she didn't miss a trick. Well, it's like this. After she put on her little act and I told her no deal, I left her in the den while I went to take a shower, mentioning before I left that she knew the way out. Instead of leaving, she got plastered. She'd been smoking cigarettes and drinking bourbon like a crazy woman as it was, and I couldn't stay silent on the subject of a pregnant woman risking her baby's health with tobacco and alcohol. Maybe she took it as a challenge. I don't know what went through her mind at that point, but after I left her alone she drank until she passed out.

"I was lying down when Marion let me know about it. We put Shannon to bed in the guest room. Incidentally, it was Marion who undressed her. Once I got her on the bed, I left the room. About two o'clock in the morning I woke up to find her in *my* bed. She was naked and all over me, apparently making a last-ditch effort to have things her way. I think she finally got the message when I told her to get the hell out of my bedroom. I remember her saying that she would get back at me for the insult. Apparently your coming along was her opportunity.

"Melissa, that's the whole story. Instead of driving up here to the cabin so I wouldn't have to see her again, I should have gone directly to your place, wakened you up and told you everything. But as selfish and self-centered as I know Shannon to be, it never occurred to me that she might talk to you and try to ruin things for us." His voice became softer. "Maybe she succeeded. Did she?"

To Melissa's chagrin, she began crying. Not loudly or with shaking shoulders, but with burning, silent tears drizzling down her cheeks. She wiped them away, but they kept coming.

Wyatt got up, walked around the table and pulled her from her chair and into his arms. "I'm sorry," she whispered thickly with her face buried in his shirt. "I don't know why I'm crying, other than that I'm feeling so mixed up."

"How could you be anything else?" Though there was a bitter curl to his lips, he spoke gently. He would like to hold her like this for eternity, or at least for a good long while. But he could sense how troubled she was and that she still hadn't come to terms with the past, both distant and recent.

"I've been miserably unhappy all week," she whispered tearily.

"So have I, honey. Look, why don't you come and sit in the living room and let me fix you something nice to drink that will relieve some of your tension."

Sniffling, she nodded. Wyatt took her hand and led her to a comfortable chair near the living room fireplace. "Just sit there and relax," he said quietly. "I'll be right back."

He returned in a few minutes with two steaming mugs, one of which he placed in Melissa's hand. "It's hot, so be careful," he said.

"Thank you." She could smell some kind of liquor in the drink, maybe brandy, but she didn't care what he'd put in it. It tasted good and warmed her tight throat clear to the knot in her stomach.

He sat in the chair closest to hers and sipped his own hot drink. Then he said in a low, tense voice, "If I ask *you* a question, will you answer it honestly?"

"I—I'll try." It was all she could promise. With her hands trembling, she lifted the mug to her lips.

"You know how I feel about you—I've said it a dozen times—but how do you feel about me? What I'm asking is, do you love me?" Why else would she be here? he reasoned. Yet he needed to hear her say it.

Melissa's eyes filled again. "I...think I do."

Closing his eyes, Wyatt felt relief pour through him. Thinking she loved him and saying so was a giant step forward, in his book. Still, he hadn't missed the reluctance in her voice. She must not be overly thrilled at finding herself in love with him again.

He took a big swallow of his drink, all the while watching her. Though she periodically wiped her eyes, she was gradually emptying her mug.

Without a word, he set his aside and got up to build a fire. Now Melissa watched him. She had admitted—or almost admitted—that she loved him, and she wondered if he weren't building a fire to delay giving a response. Her mind was a little loopy from the hot drink, she realized, but there was no question that it had relieved a lot of her tension.

When there were flames dancing in the fireplace, Wyatt returned to his chair. Sighing, Melissa snuggled deeper into hers, drawing her legs up under her. The warmth of the drink and of the fire were making her feel a little drowsy, and she laid her head back to ponder the differences in the same story told by Shannon and Wyatt. *"Believe Shannon or believe in me. Believe in me... believe in me."*

"I want to believe in you," she said, as though there'd been no lapse in conversation. "I hope you understand that."

"I'll tell you what I understand, Melissa. I understand how badly I hurt you six years ago and that it destroyed your trust in me. I understand that the two of us meeting again, unexpectedly the way we did, was a shock you're still feeling. I understand that meeting and talking to Shannon just when you and I were finally overcoming the past brought it all back again. Do I blame you for reacting as you did? No. Am I resentful of your reactions? I'm resentful, but not of you. Shannon has a lot to answer for, but I believe what goes around comes around. I paid for my sins and Shannon will pay for hers."

He chewed on his lip for a moment. "Don't get me wrong. I'm not wishing her any bad luck, and knowing her the way I do, she might go on for years without paying the bill. But sooner or later her selfish disregard for everyone else will catch up with her.

"Melissa, I don't know what else to say. I can't change the past. God, if only I could. We lost six years, you and I, six years that we should have spent together in living, loving and having babies." He saw the tears spilling from her eyes again. "Please don't cry."

"I...can't help it. Wyatt, do you really consider me a hard person? You said so once. Maybe twice."

He smiled. "With me, yes."

"I don't want to be hard. All I've ever hoped for was..." She stopped, because she honestly couldn't remember what her hopes were, other than finding out who murdered her father and attaining some financial success. But nowhere in her mind could she locate any long-term personal hopes, certainly none that included falling in love.

And then, looking at Wyatt, she knew why. She had never stopped loving him, even when she'd been angry and hurt and swearing she despised him. And he had never stopped loving her. How could she have been such a fool not to have figured it out before this? Not to have *believed*?

"Our lives took some very strange twists," she murmured.

Wyatt nodded. "A little stranger than most, I think. But it's all in the past and best forgotten. For me, anyway. Something wonderful came out of my marriage—Timmy. I wish my father were alive to know Timmy. For Timmy to know him." His eyes rested on Melissa. "He was with me this last weekend. I'll have him again in two weeks. I'd like you to meet him."

"I'd like that, too."

There was something in her voice that told Wyatt the worst was over. Rising, he knelt in front of her, took the empty mug from her hand and set it on the floor. Then his hands wrapped around hers. "I love you, Melissa. I've loved you since high school, and I'll love you in the same powerful way the day I draw my final breath."

She was crying again, this time with great gulping sobs. "I've been...a...terrible fool." Pulling her hands from his, she threw her arms around his neck. "Wyatt, please, please forgive me. I love you, too, so much."

At last, he thought, giddy with relief. Kissing her damp, teary face, he realized his tears were mingling with hers. "Melissa..." He pressed his lips to hers, and her passionate response ignited the flames of arousal in his body.

"Oh, Wyatt," she whispered. "I want you. I need you." Taking his face in her hands, she kissed his mouth until they were both breathless.

Wyatt pulled away then, standing to bring her to her feet. He kissed her once, then bent over to wrap one arm behind her knees. With a growl of utter possession, he scooped her up and strode from the room.

Melissa buried her face in the curve of his throat and closed her eyes for the trip to his bedroom. "I love you," she murmured. "I love you." It felt so good to say it, but even better to feel it. Releasing the past was like stepping from darkness into bright sunlight. Why had she clung to those old hurts for so long?

In Wyatt's bedroom they undressed quickly and lay down together. There was joy in their kisses and caresses, and in the freedom of expressing their love for each other. Then the joy turned fiercely ardent as they made full and complete love. They cried out together and Wyatt vowed it would always be this way for them. Sated, they held each other while their racing hearts and labored breaths returned to normal.

"I will never forget today," Melissa murmured softly.

"Nor will I," Wyatt said, his voice husky with emotion. He raised up to look at her, gently pushing wayward tendrils of hair from her face. "You're so beautiful, Melissa. I love looking at you."

She raised a hand to touch his face. "I can say the same." She smiled ruefully. "I'm sorry I was so difficult."

"No more apologies, my love." He took her hand and brought it to his lips for a tender kiss. "Will you marry me?"

Her eyes closed for a moment, then opened with an adoring light in them. "Yes."

"Thank you, God!" he said ecstatically, and pulled Melissa into a fervent embrace. "We have a lot of plans to make. I'd like a long honeymoon." Peering into her eyes, he asked, "How do you feel about long honeymoons?"

She laughed joyously. "I'd love the opportunity to find out."

"I've been thinking about Europe...Paris, in particular."

A beautiful, dreamy smile lit her features. "Paris sounds wonderful." Again she touched his face. "But anywhere with you would be wonderful."

The telephone rang. "That'll be Joe," Wyatt said, reaching for the bedside instrument. "Hello?"

Melissa chuckled quietly. Wyatt's end of the conversation proved beyond a shadow of a doubt that he had sent Joe away because she had arrived. When Wyatt signed off, she said teasingly, "So Joe had things to do, hmm?"

Laughing, he snuggled down beside her. "Not Joe, sweetheart. Me." His voice softened. "And you. Guess we got them done, didn't we?"

"Guess we did," she said with a contented sigh.

Epilogue

There were important decisions to make before their wedding, most of them Melissa's and most revolving around her business. Wyatt could leave the ranch without worry, but Melissa was such an important component in the success of the café that leaving it for a long honeymoon could cause a tremendous setback in business.

They saw each other every evening and discussed the problem from various angles. The sad truth they kept bumping into was that neither of them knew anyone capable of taking Melissa's place.

There were other problems to discuss, as well. Melissa had called her mother with the news of her impending nuptials. Nan was happy for her, and they laughed and talked for nearly an hour before Melissa got up the nerve to ask, "Will you come for my wedding, Mom?"

A heavy silence ensued, then Nan began hemming and hawing about the long trip and her failing health, and Melissa knew that her mother was still adamant about never returning to Whitehorn.

That evening she told Wyatt about it. "So she won't be at our wedding. I know why she won't come to Whitehorn, Wyatt, and her reason has nothing to do with disliking travel or her health. It's because everyone believed for years that Dad deserted us, and that hurt her so deeply she simply washed her hands of the town."

"Gossip can be deadly," Wyatt agreed.

Another hurdle for Melissa to overcome was the all-but-nonexistent headway the law was making in the investigation of her father's death. She discussed it with Wyatt.

"Nothing's happening," she said with a frustrated sigh one day.

"Make something happen, honey."

"How? What do I know about murder investigations?"

"Hire someone who does know. Hire a private investigator."

Melissa's eyes brightened. "I thought of that before. It *is* a good idea, isn't it?"

"I think so."

And so she began a search for a PI. In the Whitehorn library she went through all the telephone books she could find and made a list of possible private investigators. One in particular stood out. The ad stated humorously: Have Experience, Will Travel.

Gearing up her determination, she placed a long-distance call to Nick Dean, Private Investigator, who sounded cordial and pleasant on the phone. Melissa explained why she was in need of his services, and Nick agreed to take the case, although he couldn't give her a definite date of arrival because of his current workload. "Sometime within the next few weeks," he told her. "Is that all right?"

Melissa thought for a moment, then said yes. "Just so we get to meet and talk before my wedding in November. After that, I'll be away for some time." She put the phone down feeling better about *that* problem.

But there just didn't seem to be any solutions to the others. She wanted her mother at her wedding and felt bad that Nan wouldn't be there. Plus, she couldn't leave the café for an extended leave and enjoy herself. She knew she would worry every day of the honeymoon and probably end up ruining it.

She and Wyatt had dinner in her apartment on a Wednesday evening, but Melissa was just barely eating. Wyatt noticed and frowned. "What's wrong, honey?"

Laying down her fork, she put her elbows on the table and her chin on her folded hands. "Wyatt, I have to ask you something. How much do you love me?"

He stared for a second, then chuckled. "Well, let me see. In pounds, about ten trillion. In size, about the dimensions of the universe. In—"

"Stop it," she said with a laugh, which faded into sobriety almost immediately. She spoke falteringly. "Would you be terribly disappointed if we didn't take that long honeymoon right after the wedding?"

He laid his own fork on his plate. "Is that what you want?"

"No, but how can I leave for a long time without someone I trust implicitly being in charge of the café?"

He spoke slowly. "I suppose you can't."

Melissa reached across the table for his hand. "Wyatt, we could go next year, possibly sooner. I can train someone to do what I do, but it will take time."

His eyes contained so much love that her breath caught in her throat. "I will never refuse you anything, Melissa. If you feel that we should delay our honeymoon, then that's what we'll do. Something's been on my mind, as well. I've been a little concerned about being away from Timmy for so long right now. It's probably best for both of us if we delay our honeymoon for a while."

She smiled at her beloved. "I understand and agree." After a slight hesitation, she said rather meekly, "There is one other matter."

"What's that?"

"I'd like us to be married in California so my family can be there. We could take Timmy with us, if you wish. Oh, Wyatt, I'm such a burden to you, and I don't want to be. It's just that—"

He got up and walked around the table, holding out his hand to her. "Come here."

She got up and he pulled her into his arms. After a long, delicious kiss, he looked into her eyes. "Listen to me, kiddo. You will never be a burden as far as I'm concerned, understand? I love everything about you, and I intend to help rather than hinder you when you're faced with a problem.

I don't give a damn where we get married, as long as we get married. Got it?''

Her smile was a yard wide and very excited. "Got it. This is wonderful. *You're* wonderful. I'll call Mother and—''

"Call Mother in the morning. Right now I'd like you to prove how wonderful you think I am.''

Archly, Melissa glanced at the table. "What about dinner?''

"Dinner can wait, baby." Taking her hand, he led her from the kitchen. She smiled all the way to the bedroom.

Wyatt picked up the phone on the third ring. "North Ranch."

"Wyatt, this is Wilbur Kiley."

Wyatt went into alert mode. "How are you, Wilbur?"

"Very well, thank you. Wyatt, Shannon asked me to make this call."

"Oh?" Wyatt's stomach tensed.

"She got married last night...to Rick Malone. Listen, Wyatt, I know what she tried to do to you and your lady. She broke down and confessed the whole sordid mess to me a few days ago. I know I spoiled her something awful after her mother died, but she's not all bad and well...I just wanted you to know you're off the hook. The baby is Rick's. They both told me so."

Wyatt went weak with relief. "Thanks, Wilbur."

The older man sighed in Wyatt's ear. "Well, Rick Malone is no Wyatt North, but maybe he's the kind of man Shannon needs. I'm pretty certain he'll keep her on her toes."

"Will you tell her I wish her well, Wilbur?"

"That's mighty generous of you, Wyatt. Yes, I'll pass on the message. You have Timmy this weekend, don't you?"

"He's here. I put him to bed about an hour ago."

"He's a fine boy, Wyatt."

"Yes, he is."

"Which brings me to the real reason for this call. Wyatt, would you like to have full custody of Timmy?"

Wyatt's jaw dropped. "My God, yes. But Shannon—"

"Rick prefers not raising another man's child, Wyatt. I've been trying very hard not to judge the fellow, nor my daughter for conceding to his wishes, especially since I was so certain you would jump at the chance of having Timmy full-time."

Wyatt thought his heart might burst through his chest with excitement. "In writing, Wilbur?"

"In writing. Shannon asks only that she be permitted to see him at specified intervals."

"Well, of course she could." My God, this was fantastic. Wyatt didn't know how he was managing to speak normally when elation was making his head spin. Timmy could live at the ranch. Timmy could go to school in Whitehorn. It was a dream come true for Wyatt, and he hadn't even asked for it.

"I understand you're getting married, Wyatt. Congratulations. I hope you and your bride will be very happy."

"Thanks, Wilbur. I appreciate it." Melissa had fallen in love with Timmy on sight, and the little boy had taken to her, as well. Wyatt knew that she would be as thrilled with full custody as he was.

"Let's stay in touch. We do have Timmy in common, and I would like to see my grandson on occasion."

"You may see him whenever you wish, Wilbur. You have an open invitation to visit the ranch."

After they hung up, Wyatt sat back in his desk chair, stunned. He'd just been handed the most precious gift he could have ever imagined—his son, full-time.

Smiling, he picked up the phone and dialed the Hip Hop's number. The last loose end in his life was tied up, and he wanted to share his euphoria with Melissa.

"Melissa? Have I told you how much I love you?"

She laughed teasingly. "Not for several hours."

"Listen, sweetheart, something incredible just happened." Quickly he related Wilbur's call.

"Oh, Wyatt, everything's perfect, isn't it?"

"Yes, my love, everything is perfect."

And it was.

*   *   *   *   *

Montana Mavericks

continues with

OUTLAW LOVERS

by Pat Warren

Available in January

Here's an exciting preview....

One

All small towns have their secrets, Nick Dean thought as he drove along the highway heading toward the ranch. And some more than others. The town of Whitehorn, Montana, seemed to have more than its fair share, or so he'd discovered these past few days.

People were willing to gossip about Charlie Avery, the man who'd disappeared twenty-seven years ago and whose bones had been discovered on the nearby Laughing Horse Reservation. Nick had listened with interest to the townspeople, but hadn't heard anything that would lead to the killer.

As he straightened the vehicle after going around a curve, Nick suddenly felt the jolt of a tremendous explosion. Fire burst forth, flames shooting out from under the hood as his Blazer came to an abrupt stop. The driver's door shot open and Nick was thrown out, hitting the cold ground, then rolling down the embankment. He had no time to prepare himself, no time to brace against the tumble and roll into the fall. As he plunged down the hill, he heard another roaring eruption.

He didn't see the black smoke billowing up from the wreckage. Before his body rammed into a cluster of prickly bushes, Nick Dean mercifully passed out.

Sara Lewis was relieved to be heading for home. It had been a long day, and the weather was threatening. The snow flurries were getting larger and she feared an early storm was on its way. She wanted to get back to the reservation soon. Tomorrow she had—

Sara instinctively stepped hard on the brakes as a tall figure loomed just ahead of her. From the headlights, she could see that he was having trouble staying upright. If it hadn't been for his red jacket, she might have missed him altogether. Pulling off the road, she stopped by a thick copse of pine trees.

She jumped out of the car and rushed over to where the man had fallen.

Dried grass clung to his thick blond hair and there were scrapes and bruises on his angular face. A large gash on his head was bleeding and his jeans were dirty and ripped. "What happened?" she asked quickly.

The man was having trouble sitting up. But he wouldn't stop trying. "Blazer," he finally managed to answer. "Caught fire."

Sara looked around but couldn't spot his car. "Where?"

He motioned vaguely. "Highway. Gotta get help. I started walking. Fell." He moved to push himself upright but the effort was too much.

"Here, let me help you." Sara moved to his side and slipped one arm around him. "Let me drive you the hospital and—"

"No! Explosion. Can't risk it. No hospital." Nick reached a shaky hand to his forehead and saw that his fingers came away bloody.

"Then where would you like me to take you? The police station?"

He looked up, his blue eyes suddenly wild as his hand reached to grip hers. "No, please. I don't know what happened or who did it. My head . . ." He lowered his head into his other hand. "Hurts so much."

Sara tried to assess the situation. The man was a stranger—she knew pretty much everyone in Whitehorn, and there was no way she could have missed him. Even disheveled and bloody he was very attractive. But she couldn't leave him here by the side of the road, bleeding and nearly incoherent, with snow coming down fast and furious and the temperature below freezing already.

Sara came to a decision. She'd take him home—her house was right behind the tribal police station. Too, she'd taken a self-defense course and the man seemed in no shape to harm her physically. And once in her house, she could call her friend, Dr. Kane Hunter, for advice on how to care for the man's injuries.

"Come on," she said. "Let me help you into my car. We've got to get you out of this cold." She braced herself to accommodate him, trying to avoid his wounded shoulder.

Nick groaned but made it upright, leaning heavily on the woman as they headed for her car. Once inside, he leaned back, shivering, and clutching his arm.

He'd feel a lot better if he could figure out what the hell had happened. He'd had the Blazer serviced before leaving Butte and hadn't had any indication of a problem until the explosion.

Who would try to harm him and why? Was it something to do with his investigation into Charlie Avery's murder?

He saw the sign for the tribal police as Sara pulled off the road, and tried to sit up. "Where are you taking me?"

Sara heard the fear in his question. Was he afraid of the police? "Are you in trouble with the law?"

"Not that I know of."

As she drove on, she wondered if she'd made a colossal mistake by taking this stranger to her home. But she'd always taken in strays and tried to help others. And this man certainly needed help. She pulled as close as possible to the front door then turned to him, aiding his exit from the car.

She maneuvered the man into the house, taking most of his weight as she led him to the couch.

Nick collapsed wearily as the woman went to get her medical supplies. He winced as she began drawing off his jacket and examining his wounds. To avoid the pain, he looked at the woman before him.

He must really have been out of it not to have noticed how beautiful she was. She was tall and slender, but with plenty of womanly curves beneath her sweater. Her eyes were large and so deep a brown they were almost black. He saw intelligence there and an enviable serenity, with just a hint of nerves. Her skin was the color of rich coffee with cream and absolutely flawless. And then there was her hair, thick, shiny and black, and so long it fell to her waist.

Maybe he'd died and gone to heaven. "Who are you?" he asked, weaving a bit.

She smiled and her face softened. "Sara Lewis." She wondered how much he remembered, of the accident, of how he'd gotten here.

Her voice was low and husky, sending shivers down his spine. Sexy. He liked it. "I'm Nick Dean."

Sara gave him another smile as she unbuttoned his shirt with fingers that were suddenly unsteady. He was so large, his shoulders so muscular. He was dressed like a rancher and looked as if he worked outdoors. She tugged his shirt from the waistband of his jeans, and saw that his stomach was flat, his waist narrow. She found herself very close to him. Close enough to smell the decidedly masculine scent that emanated from his smooth skin.

Sara cleared her throat, feeling uncharacteristically nervous. She concentrated on his injuries, carefully cleaning them with antiseptic and then bandaging them.

"Where were you heading?" Sara questioned Nick to keep him alert and aware.

"I'm a private investigator. I'm looking into Charlie Avery's murder. His remains were found recently and his daughter hired me to help find her father's killer."

"I remember. The bones were found about twenty miles from here."

"From here?"

"Yes, you're on the Laughing Horse Reservation." She watched the knowledge register.

"Are you an . . ."

"An Indian, yes. Or a Native American, as some prefer." She tossed her long hair over her shoulder challengingly. "Are you sure you don't want me to take you somewhere now that you know that? I might have a tomahawk tucked in my purse."

He frowned again. "Why would you say that? Don't put yourself down, or your people. And don't resort to clichés. You're Indian, I'm not. So what?"

Sara was nonplussed. She'd never heard any white person, man or woman, dismiss cultural difference so casually. Perhaps it was his concussion. She'd have to see how he reacted in the morning. Ignoring his remark for now, she asked, "Would you like a nice cup of tea with honey and lemon?"

He almost smiled. "That's exactly what my mother used to fix for me when I had a cold."

"Mine, too. Perhaps we're not so very different after all." Sara started for the kitchen, but his next comment stopped her.

"Oh, yes, we are," Nick said to her retreating back.

She swung about, raising a questioning brow.

"I'm a man and you're definitely a woman." This time he did smile. "I may be in shock, but my eyes are working just fine."

Taken aback once more, Sara quickly left the room.

What had she gotten herself into, now?